The Degenerates

Raeden Richardson

_t_

TEXT PUBLISHING MELBOURNE AUSTRALIA

CW01394853

The Text Publishing Company acknowledges the Traditional Owners of the country on which we work, the Wurundjeri people of the Kulin Nation, and pays respect to their Elders past and present.

textpublishing.com.au

The Text Publishing Company
Wurundjeri Country, Level 6, Royal Bank Chambers, 287 Collins Street, Melbourne Victoria 3000 Australia

Copyright © Raeden Richardson, 2024

The moral right of Raeden Richardson to be identified as the author of this work has been asserted.

All rights reserved. Without limiting the rights under copyright above, no part of this publication shall be reproduced, stored in or introduced into a retrieval system, or transmitted in any form or by any means (electronic, mechanical, photocopying, recording or otherwise), without the prior permission of both the copyright owner and the publisher of this book.

Published by The Text Publishing Company, 2024

Cover design by W. H. Chong
Cover image by Mark Chu
Page design by Imogen Stubbs
Typeset by J&M Typesetting

Printed and bound in Australia by Griffin Press, a member of the Opus Group. The Opus Group is ISO/NZS 14001:2004 Environmental Management System certified.

ISBN: 9781923058040 (paperback)
ISBN: 9781923059047 (ebook)

A catalogue record for this book is available from the National Library of Australia.

FSC
www.fsc.org
MIX
Paper | Supporting responsible forestry
FSC® C018684

The paper this book is printed on is certified against the Forest Stewardship Council® Standards. Griffin Press, a member of the Opus Group, holds chain of custody certification SCS-COC-001185. FSC® promotes environmentally responsible, socially beneficial and economically viable management of the world's forests.

PRAISE FOR RAEDEN RICHARDSON
AND *THE DEGENERATES*

'*The Degenerates* is going for broke.
It's that rare thing: a wholly original novel told
in fantastically propulsive prose, rollicking, robust,
swerving between the comically weird and the direly
tragic, taking risks, talking dirty, and ending in a
vision that will reduce its dazzled readers to tears.
Melbourne has never been so lurid and hallucinogenic,
seen through the grimy lens of a hidden garage in
Degraves Street: more goon than any Goon Squad,
more hoon than celebrations of the AFL Grand Final
of 2017, more goon-bag realist in its bold and wildly
confident hyperrealism.' GAIL JONES, AUTHOR OF
ONE ANOTHER

'*The Degenerates* is vivid, wild and even prophetic.
It left me in awe. Raeden Richardson is the real deal.'
ROBBIE ARNOTT, AUTHOR OF *LIMBERLOST*

'Outstanding—an epic tale full of vivid characters
and told in a unique voice. *The Degenerates* is
sad and funny and beautiful and strange.' CHRIS
WOMERSLEY, AUTHOR OF *ORDINARY GODS
AND MONSTERS*

'*The Degenerates* is a buoyant, macabre,
subversive love song to the art of storytelling, a
playful, visceral flight of language that rises from
the muck of commerce and the decay of bodies
into utopian narrative glory. The joyful darkness
of Richardson's inventiveness reminds me of
Trainspotting, *The Horse's Mouth*, and *The God
of Small Things*.' KATE CHRISTENSEN, AUTHOR
OF *WELCOME HOME, STRANGER*

'This extraordinary novel so radiates with vitality that one feels as if its pages are somehow emitting the material of real life. *The Degenerates* is as much a story—one that is simultaneously entertaining and purposeful—as an argument for the value of storytelling itself.' VAUHINI VARA, AUTHOR OF *THE IMMORTAL KING RAO*

'Raeden Richardson creates a world much like ours but filled with dark magic and coincidences of the wildest kinds. Ants carry unlikely wisdom. Stardom is just a step away. The dead never leave. Richardson's prose is filled with glittering moments, his plot with dazzling twists and turns. *The Degenerates* is a brilliant and transporting debut.' MARGOT LIVESEY, AUTHOR OF *THE ROAD FROM BELHAVEN*

'*The Degenerates* is polyphonic, inventive, and daring. It's sweeping, expertly spanning multiple eras and lives, transporting the reader from Mumbai to Melbourne to Brooklyn, and making for an immersive global novel. There's something ravenous about Raeden Richardson's voice. It consumes everything in its path to forge an entirely fresh language. The result is a book that contains both the profane and the sacred, the vernacular and the transcendent.' SANJENA SATHIAN, AUTHOR OF *GOLD DIGGERS*

'To call *The Degenerates* ambitious would be a gross understatement. Raeden Richardson contends with nothing less than Buddhist samsara and the nature of existence itself, emulating the distinct surrealism of David Lynch. He pulls out all the stops of language and storytelling, achieving a debut that is as much a sage meditation as a novel.' ROBIN HEMLEY, AUTHOR OF *OBLIVION: AN AFTER AUTOBIOGRAPHY*

'It's rare to find a novel that moves as confidently yet unpredictably as *The Degenerates*. Raeden Richardson writes like a composer scoring a symphony, with such grace, fluidity, and musical control you almost feel you can see the notes rising off the page. Each of his characters possesses a wholly unique interiority, and through their minds, he communicates a vision of a world in which dissolution and creation—the degenerative and the regenerative—are inseparable from each other.' KEVIN BROCKMEIER, AUTHOR OF *THE BRIEF HISTORY OF THE DEAD*

Raeden Richardson grew up in Melbourne and graduated from the Iowa Writers' Workshop. His writing has appeared in *The Sydney Morning Herald*, *Griffith Review*, *Kill Your Darlings* and *New Australian Fiction*.

To my mother, who came from afar,
and to my father, who showed us these streets.

O compassion on these suffering conscious beings
Who wander in the life cycle, darkened with delusions.

PADMASAMBHAVA

Nasbandi

ALL THOSE YEARS AGO, in that sweltering city by the sea, Somnath Sunder Sonpate leaned against a bullock cart, scratching his nipples, which had turned red, as of recently, with an itchy rash. He waited on the pavement outside Readymoney Mansion, wriggling his crimson fingernails into his pockets, as lilting lullabies from the stone balconies echoed through the pigeon netting and into the skulls of the street dwellers. It was past midday: Preeti, the street beggar, took her next perch by the barbershop, mumbling for alms, smiling her tongueless smile and sliding her hand to her belly, which was fat with child. It was 1976: the brokers from the stock exchange hurried down Dalal Street by the hundred, voices raspy from all their trading, squelching over betel stains and coffee spills, dirtying their leather shoes as they sought out teawallahs and boiled-egg specialists. Sometimes Somnath sat with Preeti, sharing scraps of chapati or handfuls of rice and daal, until a businessman whistled, clicked his fingers and tapped his feet. 'All apologies, dear Preetibai,' Somnath would say, before scurrying across the pavement, armed with a canister of polish and his prickliest brush, and working with every ounce of zest, a pukka three-paisa performance, spick-spanning the businessmen's shoes to become the best shoeshiner in all of Bombay. Today, see, was no different: Somnath relished the scent of the shoe polish, the songs of the Readymoney children and the clatter of coins into his bucket, dulling his irritating itchiness with his honest, hard work.

Somnath had come to Bombay to make first a fortune and then a family. When he turned fifteen he left his good-for-nothing childhood and in the two years since arriving in the city he had become busy-busy and many-headed:

shoeshiner, three paisa per shoe
streetsweeper, four paisa per pavement
taxi cleaner, ten paisa per car
taxi dryer, na complimentary
window washer, twelve paisa per building
motorcycle mechanic (most lucrative), one rupee per repair

He had graduated from one trade to the next, all in the five hundred metres from St Thomas Cathedral to Flora Fountain, collecting rupees in the wicker basket he kept under his cushion when he slept. On these streets, yaar, money was god. No Bombayite could care to know the lowly bloodline of Somnath's father, or his father before him, so long as he got the job done. Most days, he waited at the doorstep of the most magnificent building on the street. It was the grey-stone, maroon-latticed, ivy-encased abode built by Cowasji Jehangir Readymoney, the city's most prominent entrepreneur, whose children etched 'Readymoney Mansion' above the archway where Somnath waited for his day's first shoeshine. In the afternoons, he inspected the motorcycles lined along the law firms and if he found a dent, or rusted axle, or clogged exhaust, he knelt by the vehicle and started fixing, timing his repairs so the clerks would return, at first aghast and then enamoured with this sharp-eyed coolie. 'But how much, ah?' the clerks would ask. Unlike the other mechanics who charged five-six rupees, who spoke-spat their quotes between their betel-black teeth,

Somnath would hold a single finger aloft—'But a single rupee? Such a top-notch coolie, this boy!'—and offer a precocious smile, winning both their money and their trust.

After the day's work, Somnath would hurry past the towers of novels at Flora Fountain, by the gilded faces of authors embossed on the covers of English imprints, and catch the fast train at Churchgate, heading north to Grant Road. The Anglicans ran night school from a shut pharmacy—thirty paisa per lesson, but free for the slum girls and their maas. Each class, a sister dictated the poems of Keats and Byron for them to pen on parchment paper. Over the months, they had learned to write cursive paragraphs in proper British English, to read without touching the page, to tally lists and make receipts. But undoubtedly Somnath's favourite project came at the end of his first year at night school, when the sisters asked the students to label their future family trees: wife/mother, son, daughter, grandson, granddaughter, great-grandson, great-granddaughter. This Somnath sketched most carefully, tensing his toes in concentration as he wrote, scrawling lineages down every page of his notebook, penning 'Somnath Sunder Sonpate' at the top of the chart in his finest cursive as his forthcoming sons spilled from page to page. There was nothing more worthy than an heir, yaar, and nothing more desirable than a hustling, bustling bloodline. If one day he should have his own empire, he would need more sons than fingers and toes. Night school lessons ran until ten, payments sliding into the wooden box on the druggist's counter. Unless the police arrived: a silhouette across the dusty window; a bang-bang against the roller door; a whisper from the sisters to toss their books under the shelves, switch off the lamp and begin reciting their prayers. 'We are not illegals,' said a maa to her whimpering daughter. 'We are not enemies in the Emergency. All madness, my sweet. All idiocy. These policeboys will do anything to fill their quotas, I tell you.' Tonight, some hours after curfew, Somnath hurried by the idle taxis around Grant Road, scratching his singlet and clasping his notebook with his scores of sons peppering the pages. He ran the many miles down to Dalal Street, past the curtained windows of Readymoney Mansion and along the alleyway at the rear. When he reached the banyan tree, he unfurled his blue tarpaulin and strung it between a branch and the drainpipe, sliding off his belt to tie it in place. He ambled across the alleyway and put his notebook on the pile under Preeti's head. Though they exchanged the most minimum of words, their long days on Dalal Street had made them the unlikeliest of friends. As she lay on her back, resting his pages on her mountainous belly, the wet ink met the moonlight and she seemed to sleep beneath shining rivers that ran to safer places. Then Somnath went back to the banyan tree and pooled the day's paisa in his basket, sweeping his hand through his earnings. Six more months, yaar, closing the lid and rubbing his red chest, and he could try for a flat in Byculla. Twelve more months, yaar, calming his itchiness with his soft, slow breath, and he could try for a wife.

'But wake up, untouchable,' said the beggarwallah, clutching Somnath's leg with his stubby fingers, 'and touch these nuts, ah. What all will you do when my good nephew outworks you?' The stink of fruit wine pressed into Somnath's face; he dug his thumbs into the beggarwallah's empty eye sockets and pushed him away. The old man chuckled, stumbling down the alleyway until his feet met the mound of books beneath his sister's back. Soon he started snoring and Somnath exhaled, clutching his wicker basket to his chest. Much better, really, than the bash and crash from months earlier, the scolding and howling and moaning, when Preeti first showed with child. 'What all have you done?' the beggarwallah had said, grabbing her budding belly. 'What dirty man's work is this?' 'Listen,' said Preeti, pale-face and wide-eyed. 'Alone I've lain. Not a single soul.' 'Im-possible,' said the beggarwallah. But Somnath knew the truth: Preeti had always kept her distance, sleeping by herself, cuddling but papers for warmth, caressing only old pages from novels and notebooks. 'A miracle,' said Preeti. 'There's no other explanation. Believe me, won't you, my own brother?' 'Shut it up,' said the beggarwallah. And for all of her honesty, and for all of her days working hand to mouth, hand to heart, saving her paisa for her brother, these were her last words: 'Will you just listen? Please?' 'Enough,' he said. 'Such miracles belong in the Vedas, fit for royals, for heroes. Not from the street. Not from the poor. Not from the loose mouth of a no-good whore.' Like that, he took out her tongue; she howled and bled on her bed of books. Never had Somnath heard such a painful wail. But all these weeks later, the beggarwallah spent his mornings stumbling down Dalal Street, speaking where she was speechless, wrapping his hands around her belly as if weighing a promising mango. Every burden, every sign of suffering, meant better business. He walked without a cane, his feet intimate with every crack in the road, his two vacuous eye sockets, wounds from his own beggarmaster many decades earlier, shining like Krishna's holy pearls. 'Touch this truth, untouchable,' he would say, as he passed Somnath outside Readymoney Mansion. 'One day my good nephew will chase you back to the village.' Somnath would shudder, staring sadly at Preeti working so devotedly, not for one, not for two, but for three forsaken people, until he found some windows to wash or some time to sweep the dark and dirty street.

'But a whole tiffin, Preetibai, too much for me to eat on my own,' said Somnath, on the last morning of his itchiness, which had spread from his nipples to his collarbones. 'Please take.' She turned her head, continuing her hand-to-belly routine, and opened her mouth, slipping her half-tongue between her rotten teeth. Somnath folded the chapati, tore it in two and pressed it over her gums. She nodded her thanks, a blessing too, and turned back to the pavement, eye-level with the brokers, all suited and booted, on break from their offices as the clock struck midday. Somnath made his rounds, polishing shoes and inspecting motorcycles. In another hour all the businessmen left Dalal Street and the coolies reclined under the shop awnings. But just as he was walking back to the bullock cart, a ruckus started down the street. He froze. The coolies turned their heads. Lines of navy-blue shirts and shorts, rows of policemen, circled Flora Fountain and the book-wallah's lots, stalking the towers of novels, toppling paperbacks to the curb, cracking the concrete with their batons. 'Citywide beautification is now in progress,' said a tinny voice through a loudspeaker. 'Nation-wide regulation. Discipline makes the nation great.' An inspection, see, and the streetpeace imploded. The shoeshiners scrounged their coins into pockets, rolled their mats under their arms and kicked their pedestals to the curbs. The barbers flicked their beedies to the pavement, upturned their wooden stools and ran out of sight. The taxiwallahs leapt into their cars, revved their engines and tooted away. A roiling mass of coolies streamed down the street, fleeing the police-men hunting for documents and permits and identification cards. Somnath turned to run, caught in the currents of unlicensed men, when Preeti yelped from her perch. She had collapsed, knocked to the concrete not by some fleeing coolie, na, but her own incontinence: her legs and ankles glistened and a puddle eked from her crotch. 'Good friend,' he said, 'now is no time for toilet duties.' She gasped, clutching her spectacular belly: a birth, really, at this mad hour. Somnath knelt and held her as the street filled with cops, the thwacking of their batons like the slicing of reeds in a field. 'You there, boss, you can rest easy,' said a policeboy, his hair shaved close to his skull. 'She is birthing, what to do?' said Somnath. 'Most definitely we can handle such matters,' said the policeboy. 'And you, buddy? Birthing, or what?' 'No, just visiting from the village.' The policeboy grabbed Somnath's wrists, twisting his hands in circles for inspection: streaks of boot polish, flecks of oil and fingernails blackened with grime. 'So this visitor has been working. And where are your papers?' 'Papers?' 'Where is your registration? Shoeshiner, drug-dealer, money-stealer, overall entrepreneurial endeavours. What else, ah?' 'Please,' said Somnath, 'no trouble, okay?' The policeboy wrung Somnath's arms and slid the baton between his shoulder blades. 'Must clarify your story,' he said, breathing into his ear and pushing him down the road, away from gasping Preeti, the vacant balconies of Readymoney Mansion, the mounds of toppled novels, and out, far beyond Flora Fountain, where a lone white caravan awaited.

'Tell the doctor your age,' said the policeboy. 'Seventeen.' 'And your name.' 'Som.' 'Full name.' 'Somnath Sunder.' 'Surname too.' 'Somnath Sunder Sonpate.' The policeboy scribbled on a document and lowered his pen. The caravan stank of formaldehyde and the windows were curtained with black sheets. A metal table stood in the corner of the room, two leather cuffs dangling off the end. The doctor leaned over a desk, chewing a wad of gum as he polished his silver instruments, his arm-hair bristling under his blue coat. 'Place of birth,' said the policeboy. 'Vita,' said Somnath, 'Western Maharashtra.' The doctor swivelled around, burst his gum and said, 'He is a Vita-born Sunder. He is a Dalit.' Somnath reached for the door, but the doctor thwacked his wrist with the policeboy's baton. Somnath fell to his knees, clutching his hand to his chest. 'Disobedience,' said the doctor, 'is a typical trait of the untouchable.' 'Well, ah, lucky for you, Somnath Sunder Sonpate,' said the policeboy, shifting nervously in his oversized shirt, tapping the page in his hand as he spoke, 'a trilemma presents itself. Options, *three*, by which I mean *one way* to escape *two* horrible fates. The first option, least desirable, most contemptible, this hardworking coolie lands in Yerawada Central Jail, stuck with the goondas and terrorists and student-union anarchists. Somnath Sunder Sonpate, hardworking coolie, living in shit, cramped cell, piss on the feet, piss in the ghee. Option two, also lesser desirability, hardworking coolie locked in a truck, sent back to Vita with its plentitude of dirty, grimy children and bone-dry crops. Want to eat the famine, Somnath Sunder Sonpate?' The policeboy turned the pages of his document, past the signatures and biodata, to a diagram with English labels: the sketch of a penis, a perforated line above the hairless testes, the vas deferens curled out of the skin, like laces yanked out of a shoe. The tubes were soldered shut. 'Or nasbandi,' said the policeboy, 'option three, best option in my professional opinion, state-recommended, doctor-endorsed, easiest of all, a gift, ah, true American freedom: precise procedure, simple snip-snip, nothing to change habit or desire, will boost sexual performance, maximum satisfaction for wife and mistress, true bamboozlement for all.' Somnath shuddered. Pain shot from his nipples to his belly and he groaned. 'What's the issue?' said the policeboy. 'Na,' said Somnath, shielding his hands over his crotch. 'But dekh bhai, just see, nasbandi is safe as cement.' 'I will go back to Vita. Put me in the truck,' said Somnath. 'Spoken like a true traitor of the state,' said the doctor, spitting out his wad of gum. 'Does this dirty Dalit want to be punished? Does he want to be taken before a court of law?' 'Send me to jail, sir. I'll accept. Please and thanks.' 'Just take the doctor's gift, yaar,' said the policeboy. 'No trouble. Vasectomy is easy for all, okay?' Somnath grabbed the documents and tore them apart. He sprung to his feet and banged the caravan wall. The police-boy cracked Somnath's shoulder with the baton, but he managed to find the door latch, fiddle the lock open and breath the balmy air of the street. He moaned across the road, his voice echoing off the shop-houses in the darkened street—and then he buckled, collapsing to the floor of the caravan. The doctor stood over him, sheathing a syringe in his pocket. 'Take him to the table. Full restraints may be required.'

When Somnath awoke on the table, his trousers were folded by his shoulder and his underwear had turned yellow-orange-red. 'India thanks you,' said the policeboy, rubbing Somnath's hands, which were numb, see, totally wooden. Slowly, he rocked forward on the table, his thighs twitching. The policeboy pressed the salvaged papers, covered in new signatures and adhesive tape, onto the doctor's desk. 'Two more by today-evening,' said the doctor, unfurling a ten-rupee note. 'You will find me in Jogeshwari. Next week I am back to Uttar Pradesh.' The policeboy took the money, picked up his baton and stepped out of the caravan, disappearing down the road. Somnath followed, his trousers tucked under his arm, lurching along, the road wobbling under his toes, his eyes filling with beady tears. With every footfall his gut warbled. A tremor rose from deep beneath his belly, from a hole he had not known until now, and the fractured moon quivered in the sky above the shophouses. Dalal Street was deserted. All the coolies were gone, na, done for: the stools piled in a corner, the carpets rolled and set on fire, the carts piled with boxes, and the only beings to see were two stray dogs on the pavement outside Readymoney Mansion, sniffing their grotty paws. His gut-warble grew and he wept without thinking, see, thinking was impossible, impractical, impotent. He was only a naive village boy. How could he have been anything more? He stood at the stone balustrades and held his stomach in his hands. Maybe a peshab, yaar, to ease the pressure, to fade, to drain away, so he peeled his underwear off his hips and grabbed his lund, shrivelled now like a snail, but his knuckles brushed his balls, exploding every nerve. The strays howled, racing towards the cathedral, hair turned stiff on their spines, and the moon faded. That man in his caravan drove on. Somewhere in the stars was an alternative, a life Somnath could never have, a lineage waiting only on the streets of his fantasies. He swayed, just see, how could this have happened? The sharp stitches pricked his fingertips. The ridge of his wound swelled and pus dripped onto his thumb. He pulled his underwear up and kept walking, aching for his own end, the wind moaning around him on the stones. He limped into the courtyard. The tarpaulin sheets were torn in pieces, the corrugated iron bent in chunks, the bamboo scorched and the cotton sheets charred to a crisp. All the books had been burned, blackened, now a smouldering heap, a cloud of stinging smoke. He stumbled into the rubble and found the lid of his wicker basket. It crumbled in his hands. Then came a murmuring, a fidgeting in the remains. 'Preetibai?' he said, swaying on his feet. The murmuring continued, a gasp, a shuffle under the last soiled sheet. He unfolded the dirty linen and found a baby, rustling in the rubbish, a baby girl, see, with ruddy cheeks and fat fingers, not yet dead. He rolled her out and held her by the feet, circling the courtyard, shaking his head left right, left right, the pavement firming under every step. He sat gingerly under the banyan tree, his face smeared with salt and grime, thudding his head on the trunk. No good could come of this. Suffering only authored more suffering. 'All apologies, poor girl.' He smothered her mouth against his chest, crushing her into his ribs, but she latched onto one of his red nipples. A streak of milk leaked down her lips. She began to feed. His grip loosened on her head and she suckled until she took her fill, easing his convulsions, slowing his panting and drawing him along into sleep.

'Citywide beautification is now in progress,' rang the loudspeaker through the pre-dawn streets. 'Discipline makes the nation great.' Embers lit the courtyard and scraps of paper swirled on the breeze. As the voice echoed around the buildings, the baby shivered against Somnath's chest, thrusting her cheek to his ribs as she twitched with the morning cold. He found a dirty shawl and the remains of a linen bag and wrapped himself in a makeshift saree. He swaddled the baby tightly and left the courtyard. The voices rang louder, boots thudded in the alley, and Somnath limped away from Dalal Street, heading east towards the rising sun. 'Stop there, beggarwoman,' yelled a policeman, 'I told you yesterday these are not your streets for birthing. No place for ama to make a nursery.' Somnath scuttled, faster and faster, in spite of the knot tightening in his belly and the bile rising in his throat. He ran past the shining stairs of the Asiatic Museum, the polished cars in a semicircle around the park and the line upon line of unattended motorcycles. The officer shouted for added support, and soon five and six and seven pairs of police boots pounded in Somnath's wake. He veered towards the naval yard, securing the baby with one hand and his swollen balls with the other. At the wall around the docks, he leapt on a bullock cart piled high with crates, scattering the boxes over the gutter. He scaled three metres up the concrete and over the barbed wire, landing on the green lawns of the docks. The naval yard was ghostly calm, the cargo ships waiting silently on the calm water, and when the policemen yelped from behind the wall, their threats were muffled by the fog. Somnath scuttled past the guardhouse and found an unmanned ship, a mammoth vessel with red and green containers. He snuck into the nearest one, shut the door and closed the latch. Enveloped in darkness, he guided the baby to his nipple, nursing her again as his chest swelled and tingled. Minutes passed, his vision sharpened, and her eyes opened to reveal shining brown wellsprings. 'Suppose your name is Maha,' he said, 'for your endless gaze. How can you live, baby, when most clearly you should not?' 'Hey,' came a voice, 'shut it, boy. Keep quiet.' A row of gleaming eyes, sunken and startled, stared between the barrels and through the gloom. Whole families sat silently in the dark, trembling hands clutching suitcases and rucksacks, tattered sarees and shawls. Somnath held Maha against his chest, gasping as the pain seared up his crotch. In his hands was a baby, a little lady, every sniffle a sign of the sons he had lost. Why, oh why, such a no-good consolation? And then a horn sounded, the container shuddered, and the ship unmoored from the dock, drifting out over the ocean.

Where one dream ended, another began; when the ship emptied onto Appleton Dock, Maha clung to her father's shoulder and stared across Port Melbourne to the silhouette of the city. A queue of burly factory workers waited beside the barge, counting and measuring the barrels of petroleum, and as her father limped across the planks with his hand outstretched, the salty air made her weep, a rolling howl that echoed between the trucks and startled the plump men with their clipboards and upturned eyebrows. Her father hobbled across the docks, scowling, shaking her with both hands. 'Just please shut it up,' he said. They passed sheds, piles of timber and a red and white radio tower flashing in the fog. They walked along the Yarra under the purple sunrise. The shops were still closed, the cobblestoned laneways clear and the offices shut. Her father collapsed under the clocks at Flinders Street Station, dragging clods of dirt out of his shaggy hair, rubbing his sunken eyes, staring for hours at the happy drunks outside the Young and Jackson Hotel, like a man who had fallen through the bottom of his grave. 'Alive, but not well,' he said. 'Awake, but out of place.' They climbed the steps of St Paul's Cathedral and Maha's eyes widened at the echo of the priest's voice. 'Let all these poor migrants never forget,' he said, 'that at heart we are a good Christian nation.' Then the organs boomed, the choir wailed and Maha bawled against her father's shoulder blades. He pulled her down to his chest and she wriggled over his singlet, searching for his nipples, but when she tried to feed not a drop of milk eked over her lips. 'Please, little one,' he said, as the parishioners shifted in the candlelit pews. 'Why so many tears all of a sudden?' Her father hung her under his singlet and they bounded across town to Queen Victoria Market. 'Come in off a flight, have you, boy-o?' said a man who was cleaning his clippers on his apron. 'Just looking,' said her father, leaving Maha on a wooden table and trudging into the crowd. 'Gee, looks like big brother's not in a good way,' said the man, tickling Maha's tummy. 'Youse are Indian? Paki? No worries, bub. Welcome to Melbourne. Hope she treats you alright.' The man slid a bottle of milk across the table, the glass cold against Maha's cheek, and the shock set her face in a smile. Her father returned with some bread and a few biscuits. 'Best you stay away from this child,' he said to the man. 'She is some kind of divine disappointment.' He swept up Maha, thrust the bottle of milk under his arm and hurried through the market. 'On the house, my gift to youse,' said the man. 'Kids are the future, mate. She could be the next Mahatma Gandhi, you never know. Can't write off anyone in this town.'

They squatted in a flat on Swan Street and ate brown bread with white sugar. Every morning, her father covered Maha in tartan sheets, hid her in the cupboard, then disappeared down the street. She cooed in the dark, yearning to be with him, to nestle against his chest. He would return each night with his face knotted, his fingers kneading his crotch. 'Not one doctor,' he said, 'not a single surgeon. No one has any alternative. No solution, none.' Not once did he want to play; he was only in need, it seemed, of the echoes of his lone voice. Soon he started murmuring about finding work, returning each evening with his hands smeared with oil. 'So much of loss, little one,' he said. 'My sadness, so much for them to handle. One day they will see I am not like them, not another Aussie, not another *top bloke*. From the bottom, then, I tell you. Without home or family or trust in god. But from the bottom comes patience, see, and cunning.' He poured her shots of milk, broke bread crusts for himself and limped in circles around the flat. Sometimes she woke to see him crying, or biting his lip as he hovered by the cupboard, or circling his hands over his belly. After two months, her father returned from working on the streets, pulled Maha from the cupboard, hefted her over his shoulder and hurried into the night. They walked back to Swanston Street, down by the arcades along Flinders Street and stopped before a boarded-up garage. 'Garagewallah says owner of the best chop shop has skipped town. Melbourne needs a new coolie to carry the flame,' he said, 'and no police would ever suspect me, na, this *young man so fresh off his boat*.' Her father opened the chop shop there and then, in the middle of the night. He coiled the cord of the shop vac into a makeshift cradle, placing her inside, then tightened the pneumatic lines and sealed the rubber leaks. Over the next few weeks, he took hundreds of discarded books from

Cash Converters and piled them around the basement for insulation. Encyclopaedias and atlases lined the brick walls. Physics textbooks and world histories towered around her bed. With her body heat trapped under the cement ceiling, Maha rocked from side-to-side, squinting at the spines of the novels. Every Saturday for two years, her father took her on his rounds of the city, passing cash and papers to men in black leather coats, their faces lit by the embers of Pall Mall cigarettes as they warbled in their avian accents. Sometimes they met the clients at the Melbourne Cricket Ground, where the city folk gathered to watch the footy, a rough-and-tumble, free-for-all game seemingly without rules, played by men with the torsos of weightlifters and the long limbs of marathon runners. The sport was brutal, like a gladiator contest, and as they roared from the stands, the locals' faces reddened and their weekday nonchalance faded. Oblivious to her father's wheeling and dealing, Maha left the stadium with ringing ears, her fingertips splitting as she clapped to the rhythms of the footy fans, those lifelong devotees in scarfs and beanies. At home, she curled in the shop vac cord or crawled between the repaired motorcycles, while her father ran the garage, eighteen hours a day, through migraine headaches, winter viruses and blisters on his toes. He poisoned the mice that hid in the walls, crushed the spiders with his broom and beat the possums out of her bed with his bare hands. 'It is no wonder this place is full of brutish animals,' he said. 'In a country of such degenerate men, their reincarnate forms could be no better.' In spite of all his scorn for the locals, word of this subcontinental workaholic spread in cafes and bars. First came the amateurs, in need of honest repairs for their Nortons or Triumphs. Then came the clandestine gangs, who needed to disassemble their outlawed rides and pawn the parts, who gave her father extra to break the steering lock and grind the VIN off the forks. They always paid in cash. Trust was established and her father's reputation grew.

Each night, after locking the roller door and swaddling Maha in her sheets, he sat against his sacks of cash, plumping them like pillows. Then he opened his newest magazine, ignoring Maha's murmurs for attention, and followed those faraway sentences further into silence.

Maha spent the next few years pressing her face to the window, staring past her round cheeks and curly hair at the silhouettes on the street. Women clasped their daughters' hands as they crossed the road. Men bounced their little girls on their shoulders as they walked. She crept upstairs to the garage and tied her arms around her father's waist, but he only huffed and shook her off to focus on his chores. She felt sad that she was not a normal daughter, that she had no mother who would listen to her, but she didn't want to bother her father, so she kept her sorrows to herself. One day, enchanted by the city beyond the basement, she took a ten-dollar note from one of her father's sacks and snuck outside, wandering for hours between the crowds of businessmen, their faces hidden in broadsheet newspapers, and past salons where women dyed their hair pink and red and peroxide blonde. She watched the girls in their lessons at the outdoor swimming pools, their sun-drenched bodies shivering in one-piece suits, and followed them to choir recitals, and picnics, and to a cafe where their mothers waited with desserts on shining plates. She waited in line and bought the treats for herself: pavlovas, lamingtons, chocolate biscuits, vanilla scrolls, hot jam doughnuts. She liked to close her eyes and let the sugar ooze over her tongue and settle on the ridges of her teeth. 'But, darling,' said the shopkeeper, 'where's your mum? You can't be loitering in here.' Maha opened her eyes; of course, she was alone in the cafe. Trudging back to the chop shop, she wondered where her own mother was waiting. When would she arrive, after all this time, and guide Maha home? Away, she thought, far away from the loneliness that lined these streets and darkened the four corners of the basement. That evening, she scrambled out of bed and wailed until the walls shook. 'Where is she?' she said. 'Mother, when will she come?' 'Please quiet,' said her father, wiping his thumb across her wet cheeks. 'Just wait. Let me show you. Here, your mother's love.' He leafed through a Yamaha manual, tracing her fingers over the letters and pronouncing their sounds, and as she copied him, the words held her in a state of grace, a kind of knowing she had never had before. Her tears dried. She opened an atlas, tracing her fingers over the borders of the continents, the curves of the tectonic plates, the shores of the widest oceans. 'Good,' he said, opening a pulp story magazine, 'better than expected. All natural ability, and more.' Over the next sleepless weeks, she sang poems, mulling each syllable over her tongue, revering every stanza she uttered. She read ancient scriptures from every corner of the Earth, the histories of divinities, of those who destroyed cities, or spread enlightenment, or faced only ridicule and torture. She learned that all beings came and went out of this form and into the next. And yet she found that books held infinite worlds within their pages, that writers were gods who wrote other humans into being, that every creator would find her readers, her true believers amid the loneliness of her life. Soon she brought her favourite sweets back from the cafes and read for hours in the dark, embraced by this presence she could not see. She munched her pastries with glee, ignoring the lives of the other Melburnians, of the other daughters she would never be.

When Maha was fourteen, her father hired three apprentices to make a team, recruited through his network of bikies from Gippsland to Bacchus Marsh. The criterion for entry into Sonpate's Squad was simple. 'Leaky lips sink the ship,' he would say. 'Trust is number one. More important than any technical proficiency.' And he wanted devotion, a love of engines that trumped any interest in girls or footy. Somnath made each applicant work outside the chop shop for twenty-two hours, hand-scrubbing the rust off old carburettors while Maha ate her breakfast and sprayed them with paint thinner. By lunchtime, most of the candidates crumpled, scattering the flock of pigeons at the newsstand or stamping their feet. 'Bloody apes,' said one. 'You'll never get away with this, you curry-muncher,' said another. But three boys triumphed. Maha's father welcomed Christos, Angus and Luke with a firm handshake, signing them up for a generous wage of twenty dollars a day, and passed the subterranean secrets of the clientele out of black loose-leaf binders and into their hands. Hiding in the stairwell, Maha sucked her lollies against her stubby teeth and stroked her bushy hair, spying the boys striding through the dark in their glowing yellow overalls. One day, a policeman knocked on the door, sending her father scampering with Maha to the basement. 'So we got word from an apprentice mechanic that there was some shady shit going on here,' the policeman said, waving a typed report in the doorway. 'You know anything about a Mister Sonpate? Seems he's quite the devil.' 'Not at all, sir,' said Christos. 'We're a youth group. We're learning how to serve by fixing up cars.' 'We'd love for you to join us,' said Luke. 'Every second midday, same time. It helps you feel connected to our lord, our saviour, Mister Jesus Christ.' 'Have you heard the good news?' said Angus. The policeman laughed, scrunched up his paper and walked

away. 'These boys,' her father whispered. 'So intelligent, so industri-
ous.' All day their bawdy jokes echoed down the stairs and their rock
music rattled through the chop shop from their tinny transistor radios.
Their Australian twang sounded so unruly, like squawking seagulls
trapped in a milk crate. But for all their oddity, Maha found herself
smiling at their curious phrases, their odd diction. Lying awake at
night, she pictured their weathered faces, contoured with scars and
pockmarks, and their mouths hiding under their beards. Like the
gangsters and the bikies, the boys' arms were covered in tattoos, and
their fingertips were raw, embedded with shards of steel wool, their
fingernails black with oil. 'It's grog o'clock,' they said in the afternoons,
cradling their cans of beer when it was time to unwind. They also
liked their powders and their little coloured pills, sharing their drugs
when the day was done, and though the thought of losing her mind
left a cold sweat on her neck, she laughed to see them so carefree.

One morning, when Maha went to take some cash for a trip to the cafe, she found her father's sacks were empty. She looked for the money everywhere in the basement, riffling through the folders and binders, knocking notebooks off the desk, before running empty-handed up the stairs. There was no sign of her father in the chop shop; like his money, he was nowhere to be found. 'I can't find him,' she said, tears smearing down her lips. 'Oh, love,' said Christos, 'you'll be right.' Luke wrapped an arm around her shoulders and smiled. 'Probably just went to clear those cobwebs in his head,' he said. 'That's all. Now, we can't piss off the boss, so we better keep working. But we'll be right here, okay?' She loped back to the basement and sat at her father's desk. On the floor, at her feet beside his logbooks, was a pile of leatherbound notebooks, maybe twenty in all, covered in import stamps, their pages blank and unopened. She restacked them, carefully. Then a folded sheet of paper slipped off the desk and landed at her feet. Slowly she opened the page. It had been torn from a pulp magazine called *Man's Tales from Near and Far*: 'THE JACKAROO, submitted by James Squid Briggs. Once there was a nurse who had two lads. She loved them as two parents love their kids, only it was just her in the house and paying the bills, for her fella was a groghead. One day she had to go into town to pay the electricity bill, so she called her lads and said, "Boys, I'm going into town, so watch out for the jackaroo. If he gets in the house, yeah, he'll tie your hands, bash you up and steal you away. The jackaroo is gacked from all the sun that's burned his brain. You'll know him by his boozy breath and his dry, calloused hands." "She'll be right, Mum," said the lads. "No need to worry about us." The nurse pinned her hair behind her head and went to town with an easy mind. But it wasn't long before someone knocked at the door and said, "Open up, little lads, y'mum is here and she's brought something for each of you." But the boys sniffed his breath. "We won't open! We can smell the grog!" So the jackaroo went to the wood shop, bought a block of charcoal, ate it and sorted out his breath. Then he came back and said, "Open up, little lads, y'mum is here and she's got a yummy treat." But the jackaroo put his hands on the window ledge. The lads saw them and said, "We won't open! Mum hasn't got calloused hands like you!" Then the jackaroo went to the beauty house and said, "I've ruined me hands. Sand away me callouses." After the beautician clipped off his callouses, he went to the lolly maker and said, "Put some soothing bee-honey on me hands." "You're out to trick some-body," said the lolly maker, and he refused to help. "If you won't do it," said the jackaroo, "I'll bash you up." So the lolly maker took the jackaroo's hands and made them soft. He went back and banged on the door a third time. "O little lads," he said, "y'mum has come home and she's brought something for each of you." The boys said, "Show us your hands!" He stuck a hand on the windowsill and they saw it was soft and supple, so they opened the door. They were scared to death and tried to hide. One lad hid under the workbench and the other in the dishwasher, but the jackaroo found the first and made short work of him before leaving: he tied him up, shoved him in his suitcase and locked the padlock tight. "Happy days," said the jackaroo. "I've got me a friend. At last." The jackaroo booked it to a gum tree near a shady creek and had a sleep. When the nurse came home, she found the door scratched up and the workbench flipped. She called for her lads but no one answered. Finally, when she reached the kitchen, she heard a muffled voice. "Mum! I'm in the dishwasher!" She helped him out and he told her the jackaroo had tricked his way in and taken his brother. Soon enough, together mother and son left the house to hunt down the jackaroo. They found him having a sleep under the gum tree, snoring so monstrously all the witchetty-grubs went burrowing under the roots. The nurse saw the suitcase athumping under his head. "Goodness gracious me," she said. "Could my little tacker still be all right?" She slid a pin from her hair and picked the lock. When she opened the suitcase, her lad stuck his head out. He was alive and hadn't even been hurt. "What a fuckwit," said the nurse. "He forgot to break your neck." Both lads hugged their mum and wept with joy. Then the nurse said, "Go and have a look for some redback spiders." The boys caught some redbacks under the rocks and stuffed them into the suitcase. When the jackaroo finished his snoozing, he stood up, yawning. The sleep had made him thirsty, so he thought he'd go to the creek, have a drink and head home to his failing farm with his new mate. But all of a sudden his suitcase made a strange sound. "What's that hopping and bopping inside me luggage?" he said. "Is it me mate who'll join me on the Red Plains?" When he opened the suitcase, the redbacks burst free and clambered all over his rig and bit him twelve times. He fell in the creek and sank into a whirlpool. When the lads saw his stiff, drowning body, they cried out, "The jackaroo is dying! The jackaroo is dying!" and they boogied around the gum tree with joy.'

As she refolded the sheet of paper, the basement swayed around her body. She scrambled to her bed, buried her face in the pillow and opened her eyes to the endless blackness, wondering what dark ideas her father entertained. Suddenly she saw herself in the jackaroo's place, bitten by spiders up her knees, over her wrists and on the back of her neck. Her skin prickled and the hairs along her arms stiffened; the more she tried to imagine the jackaroo's death, the further she sank into an endless pit: to die would mean *not* seeing the rushing water, *not* hearing the lapping of the creek, *not* feeling her flailing limbs, *not* thinking those drowning thoughts. An endless negative. Death was incomprehensible and untranslatable. It could not be seen, or felt, or even written on a page. 'Na, child, what is this?' said her father, limping into the messy basement. 'You have been looking in my things?' 'Where did you go?' said Maha. 'Madness, ah, what is this?' he said. And her father pulled the blank notebooks into a bag, pulled the drawstring tight and scowled. He pinned her wrists to the bed with both hands and loomed over her nose. His skin was covered in fine red sand. He stank of tar and petrol. 'Somnath Sunder Sonpate, busiest man in all of Melbourne. Better you don't go prying, child, not yet. Now is the time for reading. Gospels, scriptures, mantras, you have.' Maha trembled under his grip, flinching as he spoke. 'But he was so lonely,' she said. 'Why did the nurse have to hurt him?' 'No need to wander in the world of men, okay, child? Nastiness and gore, not for your eyes. Let the jackaroo go, this lowly life into the next. Else some things will destroy the fat loveliness in a girl.' Her father hurried upstairs and left her in the darkness, sniffling under her breath. She rolled over in her bed and stretched her fingers in their knuckles, watching her joints turn white and grey. She worried she

31

had disturbed her father, annoyed him with her sadness and fear. She pressed her face into her pillow and waited for her breath to slow. At least be useful, she thought. Not another burden for him to bear. Her father's untouched logbooks spilled over his desk, so she heaved herself off the bed, lumbered across the cement and counted the pages herself, adding and forecasting with a Biro pen. She learned that her father had saved thousands of dollars by avoiding taxes and registrations, that the cash was unreported, invisible, and all their incomes were fatter for it. She wondered where he'd kept his share, so she checked her calculations twice but they were all in order. Slowly she cleaned the tachometer he had saved from a Royal Enfield: she wiped the dust off the lid with her fingertip wrapped in a rag, then unscrewed the range adjustor and pulled off the glass cover. She polished the chrome bezel with all her might, rubbing in a frenzy. The drawstring bag sat at her feet, hiding the many blank notebooks with all their unwritten words. The story from the magazine was scrunched in a ball. 'I'm sorry, Mr Jackaroo,' she said. 'Today is not a happy day. We must work. We must focus.'

For the next five years, Maha rose each morning with her father and sat at his desk to count his carbon copies from the previous day. She checked the accounts in the logbooks, filed feedback from the bikies and researched their competitors in Fitzroy and Collingwood. Maha found the courage to walk the chop shop, learning every detail about the mechanical repairs. The Squad revered her, never disobeying, never slinging their bawdy jokes her way, never watching her body as she shuffled to and fro—a habit they trained whenever a woman peeked into the chop shop, or crossed Swanston Street smoking a cigarette, her hair draped over her sun-kissed shoulders. They never whistled when Maha bent under the lift to unplug the pneumatic hoses. They never slid a hand around her back to help her up the stairs. As the months passed, Maha ordered the Squad about like a footy coach, her face stuffed with lamingtons and Freddo Frogs, and soon the bikies lined the garage walls, hoping to glimpse the boss's daughter commanding her team of macho men. Her voice echoed the Australian accents of the customers. Her consonants shrank, her tone turned nasal and her subcontinental lilt faded. She spent ten years leading the chop shop, engrossed in the rhythms of the business, while her father disappeared for hours at a time. He left on the weekends, then during the week, never announcing his departure. She waited for some sign of his trust in her, some wish to bring her along, but he said nothing. He would not explain the red dust on his shoes, the sand on his hands or all the missing money. She tried to keep her bitterness in check, but she couldn't stop hounding him with her questions. 'Enough,' he would say. 'Other jobs is all. Must you be ungrateful? How to ensure our long-term success? But not for discussion, not to stress. Not in the knowhow for a little girl.'

Once, he was gone for an entire month. Maha asked the Squad, but they said they knew nothing. 'You're covering for him, aren't you?' she said, and they busied themselves in repairs. She was an adult, had he forgotten? She knew all about his finances, his schemes. And yet he wouldn't trust her: he treated her like a child. One day, in the laneway by the roller door, she found three enormous crates, sent by airmail from Mumbai, and beneath the layers of tape she found more notebooks, hundreds, their pages blank like the others, their covers humming beneath her touch. She wondered if he was involved in importing, if all their money had been squandered on some overseas scheme. 'Girl, what you doing out?' he said, hours later, dragging his tartan knapsack as he brushed by her on the road. But she grabbed him around the waist, hauling his bony body against the wall. While she had grown bigger than any man who set foot in the chop shop, he had shrunk and withered. His hair had thinned. His cheekbones bulged out of his skin. His eyes had sunk in deep, dark sockets. 'You're sick,' she said. 'You look ruined.' 'Work,' he said. 'Things in motion cannot stop.' 'But I'm your daughter. I ought to know what's become of my dad.' 'Let us not discuss that, not now.' 'What kind of man keeps silent for so long?' His eyes lolled left and right. His black lips curled and he said, 'Daughter, please, what a story is this. Have you lost your mind? You will lose it, see, impatient child. Don't go looking there.' His anger waned, and behind his eyes simmered all the exhaustion of a lifetime. Maha's mouth felt parched. She loosened her grip and he stumbled down the stairs. As she followed him into the chop shop, she realised that for so long she had revered the garage, beholding the tools and dismembered motorcycles as the icons of incredible men, but now she sensed the place was something else: a backstage, a crypt, a diorama of life, but not life itself. The workbenches had gathered dust, the hoses had lost their pressure, the yellow dazzle of the overalls had dwindled, replaced with oil and grease. 'Why can't you tell me what's going on, your own flesh and blood? If it's the tax you're worried about,' she said, 'I already know. And I don't give a shit.' 'Come now,' he said, 'back to work.' 'Well,' she said, 'your only daughter thinks your cowardice can't last forever. Stupid fool.' He turned, breathing heavily, his gaze dropping to his boots, and he said, 'Stupid is quite correct.' 'You've been so weak,' she said. 'For my whole life.' Then he said: 'Well, weak or not, this much is true…' He began to recount his life in Mumbai: the hope of an empire, the curfews of the Emergency, the doctor in the caravan, the baby in the rubble. Maha trembled as she listened. Her skin turned red and hot. The stairs swayed beneath her toes. 'I can tell you this much,' he said, pointing at his crotch. 'Indeed all scars heal, but nasbandi never fixes. This outsider, this nirvaasit, stays childless. No reverse operation. No real family. Daughter? Na. Father? Im-possible. You don't belong to me, nor to any weak man I have ever seen.'

He rubbed his jaw, panting half-breaths in the shadows. She retreated into the basement, wrapped her arms around her hips and sat in bed, rocking from side to side. Her bags of sweets tumbled off the mattress. Her bottles of soft drink rolled across the floor. Echoes of Somnath's revelation droned off the stone pillars around her. She was plain, unwanted, with no real parents she could blame for her misbegotten life, raised by a boy, a fool, who couldn't see past the money he made, obsessed with his endless odd jobs, so serious, see, that he denied his heart in the banal pursuit of more work. She slept in starts. In a dream, she found herself clutching his swollen head, and saw his eyes engorged, his chest inflated. Haunted by the vision, she heaved herself out of bed and found Somnath hunched over another issue of *Man's Tales from Near and Far*. 'You have to stay away from here,' she said. 'From me, from everything.' She carried him downstairs, away from the ageing props of the chop shop, where waited all number of possible accidents: an air hose could explode, a dodgy welder could electrocute, an angle-grinder could shatter and slit his throat. He sighed, so tired, it seemed, he couldn't argue any longer. 'Take your lunch from my treats,' she said, locking the door with a heavy chain. 'I'll see you later.' When the Squad arrived, they stopped their banter as soon as she appeared, working mutely in her shadow. The chop shop echoed with their repairs, the whirring and clattering that filled a normal day's work. The chilling aura of her dream faded. Her fear ebbed away. She remembered yesterday's delivery, the notebooks from Mumbai, and she hurried outside to bring them to Somnath, but the street was filled with tradesmen, measuring the kerb and the footpath, and the boxes were gone. 'Where are you?' she said, her voice muffled by the diggers and trucks. 'Why were you ever here at all?' Then she realised she could go on looking forever—for those boxes, for their money, for her real father. But what did it matter where she came from? She and Somnath had been together for more than thirty-four years, from one country to another, from hunger to happiness. Nothing needed to be revealed. The truth was here, if she could simply accept it. 'Let's break early,' she told the Squad. 'We'll see you tomorrow.' Then she went downstairs, unlocked the chain and opened the basement door. 'I'm sorry, Dad,' she said. 'I really am.' But the stools were on their side. The desk had tipped. The towers of books had toppled. Reams of paper were scattered across the floor. She stepped by the busted cabinet and over the broken glass on the cement. There, on his back by her bed, his bedsheets wrapped around his overalls, lay her father. His flesh had swollen from neck to ankle. The nails had fallen off his fingers. He held a sheet of paper to his chest. The Jackaroo. The words of the bastard fairytale began to blur. Death, just see, so incomprehensible, so untranslatable, and he gurgled on the floor. 'Come back here,' she said, cradling his head between her hands. 'Somnath Sunder Sonpate.' His breath paused on her forearms. His spit cooled on her thumbs. His eyes emptied, and whitened, like the blank space at the bottom of a page.

A copper came, holding his blue cap over his larynx, his bare forehead gleaming in the dark. He eased the overalls off her father's body and drew a sheet over his face. 'A big fat heart attack,' he said. 'Number-one killer. So many blokes just stress themselves to death.' Then he shone his torch at the toppled books, the broken glass, and along the thick scratches running up the walls. 'The poor guy was trapped,' he said, 'like a crab in a bucket. I'm surprised you didn't hear anything.' He kicked the bag of lollies and a bottle of Coke. 'Too much sugar, that'll get you. He must've been diabetic. Now, you alright to stay here?' She shrugged. 'You got anyone to chat to?' She tried to fit her hand in the scratches but her fingers were too big. 'Don't go eating away your blues or anything,' he said. 'I've never,' she said. 'Righty-o. Well, it's been a day of surprises, that's for sure. I didn't know this garage was still open. When Sergeant Philips gave me a buzz, I thought she was pulling my leg. We'd wondered if this was an underground den with some naughty ties, but you wouldn't have the wits to go wooing any crooks, would you, hun?' Another man arrived, a younger constable with a mullet and a pencil moustache. 'Good to see you, Stevo,' he said to the copper. 'Giving you the chop-out, aren't I?' He unpacked a trolley and heaved the body onto the tray. 'Let me tell you about the last time I saw this constable,' said the copper, strapping three Velcro cords across the corpse. 'He was gacked off his head at a disco in Coogee Beach, swinging his Toohey's singlet around his head, bopping about to Kylie Minogue.' 'I know a boogie or two, that's for sure,' said the constable, and together they hefted the trolley up the narrow stairwell. 'Take care of yourself, hun,' said the copper, waving from across the street. 'You got anything to eat that ain't all sugar?'

Maha took the overalls and hung them in the wardrobe. Then she curled on the floor where her father's body had lain. The size of her sorrow darkened her shadow on the wall. She pulled his Zippo from his knapsack, twirled the lighter around her fist and yanked a single strand of hair out of her scalp. She set it alight. Then she pulled another. And another. On and on, her scalp shining under her hand, filling the basement with acrid smoke, until nine the next morning when she opened the chop shop to find the footpath streaming with men in hardhats and orange fluoro vests. Leaving the Zippo in the gutter, she watched the cement diggers trailing to Swanston Street. Rows of squat rubber cones stopped the cars from driving up Degraves Street. The laneways were fenced off. The entire thoroughfare was blocked. The telephone rang and she held it to her ear as a jackhammer started boring into the earth. 'The pigs are redoing the tramline,' said Angus, 'and stopping all vehicles from going north or south, even bikes. We can't drive up anymore. You two doing okay down there?' She ended the call before she could admit the news about her father. Five minutes later, Christos rang. 'We won't be getting through any time soon. Or ever again, darl. Seems like they're saving Swanston for trams only and Degraves for pedestrians. The dumb old mayor wants an engine-free CBD.' It was true, read Maha, as she leafed through yesterday's *Herald Sun* in the recycling bin. There, on the front page, glowed an artist's rendering of the future neighbourhood. No cars. No motorcycles. Only pedestrians, bicycles and restaurants. Bubble tea. Burritos. Ramen soup. It had been planned for years but they had not, for a single moment, thought to listen to the city outside the chop shop. She tried for a week to keep the place running, but it was useless. The bikies, though passionate, couldn't make a public protest.

The enthusiasts, though wealthy, wanted only good service and convenience. And the Squad, though mourning her father's death, had to make their living elsewhere, in the outer suburbs, where the old garages were relocating to new warehouses. By Friday, the chop shop was dead, like a dog that had trailed its master into his grave. Maha closed the roller door, tramped over the squandered screws, around the tools hanging from the corkboard fixtures, between the bodies of bygone motorcycles, past her mouldy library, and down, down, to her basement bedroom.

A Caterpillar digger blocked the window. Layers of dust covered the glass. The droning of jackhammers filled the basement. Without sunlight, the line between night and day disappeared. Time began to unravel. The stars slipped from the sky and her mind became suspended, directionless, like an ant trapped in a drop of oil. Sometimes Christos would call, asking again if her father had left her any money. 'I told you there's nothing here,' she said. 'Of all his hundreds of thousands of dollars, not a cent.' 'We're worried about you,' he said. 'How you going to get by?' The bikies sent her fifty dollars every week and subscribed her to a grocery service. Boxes of beef jerky piled by the entrance to the laneway. In the darkness of the basement, as her thoughts reached through the decades to grasp the past, she imagined her father in his Bombay, a young man with the hopes of his own empire. She found a sheaf of papers, pulled a pen from the drawer and wrote: 'All those years ago, in that sweltering city by the sea, Somnath Sunder Sonpate leaned against a bullock cart, scratching his nipples, which had turned red, as of recently, with an itchy rash.' She imagined his motorcycle maintenance, his care for Preeti, and his fateful nasbandi. He was seventeen, an apprentice of the Queen's English, and his singsong sentences echoed in the basement as she read them aloud. She let him have his own magic. She saw him at the peak of his loss, when he discovered a baby born of a miracle. For the first time in her life, having held Somnath on this cramped page, she understood him: all the years of reticence were his way to forget the dream he had lost in Bombay. As Maha leafed through the pages, she felt the charm of the magic that was his alone, of the impossible beauty of a life not her own, of the brevity of his human form. As she read, each rolling sentence was embraced by stillness. Each scene came and went along an indivisible thread. One day the garage teemed with patrons, the next it was abandoned. One day there were revving engines and squeaking pistons, boyish jokes and bitter arguments, the next there was silence. One day her father tallied his savings and tapped his slippers, the next he was a chunk of flesh on the constable's gurney, his heart worn out from years of tension, awaiting his rebirth. Maha lay on her back and stretched her hands over the concrete. She felt the ligaments tighten in her palm and a gap spread under her fingernails as they split from the cuticles. She listened to the street and heard dinging bike bells and stamping feet. She breathed, and with as little notice as they arrived, the noises passed. She focused on the veins beating at the top of her wrist, holding and releasing heat, accumulating and renouncing power. Every sensation awaited degeneration. Here, gone. She rolled onto her side, plunging her wrists between her thighs. 'Here, gone,' she said. 'Here, gone.'

Waking from a week-long slumber, she crawled to the window by Swanston Street. It was midnight. The streetlights shone like stars along the footpaths. Crates of bricks were lined along the road. Mounds of smashed concrete cornered the trucks and utes. A fruit bat hung from the tram wires, twitching beneath its curled wings, longing for the streets beyond the city. She knew it was her father, born again into his next form, ever eager to be elsewhere, and she found herself listening to the fruit bat's story, understanding it from within, seeing all its pasts and futures in one moment. She saw cement offices, gilded railings weathered by decades of rain, rooftops crowded with Melburnians clutching wine glasses and beer bottles, and suburban backyards lit by fairy lights and fire pits. She felt the wind wisping through chestnut fur and flapping between a pair of leathery wings. She sensed the longing for the eucalypts in the Botanical Gardens and heard the twittering of the other bats in the treetops. Her mind held this divine insight: just as water contained all forms, hail, rain and fog, so too did each living being hold every state inside, from birth to death to rebirth. She opened her eyes and the bat swung on the tram wires. Then it arced southeast, between telephone lines, above rooftops, over Federation Square and towards its nest in the Botanical Gardens. Certainly, her father had been reborn. He had been rewritten into a new form for the next story. She knelt by the window with her breath racing, cloaked in the infinite sensations of her body: her pulse cooing in her wrist, her breath swooping over her lips, her hair bristling against the muslin sheet. She could know the bat in every stage of being. She could see it from the inside. As she beheld her divine power, tears hung from her human face. Slowly her mind settled. She slept.

Spurred by her discovery, Maha listened to the story of every living animal outside her window. She heard the histories of pigeons, rats and dogs, and every evening, without fail, she listened to the fruit bat clinging to the tram wire and traced its past and future between skyscrapers, over gushing creeks and across dry, parched fields. All the city's incarnations waited to be heard. After a year, the construction ended and the trams trundled up Swanston Street, spooking the critters from her window, so she left the chop shop and walked through the city, listening to them for miles. As the commuter crowds parted at her approach, she wondered if the god dreamed the people, or the people dreamed the god. In the months to come, hundreds of pairs of shoes paraded by her window: sneakers with crisscrossed webbing, stilettos with delicate gold clasps, sandals in the summer, boots in the winter cold. She looked for them on her morning walks, but their presence was so fleeting she caught only scenes of their stories—dashing to sausage sizzles at community halls, singing at birthday parties in suburban karaoke lounges, waiting outside the cinema at *Star Wars* premieres. But one afternoon, she noticed a pair of dusty feet paused outside her window, scuffed and bruised, toenails painted red, yellow and indigo, and she scrambled outside to find a young man. Instantly, she glimpsed his past: a weatherboard house in Footscray, a rusted basketball ring in the driveway, a man hurling thick textbooks across a living room, a fist on a cheek, a shattered tooth. 'You think I come to Australia to raise a poofta?' And a scramble through broken glass, up the Metro overpass, to await the Flinders Street express. A runaway. Then the young man bounded onto a tram, leaving her alone with her kaleidoscopic vision. The next day, a woman sat at the tram stop, clutching a torn envelope to her chest, combing her lustrous black hair as it noosed around her neck, and Maha saw a hair salon in Oakleigh, a bathroom stall covered in bile and blood, a grim stare from a doctor, a receptionist printing a report. Without turning her eyes from the window, Maha scribbled on a scrap of paper, ensuring that no matter the pain or the shame of the stories, she told them with all honesty. With her divine insight, she could listen to the Melburnians, comforting them through the cycles of life. She hurried out of the chop shop and up to the State Library, where she narrated the stories to a librarian, who typed them into a computer. First, she recounted her father's story, then she drafted the other urban murmurings: Vicki, who had been diagnosed with breast cancer, and Taz, who was homeless after his father found a love letter from another boy. 'You are not unknowable,' she wrote. 'I'm listening. I'll save your stories. I'll hold them forever, despite your here-gone lives.' She spellchecked the librarian's typing, wrote the address of the chop shop in the top right corner and printed fifteen hundred copies on purple paper. She slipped the flyers under the windscreen wipers of the cars parked on Bourke Street, folded them over the handlebars of the bicycles outside the Town Hall, jammed them in the mailboxes of the apartment blocks, and climbed the steps of Flinders Street Station. The clocks ticked over her shoulder, all these years since her first morning in Melbourne. She unbound her adverts. 'Mother Pulse,' they read. 'Your Lifelong Listener & Subterranean Storyteller.' She thrust her pages at the commuters, sheet after sheet until sunset, when her calves ached and the wind scattered the pages over the road. She hoped the stories would inspire, that more Melburnians would reveal their innermost quandaries, that she could preserve their lives before they ended, and that, like her, they would be free.

One misty morning, months after her visit to the State Library, Maha opened the garage door to find a letter on the hessian doormat. The chop shop address was written in flowing, cursive handwriting and a cricket stamp shone in the top right corner of the envelope. 'Dear Mama Pulse,' the letter began. 'Mark says I'm stronger than I've ever been—When the diagnosis came my way I was flabbergasted—It's not something you want to hear on your thirty-sixth birthday—but we've got a grouse solo ward in the Royal Women's Hospital—Nurses are very kind—very tactful—very graceful—There's even a view of the zoo, would you believe it?—Mark jokes that I look like Peter Garrett without my hair—but I'm radiant—I just close my eyes and look deep inside—I'm stronger now because I just get it—You know?—It's exactly as you wrote—Here, gone—All my love, Vicki.' Maha stepped out of the chop shop but the laneway was deserted. The cobblestones were clear and the boxes of beef jerky had not been moved. She read the note over. The handwriting was unlike any she had ever seen. The next day, lying on the doormat, was another letter, even longer than the first. 'Dear Mummy P,' it read. 'Today was actually Mum's birthday. I thought I should come home, say hello and all, give her a hug. Dad was there but he kept his hands off me. He wouldn't say a word or even look at me, actually. Stuck with speaking Viet the whole afternoon. So things are better in life if you accept your limitations. I agree. I mean, can you imagine me out there all night hustling with the St Kilda queens? I've still got the rest of VCE to worry about, uni after that, a career ahead of me. Better to bite the bullet. Stay home. Stay straight. Wear a mask if it means I can have what I want in the long term. You can't hide from Father in the moonlight. But I'm trying not to worry myself. I like sleeping early and waking up with the sun. Can't do that when you're turning tricks for your next pillow. So really, Mummy P, I just want to say thank you for listening when no one else would. Taz.' She searched the envelope but the sides were blank, just a pair of London Olympic stamps in the top corner. She stood in the laneway and called out to the postman with his sack of mail. He looked her over, scanned the back of the envelopes and said, 'These look legit to me. You got a stalker or something?' She hurried to the State Library and found the librarian to transcribe her words into the computer. 'Dear degenerates,' she said. 'Do not stop telling your stories. You are not alone. You have been heard.' Maha spread the purple flyers across the city by the thousands. Then she limped back to the chop shop, rereading the letters from Vicki and Taz, marvelling at these messages from her fellow Melburnians.

Other stories came, more than she could count, written on the back of napkins, scrunched sheets of newspaper and flattened paper bags. With her insight, she could see them more clearly than they could see themselves. More people were writing to her than she had ever met in her human life. They disclosed their hidden pregnancies, their unloved children, their addictions and depression. When Vicki wrote again, Maha rushed to open the letter. 'I'd already made my peace, you know?—said goodbye to Mark—to his parents—to the girls at the salon—and what would you know?—I've turned a corner—The full one-eighty—The onco couldn't believe his eyes—Remission, it's called—So I'm back, Mama—Did I tell you Mark's working a second contract at Coles as an IT technician?—He's been really stellar through it all—sold his Corvette, too—to get money for my chemo—So I'm going to pay it back to him—I'll start tonight—I'll do anything for him—get the house in order—mop upstairs and down—vacuum the sofa—iron his shirts—do a big beef roast—my appetite's not quite right so he'll have it all to himself—Absolutely anything, Mama—You hear me?' And the next day another letter slipped through the chute and onto the mat. 'I topped my cohort for the Eco exam. For Psych, too. And even Latin, which surprised everyone. Who would have thought some Viet boy would whoop their white tushes? I write a blog to vent. Gets things off my chest. And I'm on Reddit, too, because I'm curious. TightyWhiteyAzn94 (M18). Guys will pay for the silliest things online, Mummy P. Euros. Swiss Francs. US Dollars. Look me up? It can be our little secret! xx Taz.' Maha piled the letters beside her bed, running her hands over the pages, these budding verses of her own scripture. The basement filled with stories from her hundreds of degenerates. More letters arrived over the years, though Vicki's

49

handwriting began to slant, as if she were writing with her eyes closed. 'I was at home—dusting Mark's PC—and I found some emails from some bimbo he knew before we met—she's back—and she's got a set of jugs, let me tell you—but I can't be mad—I can't—It's not his fault he's married to a bag of bones who's as dry as sandpaper?—I'll strive?—I'll strive—If I can fix the house I can fix myself—hot yoga classes—hair replacements—I'm confused, so I'm writing—but that's only natural, hey? Yours, Vicki.' 'I'm in a tough spot, Mummy P,' wrote Taz. 'So I've finally finished my degree, nailed the exams and found a clerkship at Allens. But I can't move out. Not by myself. It would break Mum's heart. Dad won't say anything so long as I'm working. Keeping my head down. My toenails clean. There's this friend of mine, Joanna. Totally lovely. A white girl, a sweetheart. She doesn't know the truth so I could move out with her. Play the dating-game. I've asked people online and they say it happens all the time. It's not NYC where you can come out at Whole Foods. TightyWhiteyAzn94 (M23) is actually more of a celebrity for it. Would love to hear your thoughts, Taz xx.' The piles of letters grew so tall they touched the ceiling. She would lose herself in them. Their stories were more expansive than any single thought of her own. She spread the pages across her bed and used the tachometer for a paperweight. 'Dear degenerates,' she wrote. 'I have been listening to your voices for all these years. No matter your ailment, I'll be here. No matter what you write, I'll read it.' After delivering more flyers, she limped over the cobblestones on Degraves Street, gasped down the stairwell to the basement and exhaled over the grime on the window. Her feet ached; they felt brittle to the bone as she cocooned herself in her bedsheets. She slept through the mail delivery and into the evening, dozing through the day and into another night. And then came a thunderous rapping on the chop shop door. Maha sat up in the dark, clutching the corner of a workbench.

More raps: one-two, three-four. 'Mother Pulse?' The voice was hoarse. She hurried through the garage, wincing in the dark, and pressed her ear to the roller door. Short, sharp whimpers. One-two, three-four. She unlatched the door. A figure crept towards her, shimmering in the rain and the fog. 'Mother Pulse?' he said. He was a teenager, his sallow olive skin slick with sweat, his sunken brown eyes shining in his skull, his forearms covered in crimson scratches. He leaned against the bricks, clutching a purple flyer in his fist. 'Sorry to bother you, yeah,' he said. 'I don't know if you're taking walk-ins. Or if you'd even want to chat to a rando.' The wind whirled up the laneway, whipping his breath across her face. 'My name's Titch, yeah. Where should I start?'

Grog

'S WAKE HAD ALREADY STARTED when Titch arrived at the house. The flyscreen door was locked, but he could hear the visitors in the living room and didn't ring the doorbell in case it botched the mood. Instead, he crept down the garden path, hopped the side fence and snuck through the laundry window, spilling a bucket of soapsuds in the sink. He found the guests watching the early-season footy on the telly, as Delta,   's mum, fussed over the napkins on the table. The visitors circled between the couches and the dining room, pecking at the Doritos or Hawaiian pizza or the cauliflower casserole in the kitchenette. Their chitter-chatter lulled, punctuated by the pip-pip of the umpire's whistle and the calls of the commentators: 'Riewoldt. Crumbs it. He spins around the body—and what a start to this top-of-the-ladder clash!' The priest from St Anthony's stopped by at half-time for the sausage rolls from the oven. 'We won't be discussing this anymore, Deltaphena,' he said, sliding Delta's hand off his shoulder, avoiding her wet, grey eyes, which gleamed like rocks at the bottom of a creek. 'The parish has rules to follow. Standards to keep. And the fanfare you have here seems adequate enough,' he said. The visitors had come from as far as Dandenong and Donny Brook and even Western Australia. One aunt had caught the V-Line from Geelong that morning. The boys from Melbourne High wore their old green-and-maroon ties, slinging them over their shoulders as they cradled plates of spinach pie. 'We have any more grog?' said Bruce,   's dad, looming over the fridge with one arm stretched from the freezer to the ice dispenser, his heavy body twisting under the halogens. 'Surely we've got some more grog in this joint,' he said, jostling the tray of party-pies. 'We're the entertainers, right? We're the hosts.' As Titch slipped into   's bedroom, the old schoolmates stepped

55

aside, their chitchat caught in their throats, only looking at him if he didn't look back. A crumpled cardboard box from Myer sat on the bed, its flaps covered in looping black texta. 'Krismas Tekarashuns,' it said. Inside the box were hundreds of yellow-and-black Richmond flags, each with a tiger's head stitched in the corner.   's desk was bare but for his keys and his maroon wallet. Salvaged, yeah, and Titch held the wallet in his hand; it was heavy, like a waterlogged heart. A keepsake? 'Cheers,' he said, hiding it inside his back pocket. On the telly in the living room, the Tigers had capitulated. Sixty-eight points behind. 'Uh-oh,' said the commentator. 'Dropped mark. Lynch spins it around—party time for the Crows!' It was the last quarter, and   's godmother, a social worker from Perth, scuffled over to Titch, jangling a necklace of purple beads between her fingers. 'Are we really watching this right now?' she said. 'A couple of wins—the hype builds—they think it's their year. But seriously—Richmond? A team of spuds. How long's it been since they won a granny? Forty years? There's your unrequited love. They're hacks.' The Crows leapt further ahead, kicking four unanswered goals, and she stopped her lecture when the final siren sounded and the Tigers collapsed on the turf. 'Seventy-six points in the hole, Tiger fans,' said the commentator. 'Thought you had something going,' she said to the telly, 'but don't believe the hype.' Bruce untangled Titch from her necklace, wrapping the beads around his knuckles. 'Don't listen to her,' he said, 'don't listen to a bloody word the bloody downer bloody well says.' Titch buried his fists in his back pockets, fondling the wallet. He scanned the room and noticed the other guests were standing apart, keeping their hands to themselves. Clenching mobile phones. Massaging knuckles. Picking at callouses. Crumpling paper plates. The hush-hush was easier, like leaning against the rack after a long set of squats, and the guests had stopped their chitchat and someone had muted the TV, so all the high-fives and bum taps and interviews with the Crows players screened in silence, and nothing ruptured the film of quiet, lain over the house like a thick doona, until Bruce moaned in the hallway and said, 'I've bloody well lost the plot,' and munted on the rug. 'Classic,' said   's godmother, clutching her glass of sherry. 'Shit-faced and piss-drunk.' 'Cold beer and shame make for a chilly soul,' said the priest, rubbing the silver ring on his littlest finger. By now it was past nine-thirty. The footy was over. The Tigers were done and dusted. Sensing the rising silence in the house, the old schoolmates left to Hungry Jack's for Whoppers and soft-serve cones.   's cousins followed, eyes glazed, hair askew, dragging their parents down the garden path by the Richmond flags strung around the lemon tree, reaching their cars, where they fumbled their keys into the ignition. Titch wandered into the hallway, his back to the wall, holding a ream of paper towels from above the fridge. 'Give it here, mate,' said Bruce, ripping the towels in squares and laying them on the carpet. They turned orange, stinking of Doritos and curdled Carlton Draught. 'She'll be right,' said Bruce.

'I never reckoned you could fit so many peeps at your place,' typed Titch, tramping to the Deakin Uni dorms with his mobile glaring in his palm, 'but Delta found a way to make it happen, didn't she? TBD.' The grass was wet and the dandelions shot up from the dirt on stiff, corded stems. Inside the dorm lift was a poster for the Christian Fellowship. Another for the campus socialists. And, the biggest, for Deakin's 2017 Think Tank Challenge. 'Supported by Pronto Software,' it read, 'to find the best ideas for the biggest industry.' Titch turned back to his mobile and cycled through his home screen—blank now, after he'd deleted Facebook, Instagram, Snapchat, his photo albums and even   's contact. Couldn't have his name around, nah. Couldn't leave those little letters looking back at him. But still Titch knew his number off by heart. He stepped out of the lift, his shadow splitting off the posters as he shuffled into the corridor. In his room, he lit the two red candles on his bookshelf and slipped the money from   's wallet onto his desk, leaving the papers in the pouch without sussing them. He counted the cash. Five hundred bucks all up. 'How many do you reckon showed?' he typed. 'Pretty crowded, yeah? TBD.' He unwound his school tie, snaked it over his desk chair and dropped his rubber Casio watch in the shoebox beside his bed. 'Maybe thirty?' he typed. 'Thirty-five? TBD.' He sat in his undies, curled over the mattress, lit by the phantom flare of his phone. And then he started shaking, his chest heaving, his hips bucking, as if he was hatching from the seam of his Bonds. He clenched his mobile and pressed it to his nose, washing an otherworldly hue over his eyelids.

The pain turned the world into a screenshot. Sometimes, yeah, waiting for the bus with the whoosh of passing trucks on Burwood Highway, a whole hour would pass, Titch's body filling with static from his shoulders to his hips to the bunions on his toes. Then maybe a van would blare down the road, or a lorikeet might zip between the gum trees in the park, and he would realise he was thinking nothing, doing nothing, becoming nothing.   was done, mate. Had jumped on the tracks at Huntingdale Station. Had live-streamed it on Facebook. And yet out here the profs still held their lectures, the bus still ran fifteen minutes late, the girls still ambled to their netball practice and the uni kids still split their bongs on the Deakin lawns. It was worse in the mornings, when Titch reached for his mobile, thinking to arrange a session in the gym, only to recall that   was gone. Wasn't going to happen, mate. Titch spent his days in bed, replaying the last frames of the video. The blurry mop of   's hair. The lopsided grimace as he talked into the camera. 'I just need a break.' One step past the Myki reader. 'I hope you all get to see what you've been waiting for.' Another across the yellow line. 'I'm sorry, Mum. I am. But it'll be easy without all my mess, won't it?' And his jump over the platform edge as the train squealed down the tracks. Titch would scramble awake, run down the tiled corridor, by all the locked doors of the other dorms, and crawl under the ice-cold shower, huffing and gasping to get his body moving. But so often, as he strode from the shower, drying the ridges of his back, there came the murmuring memories. That summer afternoon when   wrote up his goals on a sheet of butcher's paper. So many specifics, so many outlines, written and worshipped like they were the means to become someone. But now, yeah, weren't all those plans really a farce? And so Titch dropped his towel and that fucking Facebook video appeared again, and he saw   downing those six Carlton Draughts and that half-bottle of Smirnoff, saw him staggering the ten steps by the purple graffiti and the Rainbow Serpent Festival posters. It made Titch ill. He curled by the bin. Munted up his Maggi noodles, the bile stinging his throat and tongue and teeth. The pain stained everything. Then he was asleep, snoozing through his uni lectures, waking in his dorm as the setting sun streaked through the window. He couldn't get the video off the inside of his eyelids. He was consumed by his own mind, like a yellow-bellied black snake eating itself. Seeing or sleeping, which was shittier? Ctrl + Alt + Prt Scr. But sleeping's uncontrollable, mate. Ctrl + Alt + Prt Scr. Titch was in the screenshot and couldn't slip out.

One day he woke in a uni lecture, his chin slumped in his hand, as the business-management prof fiddled at the lectern. Titch tried to read the PowerPoint but the fonts had melted off the slides. When he looked at his notebook, his handwriting had blurred. 'Second week's assignment,' Titch read aloud. 'Read Sir Richard Branson's *Losing My Virginity*. Explain how he capitalised on the London Stock Market crash in the late eighties and how this informed his entrepreneurship.' The girl beside him woke with a fright and edged sideways in her seat. The blokes to his left guffawed behind their tartan folders. 'Boy oh boy,' said a lad with his Nikes up on the seats, 'we've got a brainiac over here.' 'If you have any questions,' said the prof, 'please email me after the lecture.' Titch grabbed his books and his single green banana and paced out of the hall. In the courtyard, as he stood by two girls smoking darts, he reloaded his mobile. But there was only an email from his ex-father. 'Stationed in the middle of fuck-all,' it started. A mass-mail, multiple recipients. 'Just wanted to keep you folks clued in on what's going on in my ambitious life. Making bank out here. Not dead. Cheers.' His ex-father was a miner who worked in Western Australia. Titch had never met him in person. Cheers, yeah. The last time they spoke was around his high-school graduation, when his ex-father wrote to ask if Titch would join him in the Kalgoorlie mines. 'Without that spastic mother holding you back now, you can really make something of yourself.' 'Nah,' Titch wrote, 'I'm going to uni.' His ex-father called and said, 'No boy of mine is going to dick around at uni. Pull your finger out. You're going to get a job and get your own dosh. You're already sixteen, mate.' But   told Titch to apply anyway and, although his marks weren't too flash, he was accepted into the Bachelor of Commerce at Deakin University, with a special provisions scholarship for a free dorm. That was ten weeks ago. Or twelve. Maybe longer. Titch offed his mobile and walked away to Sette Bello, the Italian restaurant in Glenny with the Croatian waiters, and snuck into the toilet to take a whiz. He flushed the loo, eyeing the water gushing over the bowl. He flushed again, and again, trying to drain the water before it refilled. Might've stood there for ten minutes. If he could just turn the tide, yeah, everything would be alright. Smile for once. He stopped flushing when he noticed a gold wristwatch on the soap dispenser. Might be a waiter's. But pretty snazzy, yeah. So he clunked it in his backpack and ran out of the restaurant.

He was born Titch Antoine Clement but the only guy who heard his middle name was   , five years earlier when they met at Melbourne High. Back then, Titch Antoine Clement was the skinniest boy in the Southern Hemisphere. He could sneak up behind Mum in her yoga poses without the floorboards creaking in the flat. He could squeeze his arms and legs together, exhale the air from his chest and fit inside Mum's Dune London suitcases. He could hide in the budgie cage and in the porcelain dollhouse she kept for the tabbies and the Bengals. Once, after she'd spent a fortune on her Serenace prescription, Mum told him to sneak into Pet World on Clayton Road for some cans of tuna, so he sidled through the scaffolding outside Coles and returned after twenty minutes with a box of cans, a pair of milk droppers and a calendar of Australia's Most Famous Hermit Crabs. Titch was a pipsqueak. A little lad. 'Twiggy Titch,' said Mum every morning, when she woke him with a cuddle, tickling his chin with her short black hair to make him giggle. 'Twiggy Titch,' she called through the flat on his second day at Melbourne High, as she packed his favourite celery sticks in his schoolbag. 'Wherever is my Twiggy Titch?' She had no idea that the school was so grim. Stern, ashen faces loomed out of heavy picture frames along the walls of every corridor. The teachers were gruff and darkly sarcastic. Seniors in black blazers cackled as they thrust Year Nines into lockers or yanked the tags off their school ties. Melbourne High was a selective school. All boys. The kids could come from poor families, but they had to be nerdy to study in glitzy South Yarra without paying a cent. Titch fudged the entrance exam by copying the multiple-choice answers from Jasjit, the boy sitting next to him. Somehow he got in, and by day two Mum had to coax Titch out from behind the bookshelf. 'I know you're a year younger than all the others, but you're saving us a lot of money,' she said, 'and you've got nothing to be ashamed of. You are who you are. Your friends should know how lovely you can be.' An hour later, his new classmates spotted his pencil case labelled with 'Twiggy Titch.' 'That's a name for dick-lickers,' said one boy. 'Why you like that?' said another. 'Because you're anorexic, or what?' Like an eggy fart, the name spread round the schoolyard and couldn't be avoided. That kid who snuck between the canteen turnstiles without the mums noticing? Twiggy Titch. That kid with the baggy, oversized blazer? Twiggy Titch. That kid who took the PE tests with everyone but who wouldn't tell his BMI to anyone? Twiggy Titch. Two weeks into the year, Titch found himself summoned to the pool in a pair of purple Speedos, the silhouette of his tiny rig reflected on the water. 'You'd better be up and about, gents,' said Presto, who ran the annual swimming test, who ignored the note from Mum saying Titch was a committed vegan who shouldn't over-exert himself. Seniors rimmed the pool deck, shirts off after rowing conditioning, stretching over the seats as they waited for the trials to wrap up. Their bodies glowed in the gloom. Titch could see them, all of them, yeah, they didn't have anything to hide. The rippling veins up their calves and their quads. Their broad butterfly backs. Their corded forearms. All the bones of their boyhoods buried under their supple muscle. 'You listening, Twiggy Titch?' said Presto, and Titch stepped over to the shallow end, fixing his gaze on the depths of the pool. 'Don't give me a pin drop. This end to the other. Make it happen, mate.' A whistle shrieked. Titch fell into the pool and was glued, for a second, to the stinging surface, his lungs howling, before sucking up a mouthful of water. The seniors whooped from their seats. Presto waded through the lanes and yanked him out. 'No fat, no muscle. You're just a bag of bones going straight to the bottom,' he said. 'You got to *eat*, Titch.' At morning tea, they told him he'd have to attend remedial swimming classes, and so, feeling pretty lousy about it at lunchtime, Titch scoffed three bags of French fries from the canteen, snuck into the PE wing and dumped a two-kilo turd on the scales outside Joey Presto's office. A week later, after the first swimming lesson, Titch sat gasping on the seats around the pool, his orange life vest unbuckled at his hips, chlorinated water dripping down his legs, when to his right a real heifer of a human took a seat. He was so tubby the bench buckled under his bum. His curly brown hair clung to his cheeks. He had pimples inside his thighs. 'Who are you?' said Titch. '   ,' he said. 'That's S-k-e-*a*-t-e-r. Dad says I should start spelling it out. What about you?' Titch sat up straight, puffed out his chest and said, 'Titch Antoine Clement. Pleased to meet you.' '*Antoine?* We'll need to do something about that, Monsieur Fancy,' said   , covering his man-tits with his hands. '*Titch Antoine Clement.* Trying saying that ten times quick, hey? Bit of a mouthful.'

At first, Titch was always on the lookout for   . He waved at him across the aisle during junior assembly, copied his timetable from his locker door, and raced to the gates before the last bell so he could bump into him leaving school. Titch always perked up whenever   called 'Titch Antoine Clement' in his make-believe fancy voice. Soon enough, yeah, Titch knew where he'd be at every minute of the day, and together they shared the shyness of their bodies, the shame of hiding a waste-of-space beneath their blazers. Friends, yeah, in the beginning. Together they paddled through the pool during their remedial lessons. Together they squelched up the stairs to their different form groups, parting at the third floor with a hug and a half-smile. At recess, they walked by the hockey pavilion and the science labs, their hair still stiff with chlorine, and invented ploys to prank Presto, who still asked Titch if he'd eaten breakfast when they passed in the corridor. For Titch, who spent every night doing his alge-bra homework next to Mum as she trawled the *Age* for doggy-adoption listings, meeting   was like discovering a new part of his brain.

       didn't fill the air with chitchat. He didn't mope. He wasn't all doom and gloom about Melbourne. He ate meat—and a lot of it. 'What we're doing now will set us up forever,' he said one day, passing some chicken wings to Titch. 'If we learn a bit of discipline, a bit of ambition, we'll go pretty far, don't you think?' Not once had Titch ever thought about greatness.   taught him to be a better Melbourne High boy. At lunch they picked up abandoned bottles and threw them in the recycling dumpster. They carried lined diaries to their classes and made careful lists of all their homework. At the end of term, they drafted thank-you notes for their teachers.   learned these rituals from his father. Bruce had graduated from Melbourne High thirty years earlier, and now he asked   every night what he had accomplished for the day. Two months later, after they both aced the final swimming test, they trudged from the locker rooms, their shirts sopping against their backs, and   said, 'So what's next for the two of us?' 'Maybe we can learn the butterfly,' said Titch. 'I have a different idea,' said   . 'Why don't we try the weights?' And to Titch, this was mint: he needed a reason to keep getting up early or Mum would start asking him to make tofu scrambles and oatmeal pancakes, and grind her Clopixol into her almond-milk chai. She still called him 'Twiggy Titch' even after he'd eaten proper hearty food for a whole term, still sceptical about calorie deficits and catabolic states. He and   started on the weights the very next morning, wandering into the gym behind Melbourne High, squirming under the bare twenty-kilo barbell at the bench press. They trained at seven a.m. before the floor filled with seniors in micro tank-tops and EDM bangers with thudding baselines. Steve Aoki. Moguai. Timmy Trumpet. They met Niki, the receptionist. She said baby boys got big and real men got strong and showed them the form for Romanian deadlifts. One week passed, and another, and Titch's lifts began to improve—only the smallest gains at first, ten kilos on the squat, five on the bench, but consistently, because it was all he cared about now. Titch's diary filled with pencilled training regimes and he kept a container of whey protein hidden in his backpack. One day, he told   , he would bench-press a hundred kilos, two plates on either side; it would be his finest and strongest achievement. Titch's shoulders widened and his bum pressed against his waistband, wobbling above his lean, feline legs, and   lost his man-tits, his gut and the flab around his ankles. At home one night, Mum crept into Titch's bedroom, her fingers clawing her throat, and said, 'I always worried about sending you to that school. But money was tight, my hand was forced. And now my son is a prince of the boys' club, just another man who makes his castles in the sky, another brute who'll run away. Why can't you stay with us, where you ought to?' He didn't see how sad she was, so he closed his door, too tired to clean the goldfish tank or even have a wank. Every second when they weren't training, they were recovering. There was never an easy day. Never a kickback. 'We can picture every exercise as a trial,' said   . 'Part of an accumulation.' They hungered for that extra one-second lockout, for that extra angle of depth in the squat, for every gasp towards passing out. Titch was addicted. He liked the moment after a rep when his vision went dark, or he ripped a callous, or his fingers twitched after dropping the bar.

          was even hungrier. Once he burst a blood vessel in his eye during a squat. Once his nose bled during a stretch. Once he shat his undies in a deadlift and had to finish the session with his bare tush glistening in the downlights. 'The body dwindles, the rig burns,' he would say, collapsing across Titch's lap after a front-squat and yelling over the beat of the Avicii. 'The body dwindles, the rig burns.' It was their mantra. They scrawled it on the back of their English Lit notebooks and signed off their texts with 'TBD' and 'TRB.'
changed his Facebook name to 'Body Dwindles' and Titch switched his to 'Rig Burns.' They started swapping their T-shirts and socks back and forth, and despite the long lines of Titch's shins, the sharpness of his elbows and the boniness of his knees, he could lift far more than anyone thought. 'Titch don't need no exams,' said   . 'He don't need no homework. When he's strong enough, he'll have whatever in the world he wants.'

Then one Saturday while Titch was out, Mum found some chicken bones in his backpack. The whey, too. She left a stream of voicemails. 'We're unsafe here,' she said. 'I'd never seen it until now.' At home, a tabby slunk over his shoes, but when Titch reached to stroke its back, the cat ran away. 'How can you love someone and never know all of them?' she said. 'I've raised a Viking. You could never be just my son, could you? Never just *mine*?' Her eyes darted over his bedroom, his backpack, his growing shoulders. She rocked against the shelves, the walls. He'd never seen her have a breakdown. No idea what to do, yeah, so he called triple-zero. A cop came and sussed the flat with a doc and asked if Titch knew his mum was paranoid-schizophrenic. 'Usually comes out as a teen,' said the doc, 'so I'm surprised it waited so long. You ever seen this in your grandparents?' 'Let me ask them,' said Titch, whistling for the tabbies. 'That's enough, mate. Where's your old man?' said the cop. Titch gave them his ex-father's mobile number, and the two men spoke on the phone, umm-ing and ah-ing, a few scribbles on a beige notebook as the froglets moaned in the aquarium. 'So it seems she has a history,' said the cop. 'You familiar with this, kiddo?' 'She was always bonkers,' said his ex-father on speakerphone. 'It's in her blood.' 'Titch?' said the cop. 'She just needs to keep her friends around her,' said Titch. 'There's not much we can do unless we treat her first,' said the doctor. 'No use,' said his ex-father. 'She's a nutter.' 'What has she taken?' said the doctor. 'Everything under the sun,' said his ex-father. 'Titch?' 'I can find the prescriptions. I just give her what she tells me to.' 'Has she ever considered ECT?' 'Nah, what's that?' said Titch. 'Electroconvulsive therapy,' said the doctor. And that night,   told Titch to bring his schoolbag and lifting belt to his place. Titch finally met Bruce, who dug the air mattress out from the cupboard, and Delta, who held his hand and wouldn't let go. Next week, when   chaperoned Titch to see Mum in the Inpatient Unit at Monash Medical, she wasn't the same. She'd lost her pizzazz. Her tongue lolled out of her mouth and two tufts of hair stuck out the side of her head, like fox ears. She smelled of baby powder and sour milk. She was the youngest person in the Unit, but she didn't know who Titch was. 'We should leave,' said   . 'Fuck the docs. Fuck the pills.' The landlord cut Mum's lease, sprayed the flat with poison and cremated the cats in the park by the lemon tree.   convinced Bruce to let them keep the air mattress in his bedroom, and the next month passed by   's side. Literature studies before breakfast. Lights-out at ten p.m. Mass at St Anthony's on Sunday morning at eleven. 'But Bruce thinks it's time each of you had your own space,' said Delta, sliding the air mattress out into the living room one night. 'Best not to get distracted. I've spoken with the school. There's a spot in the boarding house.' Bruce drove Titch into South Yarra and Presto put him up in a room by the river. Six months on and there was still no improvement in Mum; though the sadness still stung, he welcomed his time in the boarding house. He didn't have to be so scared all the time. He could eat and train and study and wank whenever he wanted. And he could visit   's house when he felt down. 'So have you brought any girls back to your new place yet?' said Delta, one evening over an eggplant parmigiana. 'Me? Nah, that'll never work,' he said. Some nights,   buzzed Titch's hair with the electric clippers, and another time they dressed in Bruce's shirts when he went to Sydney for a conference. At the start of summer, Titch would sit alone on the roof of the boarding house, spying on the kookaburras along the Yarra, or smacking ping-pong balls over the oval with a tennis racquet, counting how many magpies came shrieking through the sky. But in the summer before Year Eleven,   snuck out and spent the days

71

with Titch. He brought to the boarding house a sheet of butcher's paper, sent from Sydney by Bruce, and wrote his father's expectations at the top of the poster, with texta arrows marking the steps to success. 'Dux of Melb High?'   wrote. 'Need perfect scores in English, Physics and Latin. Perfect scores in English? Need twenty-five practice essays before the exam. Twenty-five practice essays? Need to read each novel seven times.' Bruce also wanted   to get a double degree in Law *and* Commerce at Monash University. And to get his own savings account and start investing. 'Now it's your turn,' he said, handing over the texta. 'Hundy kilo bench,' wrote Titch, and he put the marker down. 'At least one of us is free to choose,' said   , taking a photo of his plan for Bruce. For ten weeks, Titch focused entirely on his bench press. Cycling through different volumes. Varying his close-grip. Pumping out dumbbell flies and cable cross and every accessory imaginable. Then, on the last day of summer, came Titch's finest moment. 'Up for the Sunday sesh, are we?' said Niki. 'It's a graveyard in here.'   was late, running over with his curls in his eyes, smearing his chalk on his Superman shorts. 'But hold on, just a sec!' he said. 'I was taking a leak!' During the lift, Titch felt a sudden fear of the hundy and the weight looming over his neck, all the summer's hype like a puddle of tar on his chest, and though he aced the first four reps, the barbell wavered on the fifth until   moved in to spot. Just the sight of him was enough for Titch to grind it out. And he did it, yeah, the hundy. 'This is the definition of strong,' said   , holding him around the shoulders. 'Herculean.' Titch rolled on the floor. His arms throbbed. Lactic acid flooded his chest. 'Titch *Antoine* Clement?' said   , lying on the floor beside him. 'We should just christen you "Ant". From here on out, you're the kind of man who'll carry ten times his own load.'

'You got any idea about watches?' Titch wrote. 'Could do with your thoughts. TBD.' He put his mobile under his pillow and rolled over in bed. There were spit stains on the mattress and his sheets were tangled at his feet. He lay on his side, picking at the eczema that had bloomed inside his elbow. He snuck to the roof of the uni dorm, padding over the concrete tiling, past the ciggies and the beer bottles, to the building's edge. The roar of the cars along Burwood Highway filled his ears. As he stood with the wind in his fringe, the sight of the dive made his eyes sting. The black tar road. The air hissing from heating vents. The indicators flaring on the sides of the trucks. The cyclists swerving onto campus. If he could have said anything at the wake, yeah, raising his hands and facing the freeway, it would have been that   always had a higher plan. While the other boys were just trying to keep their shit together,   had always wanted something more. He had two thousand Facebook friends. He pulled six hundred likes on the picture of him serving minestrone at St Vinnies. In his first week as a senior, he sat on the pool deck every day, cheering the Year Nines as they floundered up the lanes, his voice prickly from yelling, his shorts soaked from all the times he saved a non-swimmer. In Year Eleven, started Cunts With Cans, abbreviated to C.W.C. on the pamphlet in case his parents caught wind of his branding. He bought a thirty-pack of cans at Woolies and sold them at recess. Instead of paying two bucks at the canteen, the boys could have a Coke for a dollar-eighty. 'They call it undercutting, just quietly,' he said to Titch. 'It's one way to disrupt the market.' The cricketers loved it, as did the drama kids and the basketballers. By Friday of the first week,   had made nearly thirty bucks' profit and took Titch to Subway for celebratory meatball footlongs. He made a C.W.C. order page on Instagram, then enlisted some Year Nines to run around the schoolyard with a tent-sized poster. At the start,   never spent a cent of his earnings. 'Watch, I'll save twenty thousand dollars by graduation,' he said. 'Really.' Up on the roof of the uni dorm, Titch kicked the beer bottles over the edge.   's gusto wouldn't last more than a semester, poisoned, like everything else, by the grog. A few weeks later, yeah, begged his Year Nines to borrow money after he'd spent the overhead on beer. And when Delta called to ask where   got the money for his booze, Titch said he had no idea. 'It's true,' he said. 'Really.' But it was all bullshit. He'd kept track of the C.W.C. finances, knew how much they'd turned over, but couldn't open his mouth in case Bruce caught wind of the off-the-books operation. All the schoolmates knew   was getting smashed every night. Their down payments were being guzzled by a groghead. 'Cocksuckers,' one kid commented on an Instagram post. 'You think we can't smell you spooning out all the booze?' wrote another. 'Fucking faggots.'

Term two, Year Twelve: they were warming up to deadlift when   pulled a maroon flask out from his duffel bag. 'Just some vodka. My godmother says it calms her down,' he said, opening the flask and sniffing. 'Nah,' said Titch, crinkling his nose, 'that's grim.' 'I know it doesn't smell too flash,' said   , pouring the grog into his protein shaker, 'but it relaxes your muscles. Loosens everything up. Could do with some chill.' The deadlift was bullish and at the lockout,   's cheeks hollowed and the veins inside his adductors swelled and stiffened. 'Absolutely ace,' he shouted, dropping the weights. 'Well, shit,' said Titch, who had never seen the barbell pop so quickly. The next morning,   came to their bench-press session with the maroon flask, nursing it between sets, hiding it under his singlet. 'You want to slow down? It'll mess things up,' said Titch. 'But I'm flying,' said at the fourth set, his breath burning, his neck thudding against the bench. On the third day,   unracked his barbell for a squat, caught his breath and dropped into position, only for the vodka to seep out of his lips and stain the collar of his chalky T-shirt. He dropped the bar and flung his arm around Titch. 'It's nice to stop thinking for once,' he whispered. 'Don't know if I'm doing it properly. If my priorities are right. If really I'm just waiting to let the old man down.' 'You've never made a fuss about him before,' said Titch, already irked, yeah, as he picked up   's weights. 'So I've failed? Like that?' said   . 'I see.' The next week, totally forgetting his scene in the gym,   fronted to form class with a six-pack of beer in his schoolbag. 'Are you really going again?' said Titch, his voice breaking. 'Aren't you supposed to be saving? Or did you fucking forget that too?' 'Let's pretend I go on studying, that I stay on the straight and narrow,' said   . 'Then I get a job. Wow. Rest of my life, I'll just be buying shit and pining for what I don't have. Buying and pining, buying and pining. Trust me. It's never made Mum and Dad happy, has it?' Soon   hid a silver goon sack in his locker and drank up the wine with a pink straw. By July, his staple drink was straight vodka—Grey Goose, Smirnoff, whatever he bought off his older cousin. Sometimes he asked to leave Lit class for a stroll; he was tense, jittery, his eyes darting, his neck throbbing, and he came back with a calm, dazed look on his face, stinking of grog. Sometimes, yeah, it made sense: with all the pressure from Bruce,   needed to let off some steam. But then he skipped his glute activations and slipped a disc while squatting. Stopped coming to the gym and hanging after school. Titch lost sight of him, for days on end, for the first time in four years, and as he lay awake in the boarding house, watching the insects trapped in the window screen, he learned to withhold his love. This boy was a loser.   was not a loser. Ergo, this boy was not   .

By Term Three,   came to class marinating in grog, his eyes bloodshot, bottle caps clinking in his pockets. 'We should go out together,' he told Titch. 'Come to Degraves with me. No one asks for ID. The waitresses, you know, are always finding random things in the bars. Look what they gave me...' He opened his wallet, searching between the notes for a scrap of purple paper. 'Jesus,' said Titch, 'you really think I want to look at your shit right now?' 'She's for real, man. Have a read of this.' 'Some dumb ad? Nah.' A week later, Titch got a text from Delta asking if he was with   , if he could please tell him to come home, that his parents wanted to talk to him. But Titch was alone in the boarding house, listening to Tame Impala in his undies, replaying Instagram posts of Russian powerlifters. Delta called. 'Mother Mary,' she said. 'He hasn't come home in two days.' Titch pulled on his jeans and hurried to Oakleigh, where Delta was chatting to a cop outside the house and Bruce was revving their Ford. 'Hop in, Titch-meister,' he said. 'We're on patrol.' They circled St John's Reserve, around the milk bar, checking the bus stops and taxi ranks and finally—Mother Mary, *finally*—they found him under a kiddy slide at the playground, dozing in a puddle of beer, tanbark stuck to his H&M tee. 'He's been depressed,' said Bruce. 'He won't listen when we tell him to see a therapist and straighten out.' 'I've been trying,' said   , 'as hard as I can. You know how hard I try. You can't deny it, Titch.' 'Now your mother's all rattled,' said Bruce, hurling   into the backseat. 'You ever heard of text messages? Latest and greatest technology for you dumb kids.' 'Just chill, yeah, I got him,' said Titch, cushioning   's head over his thigh. 'But do you, Titch-meister? Is that a promise?'   was grounded. Couldn't go to the bar to watch Richmond play Sydney in the last home-and-away

77

game of the season. 'I don't want him out there with all the unruly types,' whispered Delta in a call. 'Can you just come over and keep him company?' Titch relented, and that Saturday he and   sat at either end of the couch, watching on telly as the Swans turned the Tigers into training cones. Buddy Franklin put on a clinic. Aliir Aliir had the footy on a string. The Tigers capitulated, one hundred and twenty-three points down with a quarter to go. 'I've had it up to here with these bloody pathetic bloody shameful clowns,' texted Bruce from the bar.   offed the telly with the remote and sunk his face in his hands. 'It's just another sign,' he said, 'that some of us are born to be embarrassed. Better we stick it out on the boundary, watching everyone else have a fine old time.' He stared at a point on the floor for five long minutes, then stood, swayed and strode to the rug, sliding it over the floorboards, upending a plank and pulling a bottle of tequila from the cavity. He measured a shot in the lid, downed it, measured another, downed it, and went on and on, measuring and downing. He tumbled onto the couch and the bottle shattered on the hardwood. Titch swept up the glass, gnawing his lip. It was like   was going down. Given up on his grades and his body. And now sliding backwards. 'We keen to kill ourselves or what? We're stressed, yeah,' said Titch, 'but this is beyond dumb. What happened?' 'I chatted to a therapist the other day. She said that I suffer from toxic masculinity. That I'm unstable. You never get to tell them you're well aware of it, do you? I'm a sicko, man. Maybe I'll end up like your mum.' 'We need to sort this shit out. Just tell me what you need.' 'The paper towels, Titch. On top of the fridge.'   rolled over to the kitchen tiles, fumbled under the sink between the detergent and insect repellent, and toppled a goon sack out of a bucket. He lay by the oven, sucking every last drop from the silver bag, burping the wine down his chin. Titch pulled   's mobile from his pocket and texted J., some waitress from

Degraves Street. 'You around? Come over? I'm at home. Alone.' He didn't think it could get any worse than the night at St John's Reserve, but Titch was proven wrong. Again. 'Don't go,' said   . 'Just stay with me. Kick back. Why you always crawling away?' 'Hi, kiddo,' wrote J., 'you want to hit the town again?' Titch dropped the mobile and left, so angry that he punched the train window as he boarded to South Yarra, and nursed his bleeding fist as he climbed the stairs to the gym. 'Are you boys together?' texted Delta. 'I just wanted to check in and commiserate. He's still technically grounded, but I know today's result is hard to swallow. Are you both at a gymnastics session?' And after ten minutes: 'But what time are you coming back? Do you have the keys?' And after an hour: 'Please pick up.' And in class the next morning: 'We haven't slept all night.' And after school: 'Please be more responsible, Titch. Just touch base with us, okay? We thought he was with you.' And by midnight: 'Honestly I'm just so worried where all this is headed.'

'We should first talk about your attendance,' said the Deakin Uni vice-provost, 'before we even start to unpack these marks of yours. Do you know the policies for our scholarship students?' The old man's glasses wobbled on his beady nose like they didn't want to be there. Titch hunched in the padded chair, his back cracking, his knees aching. 'I got it, yeah,' said Titch, 'you told me last time.' 'But this is different, Titch. You've missed three weeks of tutorials. You haven't submitted your assignments for four courses. This isn't usually how Melbourne High Boys fare. Is there something you should be telling us? Has something happened? Do you want to see the counsellor?' 'Just getting my affairs in order, yeah.' 'Do you know how many kids are dying to have the same privileges as you? They're in line, knocking at the door. I've seen them myself.' 'You haven't seen anything,' said Titch. 'You couldn't be more blind.' He ran out of the office, up to the roof of his dorm. The weak winter sun glinted off the hoods of cars in the traffic. Then the uni sent an email saying his enrolment was suspended, his degree on pause and his scholarship cut. 'Please vacate your dormitory,' it read. 'Applications for the next academic year open in January.' Titch went back to his dorm and kicked back on the bed, folding and unfolding his arms over his chest, until someone thudded on the door and a voice called, 'Please open up, or we'll be forced to break in.' The cops. Piggy Provost had called the cops. He bundled his mobile, the gold watch, a few Snickers bars and   's wallet into a bag and opened the door. It was a woman with a massive belly and a black baton. 'You're Titch Antoine Clement?' she said. 'Nah,' he said, 'that's my mate.' He legged it past her, down the emergency exit stairs, out through the lobby and onto the lawn, where he turned to stare up at his dorm, lost now in the row upon row of dull square windows, and

81

then a light glared in the frame, and he figured the cop was having a suss through his things. At seven-thirty, he walked to Coles at the back of the Glenny shopping centre. The staff had gone home and left the garage open. He searched through the packing crates. Shmackos. Fancy Feast. Blackdog Treats. He lay beside the crate and shut his eyes. Ten-thirty: the wind swirled in the garage and seeped under his skin. He sneezed. Midnight: he was shivering, his eyes glassy, his gut growling. KFC, nah, it would be shut. He climbed in the crate and opened a can of Fancy Feast. The flakes fell apart in his hands. Tasted like bloodied mud, salty on the tongue, but he downed the can and felt warmer. Downed another as the sun rose, then he limped away before the morning staff found him in the garbage. He snuck back to the Deakin Uni library and redownloaded Facebook. He could post on the Melbourne High group. Maybe drop Delta a message. But as he was scrolling his newsfeed, Titch found an ad for a new housing estate, half in Chinese characters, half in red, cursive English. 'Very clean private apartments. Three fifty per month.' A bargain. Half the price of anything else around. He searched through the Coles bag for the gold watch, balling and unballing the useless chain in his hand. It wasn't even waterproof, yeah. Already got a Casio. So he texted Sauce, the only Melbourne High boy at Deakin, and pawned the watch for two hundred bucks. 'Can I have a loan?' he wrote to   , remembering the cash from the wallet. 'I'll get you back. TBD.' By the time Titch met the landlord, a guy in a maroon sweater and torn jeans, at the back of Springvale Station, he had seven hundred dollars to his name. Enough for a month's rent and the security deposit. 'You still studying?' asked the landlord, guiding him along the corridors of the eight-storey building. 'Nah, working now,' said Titch. 'How old are you?' 'Seventeen.' 'I like you young go-getters,' said the landlord. 'Most of the tenants are from China. They've come over to study. They don't party much. And they keep to themselves. They think they should spend their money on studying hard, and so I let them.' He pointed at the semicircles of shoes around each door. Leather boots. Stilettos. Yeezys. Kith. 'Keep the place clean, yeah? No pets allowed,' said the landlord. 'Dǒng bù dǒng?' He showed Titch the flat, as wide as a train carriage, with a bedroom, a kitchenette, a little living room and a bathroom. But it had aircon and a lock on the door. Down the street were a phò restaurant and a massage parlour. Over the road was a South Indian market. He slept on the floor that night, and waking up the next morning, with the sun streaking through the power lines outside his window, he welcomed the chance to start forgetting, to find a way through the pain. He stretched across the tiles, his back to the window and his shadow skewed across the cracks. Then he sat up cross-legged by the wall, hearing the distant screech of the train arriving at Huntingdale Station, and he told himself to imagine furnishing the flat. Start with an air mattress. Then a chair and a desk, yeah. Maybe even a rug, the furry plush kind that felt good between the toes. In his bedroom he found a trail of ants, crawling single file from a hole in the skirting boards, out to the hallway and along to the balcony. The winter sun dazzled off their backs. They were tiny brown gems, one after the other, hundreds after hundreds. He dragged his legs aside and watched them for hours, wondering where they went, where they came from. They wanted a queen, yeah, not a king. He wiped his hand through the trails, sending them into chaos, and watched them regroup. They were persistent, yeah. Resilient.

'Titch-meister,' texted Bruce, a few days later. 'Tigers are playing the Bulldogs this Saturday night. We're watching on TV. Why don't you join us?' Titch found the text that evening and figured he could visit Bruce and Delta to repay ⬚⬚⬚⬚'s loan. He wandered to the 900 stop, his jacket wrapped around his shoulders, the hoodie low over his brow, as the rain drizzled on the laminated bus timetable. At their house, the Richmond flags had clogged the drain, spreading puddles between the bougainvillea. He knocked on the door but no one answered, so he let himself in through the laundry and squelched down the hallway into the living room, where the telly was blaring. 'And the Dogs win an epic battle at Etihad Stadium by five points,' said the commentator. So late, yeah. Missed the whole game. Bruce was dozing on the couch, his cheeks glistening, as Delta, in her sleep, clung to him like a koala in a blaze. At least the two of them could catch some shuteye, yeah. Titch switched off the telly. He stumbled into the kitchen. There were leftover dishes everywhere. Beef casseroles. Pasta salads. Tofu stirfry. Webs of cheesy spaghetti. The smell was rank. First he found some Mortein and sprayed down the tiles, killing the flies that had found their way inside. Then he found a bottle of detergent and crisscrossed the cutlery in the sink with soap. How much would you pay a cleaner for this job? Five hundy, yeah, that's about right. He gathered up the Tupperware containers, threw them in a garbage bag, and mopped the tiles and crunched the beer cans underfoot, counting nearly a hundred as he flattened them into discs. An old loaf of bread slept under the table, so he smacked it awake and left it by the microwave to take home. Then he stole into ⬚⬚⬚⬚'s room. The desk was covered in bottles, lined up in rows from the back wall to the computer and around the crucifix, vodka at the back and beer at the front. The beanbag was flattened into a makeshift table to pile the cardboard from all the slabs.

          must have hidden these bottles all around the house, in every nook and cranny, and only after he was gone did Delta and Bruce discover them all. But it was no surprise to Titch. He had known the truth before   's Facebook friends, and before his parents, too. He'd seen the proof that   had decayed long before he tanked his final exams or guzzled his savings. Good enough reason for Titch not to touch it, nah, no need for booze or anything else that would fling him into a fatal brainfade. Then he remembered a few years back when a Year Twelve was caught cheating on his Chem exam and slit his wrists when his rents found out. His name was Ravi, yeah, always blabbing about his top marks in the courtyard. And there were those twins from MacRob, the sister school, who walked into Port Phillip Bay when their parents divorced. The cops found them washed up under St Kilda pier, holding hands. And then there was Ace, the boy in Titch's year level, who went for a drive one day and never came back. His parents still posted ads on Facebook and in the *Herald Sun*. 'Save Ace' was the name of the campaign. But the cops last saw his car in Healesville, where the roads were winding and rocky, and he had no money to make it very far past the hills, if that's what he really wanted. All the kids knew the truth but they didn't say anything. That's how it went, yeah, and he got up from   's bed, cracking his neck. A surprise, but plenty of set-ups, same story, if they just peered long enough through the screenshot and into the shame. Brain-fades left, right and centre.   wasn't so special. Not as unique as he'd hoped to be. Titch closed the bedroom door, grabbed the loaf of bread and walked into the storm. He waited in the torrents for the bus, shaking in his wet cotton hoodie as he boarded. His Myki had a negative balance, but the driver let him on anyway. Only a five-minute ride. Then a ten-minute walk. The grocer was still open. He asked for a dosa and smashed it down, licking the lentil chutney off his fingers. He left his sopping clothes at the door to stop the rainwater seeping into the flat. Then, kneeling on the warm tiles, he pulled apart the loaf to gift breadcrumbs to the ants. They streamed around his feet, their legs shining, their antennae searching his skin, and if he listened closely, he could hear what they had to say.

His savings fizzled. The electricity was cut off and the bossman had started tallying all the dosh Titch owed for dosas. So, on Monday morning, Titch sat at a computer in Clayton Library typing up a résumé. He wrote that he had worked at Video Ezy for two years and Insanity before that. If anyone called for references, they'd find nothing because the stores had shut. They'd just have to trust him, yeah, and then he wrote that he'd started a delivery business and had volunteered with Vinnies. He caught the bus to Chaddy shopping centre. Striding into the mall, he tried to look alive, to feel up and about, like he owned himself. He rolled his shoulders back, flaring his chest against his tee. Chaddy was a labyrinth of polished marble floors and indoor bamboo groves. Groups of uniformed cleaners loitered in the corridors, hollering in Tamil and Cantonese. There didn't seem to be any shoppers. The stores were quiet, attended by staff who scrolled on their phones or hunched at the registers. Titch strode into Reiss, the closest shop, some designer store, with his footsteps echoing off the walls. The woman behind the counter raised her head, her bleach-blonde hair cascading over her navy halter dress. 'You need a hand with anything?' she said. 'You looking to hire?' he said. 'We only take résumés off the internet. You should chat with the guys at Rebel Sport. Or GNC. They'd love a hunk like you over there.' He clasped his hands behind his back, crumpling his pages of résumés. 'So do you want to try anything?' she said. 'I'm alright. Just looking,' he said. 'Well, that's chill by me,' she said, plugging a pair of headphones in her ears. At Rebel Sport, the manager told him to apply through the online portal. As did the girl at GNC and the guy at Target. He sussed his résumés but now, after all the running about, the pages were smeared with sweat and the ink was smudged. There was only one worth keeping. The morning had fucking tanked, yeah. He wandered through an emergency exit and into the frosty noon. On the metal walkway overlooking the dumpsters, he pulled his mobile from his pocket and swiped idly through his texts. 'How's it going, bud?' said a bloke, staring into the garbage, clutching a sweet potato in a paper bag. 'Better put your phone away. The magpies will steal anything,' he said, angling his head to the sky. 'You want a pick-me-up?' 'Nah, not for me,' said Titch, as the bloke unwrapped a bundle of blue pills from his pocket and crushed them in his mouth. MDMA, maybe, with sweet potato. 'You on smoko?' said the bloke. 'Nah, I'm looking for a gig.' 'Hustling, bud? Good on you.' 'Well, no luck so far.' 'Where you been trying?' Titch told him about Reiss and the rest of the brush-offs. 'You don't want to mess with those internet applications,' said the bloke. 'Otherwise, they can find you right there online. With the social medias these days, we're all crooks. Better to make an intro in person, like if you're horny and after a root.' 'I don't know anywhere that will even look at me,' said Titch. 'You tried the bookstore? I been seeing the manager around the place recently. She's hard to miss. Pretty frazzled these days. Every night I see her in the store when everyone else goes home. Might be worth asking if she needs the helping hand.' As the bloke munched away, hunks of orange flesh tumbled down his T-shirt and onto the black garbage bags. 'The bookstore?' said Titch. 'They're the craziest crew in Chaddy,' said the bloke. 'Crazy or smart? Who knows?' They bumped fists and Titch walked past the shops to the centre directory. Reynolds, it was called, at the back of Chaddy, only fifty metres from the bus stop. He smoothed his last résumé and ran to the store, tensing his abs, balling his hands behind his back. The aisles were dim, lit only by low red lamps. The ceiling was covered in paper planes and origami birds. A woman stood motionless at the back of the store, her huge orange hair spilling over her pale cheeks.

Her eyes were circled in blue and purple. 'I'm on a break from uni and I'm wondering if you might need some extra help,' said Titch. The woman stared at her black rubber boots. He inched towards her and she said, 'Do you even read?' He rattled off the Russian authors he remembered from Literature class at Melbourne High. The Tolstoy. The Dostoyevsky. The Kafka. He extended his hand and she laughed. 'You don't even know why that's funny, do you?' she said. His hand dropped to his side. He left his résumé on the counter and walked back the way he came. Slinking along the bus bay, he tried not to feel like a tryhard, yeah, but his tee flapped around his ribs and his scalp was sweating. The breeze off the carpark was bitter and dry. He sank his face in his hands and stared into the black.

Maybe he should just have another gym sesh. He bussed to Oakleigh, trained into South Yarra and wandered down Claremont Street to the back of Melbourne High. 'There he is,' said Niki at the front counter. 'How you been holding up?' And then he remembered: today was the first sesh since   's suicide. Done so well at forgetting, yeah. 'I'm alright,' he said, hurrying into the changing rooms. He sighed in front of the mirror with his hair standing up in tufts. He would be more than alright, mate. TBD. When it came down to it, he was the one lifting the weight. Not   . Upstairs, he loaded the barbell, but the plates were heavier than he remembered, awkward to grip. TBD. He swung into a squat, panted beneath the rack and slid his hands along the bar. 'Come on,' he said under his breath. 'What the hell is up with you?' Finally he arched his lats, tensed his glutes and hammies, gripped the bar with four hooked fingers and hoisted the load onto his upper back. He dropped once, waited, and rose, and dropped again, the blood streaming up his body, the veins flaring around his neck, his torso ballooning, his bum burning. He tried once more but his balance was off. The bar tumbled down his back. He hit the floor, squirming. It was only sixty kilos. He saw himself in the mirrors, his pale body glistening, scrawny and boyish, the downlights revealing the nubs of his elbows, his kneecaps bulging like a gargoyle's eyes, the holes under his collarbones more hollow than he had ever seen. Twiggy Titch. He hurried by the reception desk before Niki could ask about the sesh, ran up to Claremont Street and shivered in the wind, crunching the yellow leaves by the fence around the train tracks. He waved at a possum, but it didn't wave back, and as he limped through the turnstiles, his quads ached with cramps. The train to Springvale rumbled into the station. The doors clunked open. A text popped up on his mobile.

90

'This is Ginny, the manager at Reynolds. I have an opening. Can you email across your bank details and tax file number? Thanks.' So they wanted him, yeah, somehow. He would have to get his paperwork ready. He would have to make himself a plan. What to wear. What to pack. What time to bus to Chaddy. What to eat on his break. And finally, whispering beside the trails of ants in his flat, Titch learned that the screenshot wouldn't disappear by itself: if he started a new life, maybe he could delete his months of pain. Step one was fixing his priorities. Stop powerlifting. Focus on his zzzs. Get some real dosh into his bank account. Come tomorrow, yeah, maybe he could be a proper workingman.

Excelsior

TWO WEEKS EARLIER, at ten to ten on a Monday morning, Ginny's cell phone pinged inside her pocket. 'May 1st,' wrote Jim, her father. 'Your mum's made more than four full months of her cleanse. Past halfway! Let's hold a Sunday arvo support brunch. What do you reckon?' With her heart pulsing in her throat, Ginny left the register, hurried from Reynolds, took the freight elevator behind Sephora and returned to her perch above the Chadstone mall. Her anxiety made a knot in her chest; she rolled a cigarette, tonguing her fake front tooth as the southeastern suburbs rippled below like a spider's web. Muddy lawns hemmed kitsch houses, parking lots smothered rusted railroads and thousands of aboveground pools shone like doped-up pupils along fences and sidewalks. The suburbs were dissected by the Monash Freeway, the expressway worming south from the airport to the countryside, barricaded by miles of concrete walls through acres of woodsy fields. Convoys of trucks and diggers circled yet another fringe housing estate and the city inched past the Dandenongs towards the Red Plains, the crimson vistas lining the horizon, the site of all the tacky suburbs to come. The Red Plains conjured waves of nausea in Ginny: the stillborn construction sites, the stagnant gas stations, the frustration of spotty cell service. The outer suburbs were haunting, an imminent oblivion, and each day, as the city sprawled even further, nothingness filtered into the hearts of the guileless homeowners, like the smell of cinnamon that lured pre-diabetic kids into Krispy Kreme to line their veins with sugar. Ginny puffed on her cigarette, dulling the image of Betty, her mother, fully sober, alert once again, and for a second she escaped back to Brooklyn, to the only place she had ever been free, but then her filter singed her fingertips, gutting her imagination, and she stepped into the closest puddle, breaking her solemn silhouette.

Ginny retraced her steps to Reynolds and found Peter, her oldest employee, schmeared across the register, blinking at the ceiling, a box of paperbacks unopened at his side. He was from Perth and smoked more weed than anyone she had ever met. He had long, thin limbs, a lardy torso and patches of hair all over his neck. He called himself 'Püd' and put 'I reckon' at the end of everything he said. 'Had a cheeky ciggy, I reckon,' he said. She ignored him and hid in the backroom. 'Miss America's going gaga, I reckon,' he yelled. 'Maybe this little wannabe should just get off her *cell phone*.' And there was Nadine, the salesgirl who always listened adoringly to Püd, who lumbered through the store in a pair of four-inch stilettos and a push-up bra, who liked to insist there was no such thing as an ugly woman, only a lazy one. She spent her weekends vlogging her favourite cosmetics, sometimes texting the store WhatsApp pictures of her spray tans from inside the Myer fitting rooms. 'I'm not sure about the tone on this one,' she'd say, sharing a photo of her nacho-cheese breasts, 'but if they turn on the strobes it won't look fake at all.' Three years ago, after graduating from Melbourne University with an Arts degree, majoring in English, Ginny applied for the job as manager of her local bookstore. Having spent every Saturday, for the last decade, wandering through the struggling shop with her books balanced in the crook of her arm, she was hired without hesitation. On her first day at Reynolds, Ginny followed her employees up the aisles with a list of cafes and indie cinemas they could visit together. But they scoffed at Ginny, shunning her invitations and ignoring her Facebook friend requests. Now she just saw them as rednecks, bereft of all intelligence. They were vacuous jerks, plebs who could never conceive of a cultured life, the living proof of Melbourne's insidious oblivion.

Ginny still lived in her father's house in Carnegie, a two-storey, red-brick mansion strangled by cement—'paved', as Jim put it. Concrete lions lined the driveway like a row of soldiers. 'If we had grass,' he said, 'then every Saturday we'd be out there on our hands and knees yanking up the weeds. And concrete's trendier. It's like we're living in the future.' Jim had lush orange hair and constellations of freckles all over his body. He was the child of Greek immigrants who had worked in paper mills, abattoirs, garages and pencil factories, squirrelling every dollar they earned under their refrigerators. Jim had amassed a fortune over a lifetime landscaping gardens and refashioning old bicycles and gadgets. He'd injected every cent into the tallest house, the widest widescreen television, the loudest V8 car and the most gargantuan pleather couch. Ginny's mother, Betty, the queen of Jim's kingdom, had spent twenty-five years shambling through his house with her bottles of chardonnay, snoring through Ginny's university graduation, vomiting at her debate finals and bumbling between AA groups whenever Jim grew jealous of the deadbeats in Betty's safe space. Once, her mother had been crowned Miss Victoria and photographed in every tabloid and men's magazine in Australia, but after baby Ginny had been dug from her belly in a C-section, leaving a twisted, pink ridge on her navel, Betty lost her fame and descended into her dressing-gown-and-goon-sack lifestyle. 'Nurse told me the sun set right when you came out,' she liked to say, pressing Ginny's cheeks between two clammy palms. 'You gonna tell us when it'll rise again?' Today, four months into her mother's homeopathic cleanse, Ginny stepped out of her Fiat Hatchback and splashed through the puddles leaking from the garden sprinklers. She squelched through the house in the dark, untying her shoelaces and easing her feet onto the hardwood. After she draped her jacket over her mirror, hiding her reflection, she shed her sopping clothes and laid them over the carpet. She dressed stiffly, yanking her pyjamas over her pink stomach, clammy thighs and the hundreds of scars all over her skin. She bound her mane of frazzled hair and burrowed her face in the pillows. Her collarbones still stung from last March, when she had snuck to the roof and lain across the tiles to suntan, only for her skin to turn red and her scars to resurface. 'The prawn's back,' Betty had said, stirring a gin and tonic on the patio with Marg. 'Only edible when you rip off her head. Isn't your little sister supposed to be depressed? Should we call a bloke over for her?' Ginny had rolled her beach towel with her eyes watering. Men were but the minions of Betty's boozy realm. They were the pioneers of suburbia, basic and brutish, with no originality beyond their lives as electricians and plumbers, or their bad-faith Catholicism, or the poor sportsmanship of their untalented dicks.

Marg, Ginny's sister, lived in the next bedroom, separated by an inch-thick drywall and posters from Victoria's Secret and *The Godfather*. Marg was developing an app to track her Instagram fans; if someone stopped following her account, she could spike their ketamine spray at the next warehouse rave. Last year, on her twenty-seventh birthday, she earned a disability pension for being diagnosed with severe attention-deficit disorder, a verdict gifted by an ex-boyfriend who had started as a psychoanalyst and needed to prove to the Australian Psychological Association that he was treating real patients. Ever since, Marg spent every day at home, trialling her Nepalese lingerie, pastel panties infused with sandalwood perfume that spiced her farts and aligned her chakras. She kept a different lover for each night of the week. To maintain the secrecy of her playdates, Marg had them climb the lions on the patio, scale the drainpipe, tumble over her windowsill and tiptoe into her bed. Ginny would be lying on her rug, rubbing pawpaw ointment on her arms or counting her antibiotics, when the latticework would rattle and a shadow would flicker over her curtains. There was a certain loyal rhythm to Marg's weekly routine: Monday wore wingtips that squealed when he jumped off the statue; Tuesday wore sneakers with no laces; Wednesday wore heavy workman's boots that flecked mud on the window; Thursday wore football cleats that clapped down the driveway; Friday went barefoot, just a hurried scraping as he climbed; Saturday wore loafers with squeaky rubber soles; and on Sunday, Marg's day of rest, Jason McDonagh parked his red Nissan GT-R, left the neons pulsing under the grill, ran up the driveway without locking the doors, shook Jim's hand and leapt upstairs into his girlfriend's arms. Not one of her lovers seemed to know about their place on a roster, had never sniffed out a rival root-and-boot at a Cranbourne shooting range, or a Chapel Street nightclub, or a Broadmeadows boxing ring. How Marg protected her secrecy was a miracle; the dating pool in Melbourne was so small, the Antons so recognisable. The reverse harem might have owed to her avant-garde polyamory, although one morning when Ginny gave her sister two collections of feminist essays, asking over a bowl of Coco Pops if she would consider herself *sex-positive*, Marg hardly stopped chewing to say, 'Gross, sis. Just keep out of it. I'm clean. And the doc says you can only get the swab twice a month.' After Ginny dumped the books back in Reynolds, doubting anyone had noticed their absence from the store, let alone their presence, she wondered how her sister could live without trying to understand herself. There were so many things to learn, she thought. What else was the point of life?

The first lesson Ginny had learned, sometime in her childhood, was that invisibility would be her only means of survival in the Anton house. Maybe it started in Grade Two when she wet the bed and found her mother stumbling in the hallway as Jim started the laundry. 'Never happened once with Marg,' said Betty, pawing the slobber off her chin. 'Everything was alright before this one came along.' At birthdays, Ginny knew to avoid the camera, exiting the frame while her mother harangued her cousins on the patio, and at Christmas she dressed as Mr Claus, because no one needed to buy Santa presents. If she smiled, Betty was reminded of her failed career, so Ginny kept her face in a perpetual frown. Speaking provoked Betty's slaps and pinches, so Ginny learned not to say a word. She ate breakfast and dinner in her bedroom, avoiding the family's Saturday evenings around the fireplace and their Sunday mornings by the pool. Throughout Grade Five, potential adopters toured through her bedroom, watching Ginny with watering eyes, kneeling on the carpet and jangling her toys, before muttering to Jim in the hallway, never to return. Her parents never answered her questions, so she learned to stop asking. Alone at night, she whispered to her battered plushies, hosting seances and exorcisms and executions, playing for hours until the sun rose at the end of the cul-de-sac. Those years of sleeplessness made her hair split in the shower, put purple bags under her eyes and caused sinus infections and earaches. She became numb to the world, as if she were watching from outer space. She wore sunglasses and sunhats all year round; she longed to look without being seen, to hide her dark eyes and fiery hair from the world that worked against her. Then came Melbourne Girls' Grammar and the irksome rituals of high school; although she tried to hide in her sci-fi novels, her classmates dragged her to their parties, unveiling her to the boys like an alien egg they hoped would hatch at their command. One New Year's Eve, her peculiar silence emboldened a kid from Melbourne Grammar to undress her behind his father's rowing shed, and in the seconds of one short-lived fuck, all her years of invisibility ended. The boys wrote about her on a blog named 'Chucky Ginny'. She didn't sleep for weeks, lying deathly still on top of her sheets, seeing the monster they all feared: a dropkick rando with dero scars all over her doughy rig. After trying to eat a bottle of antidepressants, and botching even her overdose, she went crying to Jim. 'But you don't have to try to be invisible,' he said. 'You don't have to feel lonely. You're part of a family, remember? And a very proud family at that.' But there simply had to be another way. Loneliness, she told herself, was the key to freedom, the underlying inspiration needed to leave. One day, the whole sad house would sit snugly in her rear-view mirror. Persistently and patiently, she took the necessary steps towards independence: at seventeen, when she quit the all-girls netball team; at eighteen, when she bought her JouJou Jack Rabbit; at twenty-one, when she became the manager at Reynolds; and at twenty-four, the most monumental stride of all, when she walked the streets of New York for the very first time.

More than four months earlier, in the middle of summer, Marg lassoed Ginny into her room, sweeping her fashion magazines and kickboxing pads off the bed, and loaded an itinerary on her mobile. 'Let me lay this down for you,' said Marg. 'First we do New York City—I've snagged a cheap hotel near the university. We can get around everywhere on foot, there's a pass that lets you do the Freedom Tower and the Statue of Liberty and then do a Broadway show, all for a hundred bucks. Then we should do Niagara Falls, but on the Canada side, because we're not made of money. But how bananas will it be? You get a boat right up to the waterfall and they let you keep the raincoat. And then we should do Las Vegas, do the casinos, do the musicals, maybe even do the strip clubs. Call it a cultural exploration, yeah? And then we hop back to New York and jet-set home.' Ginny's head was pounding. She dimmed the lamp and turned off the fairy lights around the bed. 'Are you keen or nah?' said Marg, patting Ginny's shoulder with a firm palm. 'Dad gave me the creativity licence.' Ginny left the room, rubbing her shoulder with unease, and paused on the landing, where she heard Jim yelling from the kitchen. 'He's world-renowned, Betts. He's saved so many marriages—and lives,' he said. 'Just give this detox a crack, okay? Maybe your big fix will come out of left field.' She hated seeing them try so hard; better to be far away when it all went up in flames. And so on the twelfth of January, she bundled into Jim's ute with Marg, while Betty mumbled in the front seat, her head lolling in her headset as she listened to *A Naturopath's Guide to Liver Rebirth*. 'Turn right on the freeway and head north,' said the ancient GPS. 'Past Chadstone. Past Toorak. Past Richmond. Through the Domain Tunnel. Then stay north to Tullamarine.' The freeway to the airport was agonisingly crowded, a constipation of cars lodged bumper-to-bumper for miles. The kangaroos on the hillsides sat munching the grass with indifference. 'Now, young ladies,' said Jim, smiling into the rear-view mirror, 'promise me you'll call us every day.' 'We're adults,' said Marg. 'We'll do whatever we want.' 'I know that,' he said, 'but I'll miss you. And I should be keeping tabs on you both.' After two hours, when they reached the Departures wing, Ginny unsheathed her new passport from the Australia Post envelope and soared to the security check, leaving her family with the luggage cart. Out the window of the plane, the city shimmered and shrank, the pink skies swallowing the brown fields like skin healing over a scab. 'Why don't they put a calorie count on these packs?' said Marg, poking through the airline meal with her plastic fork. Ginny rolled towards the aisle, cocooned in her Qantas blanket, but sleeping was treacherous; her eyes kept flitting from one screen to the next, catching the other passengers' films, tiny windows into other lives. Never in her life had she allowed herself to feel excited. Perhaps, she thought, she might indulge herself just this once. 'We've got to be the first ones out to Duty Free,' said Marg, nudging Ginny in the ribs. 'Stay with me, sis.'

'But, ma'am,' said the attendant at JFK, 'you're not going to Manhattan. That's near *Long Island* University, in Brooklyn. You better take the subway.' 'You kidding me?' said Marg. 'We paid good money for this. Who's your supervisor?' Ginny shepherded Marg towards the AirTrain and they passed a row of Hassids grumbling for a cab, two Latinas in pantsuits lugging a pooch in a crate and a thirty-foot logo suspended from the ceiling. 'The Great Seal of the State of New York,' it said. 'Excelsior. Ever Upward.' Hours later, lugging three suitcases, a Gore-Tex sleeping bag and Marg's handbag stuffed with toiletries, Ginny emerged from Jay Street-MetroTech station between a drugstore and a halal truck. 'Let's take cabs from now on,' said Marg, trailing in her wake by a dude snoring inside an upturned fridge. Ginny had never felt cold like this before. If she stayed still for a second too long, she would freeze. Marg shivered, her teeth clattering, and after checking into the hotel, she doused her fingers under the water from the kettle. 'I only brought denim,' she said. 'Didn't they say it was going to hit thirty degrees?' Ginny pulled her polka-dot sundress over her jeans, and a leather jacket over that, and found two pink rubber gloves in the sink. She stood before the bedroom mirror like an alien from Mars—or, maybe, from some antidopean town that no one ever escaped. 'How are you for energy?' said Marg, collapsing on her bed. 'I thought twenty hours of sitting around would perk me up.' Ginny opened the fridge, but it was empty. 'Can you find some food?' said Marg, yawning into her pillow. Ginny knelt by her suitcase. The carpet bristled under her shins. The door rattled on its hinges. The city was here, calling her, inside this very room. Irresistible, she thought. How could she deny it? She smiled at Marg, but her sister was fast asleep, so she unlocked the door and tiptoed down the corridor.

She ran by Junior's on DeKalb Avenue, where the wind wisped the steam around the dazzling golden sign. The C train took her uptown, under the East River and into Manhattan, and she hunched inside her collar, avoiding the eyes of the people in the subway until she got off at Spring Street. A blonde couple sat in a dumpling restaurant with their faces buried in their books. An Arab man smoked a cigar from an apartment balcony, watching her pace down Elizabeth Street by the Japanese Mormons hawking pamphlets from their black backpacks. There was a bar at the corner of Broome Street called the Randolph. The bouncer looked her over twice and said, 'You one of those alternative models, huh?' The Randolph was dim, lit only by tapers, and murmured conversations warmed the bar with an elemental heat, as if she were hiding in a cavern in the earth's core. She ordered a vesper and found a booth. 'Can I join you?' she said to the guy in the corner. He looked her over, squinting at the coarse skin on her neck, without saying a word. 'Well, it's nice to meet you,' she said, slipping into the banquette beside him and lumping her bag in her lap. The guy leaned towards her, sighed and unsheathed a golden penknife from his breast pocket. He started filing his fingernails; they glowed a striking green. She pushed the vesper across the table and he fingered the stem of the glass, smirking. His teeth were jagged, his skin indented with acne, and he wore black-rimmed glasses beneath a widow's peak. He twirled the glass over the table, revealing the geometric tattoos that dotted his wrists and slid under his sleeves. 'So, you going to tell me what's good?' he said. 'My name's Ginny.' 'Tight,' he said. 'Call me Klein. The one and only.' 'Lucky it's so warm in here.' 'Warm for some, I suppose. Now tell me, honey, how in God's name did someone like you end up in a place like this?' 'I'm travelling.' 'From where?' 'From Melbourne.'

107

'Florida?' 'Australia.' 'Well, shit,' he said, reaching into his pocket for a vial of luminescent green fluid. 'You want a nudge?' 'A what?' 'A little manza.' 'I'm okay, thank you.' 'It's chill. Proven to help with jetlag and dis-orientation.' 'I'm fine.' 'Don't be a dweeb, honey, it's what we all do here.' 'Maybe you can give me a recommendation,' she said, 'for my first night in America.' 'Maybe you could try the Box.' 'Let me google it.' 'Don't waste your time,' he said. 'It's the most exclusive club in the world.' 'Well, where is it?' Klein unscrewed the lid of the vial and dipped his penknife in the manza. A sharp smell filled the booth, the tang of ripe apples. 'You know what they say about the Box?' said Klein, digging the penknife under his fingernails and gasping. 'You go in a mensch and you come out a monster. It'll change you forever. It's a bardo. One of those in-between spaces that should never have existed. When the millennials find out, they'll shut it down forever.' He fixed the lid back on the vial and chuckled, catching Ginny's steadfast gaze. 'You'll find your devil in there,' he said. 'Well, are you going to show me?' she said. 'You don't want to go, honey.' 'But of course I do. Excelsior.' 'What?' 'Ever upward,' she said. Klein cackled. The table trembled. 'Well, maybe we can help each other out,' he said. 'A mutually beneficial arrangement. Ain't no ordinary American men like me getting in. An Aussie starlet, dancing at the Box on her first night in New York? Let's see.' He gathered his wallet, his vial of manza and his golden penknife, and then he led her from the booth and onto the street.

'First test, honey,' said Klein. 'Can you really keep up?' He clutched her wrist as they crossed from Mercer onto Canal: past critters hiding in mounds of snow and sodden cardboard boxes, past the green maw of the downtown subway entrance, past a boarded-up massage parlour, past the pedestrian traffic signal counting down, past the Chinese ornaments glowing red like mutant bats above mom-and-pop stores, past frosty wires bolted with iron into ancient tenement brickwork, past a grifter leaned against the skeletal scaffolding who said, 'You wanna buy the world?' and unveiled a crystal globe studded with emeralds, past the rows of glass pipes moulded into elephants and spread across black card tables, past a Samoyed dozing on a bench, its white fur whiffling in the breeze, past a tarot reader shuffling her Minor Arcana by a lamp, past wooden stools chained to the pillars of the former municipal building, past fishmonger stalls stinking of the day's tuna and trout, and past wooden barrels brimming with cumquats and dragon fruits. They turned north onto Chrystie Street, where the crystal spire of the Chrysler building peered through the clouds, as their feet thumped over metal trapdoors hiding bunkers and bomb shelters, as floodlights above the basketball courts swamped their faces, the glacial concrete reverberating with cries and curses and tribal punk cheering, the rhythmic drumming of Air Jordans, the walloping of sodden basketballs. Klein's fingernails glowed through their mad dash, unlikely fireflies in the January night. Ginny stopped, panting in a cloud of steam, her hands on her knees, and Klein said, 'Look alive, Miss Australia, our show ain't started just yet.'

A stencil print on the roller door read: 'Active Driveway, No Parking Anytime.' The walls were crumbling red brick. The dirty awning tilted overhead like an unwashed tablecloth. A queue of people stretched along the brickwork, parallel to the road, where a woman painted her toenails across the dashboard of a purring Lamborghini. Her legs made a triangle over the windshield. The crimson polish settled on her toenails and she fidgeted with her lace choker, turning the pages of a book. *A Streetcar Named Desire*, thought Ginny, glimpsing the front cover in the glow from the phones on the road. A man in a durag stood at the roller door, rubbing his thighs through his black trousers, humming a distant tune that escaped her ears. Klein sauntered to the bouncer, curling his fingers. 'K,' said the bouncer, 'I heard a nasty rumour that I could bum a cigarette off of you.' 'All rumours start somewhere,' said Klein, slipping a rolled cigarette from his pocket. 'Now, I got a friend in town tonight. An Aus-tra-lian. You think there might be room for the two of us?' 'Let me ask Sylvie. You man-spreading tonight?' 'If it's moving,' said Klein, 'I'm selling.' The bouncer slunk into the club and reappeared with the doorwoman. She was seven feet tall and wore charcoal wings, a feathered top hat and a lace corset. 'Who do we have here?' she said, caressing Ginny's hands. 'Are these gloves Italian?' 'Aussie,' said Ginny. 'We've had them up and about for more than a decade.' *'Up and about,'* said Klein, wrapping his arm around Ginny's shoulders. 'Why don't you come in?' said the doorwoman. 'Welcome to New York.' The bouncer unclasped the velvet rope and bumped Klein's fist. A man in a tuxedo scampered from the line and yelled, 'But I'm from Sydney, love. Been out here for hours, freezing my arse off!' 'Sorry,' said Ginny, 'I'm new.' 'Help me out, would you?' said the bloke. Klein elbowed him into the wall and unsheathed his penknife. 'Fuck you, mate-y,' he said. 'Tonight's for two. Only.' He fixed his bangs, striding into the Box as Ginny edged out of his grasp, her eyes blanketed by the shadows of the club; she had followed the city's irresistibility from Brooklyn to Manhattan and down into the dark. 'So, I'm a thug before I'm a faggot,' said Klein. 'That's what they all said about me in middle school.' 'Maybe I should go back,' she said. 'Back to what?' he said. 'Your tourist trap?' Ginny pictured Marg, sprawled on their queen bed in her beige panties, whistling through her two front teeth, the halogens gleaming on the taut skin of her abs, the impending countdown of her phone alarm ticking towards Day One of Doing New York. 'But first take a look,' said Klein, pressing his fingers to her lips. 'You at least need a proper tour.' The club must have been two hundred feet long, with a wooden stage at the furthest end and circle mirrors along the walls, like the portholes of a submarine. A gold-leaf faun glittered on the ceiling and red phosphorescent flowers snaked down from the balcony, glimmering as she ran her fingers through the buds. A single disco ball spun nonchalantly above the revellers: women in lace teddies, men in suspenders with oiled moustaches, angular jaws and aristocratic noses—and *Ginny*, yes, bopping languidly to the trumpets, traipsing behind Klein, who prowled through the Box at ease. He stepped up the staircase, balancing an elbow on the banister as he unscrewed his vial and plunged his penknife in the syrup. 'You never explained what that is,' said Ginny. '*Manzantyl* is the technical term. You don't have manza in Australia?' said Klein. 'I'd have to ask my sister. Do you get high on it regularly?' '*High?* Ginny, please, this ain't for getting high. It's for living. No one survives a night at the Box without the cover of a *man*-hole.' 'What do you mean?' 'Well, some dude from Connecticut tried to spend a whole night here stone-cold sober. He couldn't last the first act. Had his white ass hauled back to Stamford in a cab and never came back. But I mean, sure, if you want to suffer an ordinary life, no one is going to stop you.' 'But what does it do?' she said, spinning the vial in her hands, refracting the cherubs on the ceiling. 'Only you can decide that,' he said. She laid her wrist in his palm and his fingers closed in a vice-like grip. He nipped the penknife under her cuticles and the manza glowed along the blade. A jolt shot up her forearms and a warm flush seeped up her neck. Her nose tingled. Her eyelids shrivelled into her skull. 'It's about to start,' said Klein. 'Ginny's first motherfucking show.'

A purple glow spread through the club and three figures stole into the crowd. They were clad in orange hazmat suits and carried huge silver nets. The spotlight arced down the balcony, illuminating the audience below: women in flowing summer dresses and men in tinted sunglasses, floral shirts and salmon shorts. The stage curtains opened, revealing a cobbled street, divided by a streetcar line, with a spiral staircase connecting two floors of a duplex. A woman ran screaming across the bedroom, her dirty blonde hair coiled in a rhinestone tiara, her satin gown glinting under the gas lamp as she panted at the mirror, clutching a broken wine bottle to her chest. A man stumbled into the room, his red silk pyjamas billowing at his ankles and wrists. He was burly, tanned, with a paunch like a bowling ball and a flat mullet down his neck. 'Oh,' he said, 'so you want some rough-house?' She swung at him, and he laughed, gripping her wrists, sending the bottle clunking onto the stage. 'Alright,' he said, 'let's have some rough-house!' He kicked the bottle beneath the staircase and pushed the woman over the bed, wringing her neck in the meaty fulcrum of his elbow. 'We've had this date with each other from the beginning,' he said, unravelling her gown and untying the knot at his waist. He dragged his trousers to his knees, his underpants too, and out lolled his penis, a veined, ochre stump. The woman clutched the man's waist, pinning him in place, and the green footlights flared once, then again, and the woman quivered, bucking to her own rhythm. Her eyes slipped to either side of her head, her nose melted into her mouth, her lips darkened from pink to purple to the colour of moss, two feelers sprouted from her back, and she became her true form, *Idolomantis diabolica*, Devil's Flower Mantis. She held him in her mandibles. His head slid off his shoulders, spraying crimson across the streetcar tracks

113

as his hips pumped beneath her grip. The curtains closed. The audience clapped from every corner of the club. Ginny whooped with glee, revelling in this dream she had conjured on her own, nodding without knowing the origin of her fantasy. She found herself clutching Klein's shoulder as the dancefloor brightened, the trumpets blared and the disco ball descended in revolutions between the rafters.

Hours later, after Klein asked for her *cell*, taking her number and leaving with a kiss on both cheeks, Ginny skipped from Jay Street to the hotel, brimming with joy. Somehow, after just one night in New York, she felt as much of a local as anyone else. The city had welcomed her arrival, had made this trip not a holiday but a landing, and she wondered for how many years she had longed to fly away from Melbourne. At five a.m, as she hopped up the hotel staircase, a surge of lightness sprang from her heels to her hair: there were still another seven days to spend with Klein. 'Where did you get off to?' said Marg. 'A nightclub.' 'What's it called?' 'The Box.' 'How was it?' 'I'm a new person,' she said, plucking the gloves off her fingers. 'Good for you,' said Marg. 'Who was the DJ?' 'The DJ?' Ginny collapsed onto her half of the bed, giggling madly, so loudly that her laughter rang up the ventilation shaft. Marg wiped Vegemite off her lip-gloss and said, 'Well, someone's chatty all of a sudden.' Ginny awoke that afternoon with two messages on her cell: the first, from Marg, inviting her to do the Statue of Liberty and the Brooklyn Bridge; and the second, from Klein: 'I'm making dinner at home. My roommates are back from Austin and New Haven. They're curious to meet you. Come to Greenpoint?' She undressed, ran the shower and eased under the hot water, cracking her knuckles and rubbing her throbbing earlobes. She knelt on the bed before the open window, as steam caressed her thighs and licked the air over the sidewalk. If she abandoned all plans for their time in the States, this holiday could become real life, unpredictable yet wholly authentic. If she just dumped Marg's tacky tourist itinerary, she could be whoever she pleased. Her excitement grew and a smile widened her face; where once she would have stopped herself, weary of another disappointment, now she lingered in the moment. Klein embraced her at the Graham Avenue subway station, his silver nipple rings pressing through his transparent silver jacket. 'You'll never believe this,' she said. 'I haven't hugged anyone in ten years.' 'Well, we do love melodrama, don't we?' said Klein, pinching her cheeks. 'My roommates heard all the details of our night and they're in love with you already.' The entire apartment was really one long room, a railroad sectioned by drywall, with a narrow corridor running from the toilet to the kitchen past all the bedrooms in between. An old radiator heater rattled in the living room. A rickety fire escape wobbled outside the window. The rooms separated the space, but they didn't divide; every comment was part of one shared conversation. Shelly was Mauritian, bald, six-foot-four, an androgynous, ropey figure in a slim black nightie. Their deep baritone voice resounded from behind their dentures as they lounged on the ottoman, humming a set of scales. 'Move to the Empire State,' read the tattoo on their chest. 'Be a superstar.' In the town where they had grown up, not a single person had ever touched a saxophone, and now they were auditioning to play the Lincoln Centre. The other room-mate, Gordon, was an intern at the *Paris Review*. 'Technically he's only a volunteer reader,' said Klein, measuring another schmear of manza, 'but he tells the girls he meets that he's an editor.' 'It's very highbrow,' called Gordon from his room, where he was folding a red apron and a pair of red Speedos. 'We mostly take American literary fiction, the pinnacle of realist storytelling. It's how great stories are supposed to be written, you know.' 'He's working an ice-cream job on Chambers to pay his rent,' said Klein. 'It's actually gelato,' said Gordon. 'The pinnacle of highbrow,' said Klein, tapping his glasses. Ginny laughed, and snorted, and then she blushed. The frenzy came from the frantic pace, the electric wit, these mesmerising characters slowly orbiting towards her.

Throughout the night, she told them about Jim's lion statues, the Chadstone mall and the long hours at Reynolds, and they listened intently, bursting into laughter when she told them of all the lousy ways Püd tried to bed Nadine. All the while, the warmth of the manza spread up her fingers and settled between her legs. She floated off the couch, cushioned by a layer of hot air. 'Ça va?' said Shelly. 'Her life is mythic, no?' They finished their bowls of lentil salad and lay in the living room as the snow tumbled onto the balcony, blanketing the window and muffling the sirens across Greenpoint. It was her first snowfall. 'We have to celebrate,' said Klein, jiggling his vials of manza. 'But we're running low. Do we have any more Bitcoin?' Gordon scampered to his MacBook and opened Coinbase, a webpage filled with graphs, as she stared over his shoulder. 'Cryptocurrencies,' he said. 'They're the future of the economy. Unregulated. Sans borders. A global currency valuated in real time by people around the world. Prices are rising. Look.' She followed his finger to Bitcoin, which had soared twenty per cent in the last day, and, tracking through the months, she saw peak after peak, a bullish incline, a verdant tick. 'It's what we use for buying manza,' said Klein. 'We have a direct supply from Latin America if we use Bitcoin. It can't be tracked. It's making our trade so much freer. And safer.' 'But that's where he's wrong, Ginny,' said Gordon. 'It's not just the underworld. It's the whole world. Crypto is the future. No borders. No regulations. Free exchange.' 'Je suis fatigué,' said Shelly. 'Who is going to boogie with Sister Genevieve and me?' They slung the men off the couch, twirling them in their arms. The opening trill of a jazz medley lit up the room: the skitter-scatter of the cymbals, the erotic arc of the saxophone, the heartbeat of the bass going up, ever upward, the group jiving across the apartment and into the earliest hours of the next day. By the fiery light of sunrise, Ginny floated back to the hotel, hiding her glowing fingertips in her pockets, and snuck past the bathroom and into bed. 'Where the bloody hell have you been?' said Marg, bolting upright in the gloom. 'I was waiting all night. Dad's been calling.' 'I need to sleep,' said Ginny. 'You think it's safe for a girl to go out there alone? You wouldn't know what to do if some bloke started you.' A pair of Lady Liberties glowed on the nightstand and two MTA posters lay drying on the carpet by the heating vent. As Ginny burrowed into bed, one of the maps hovered off the carpet, riding the warm gust like a kite caught up, up, in its newest updraft.

And so the week passed. She told Jim their time zones were too confusing for calls, texting rows of heart emojis when she knew he was sound asleep. Then came the candlelit evenings at the bars along Graham Avenue, fistfuls of snow wiped off windowsills and hurled at faces and brows, traipsing on the subway lines as the L train rumbled down the tunnel, Monday for Shelly's calisthenics, Tuesday for Gordon's Nietzschean critiques of millennial culture, and on to Wednesday, for their second innings at the Box, and drinks on Thursday afternoon turning into Thursday night manza, and then came Friday, of course, when Ginny woke to find Marg zipping up their suitcases. 'We've got a flight today,' Marg said. 'We're doing Niagara Falls. You forgotten that too?' Ginny itched the scab inside her earlobe. She wasn't leaving New York, not yet. She would catch a return flight to Melbourne from JFK in a month's time. 'It's Dad's money anyway,' said Ginny. 'He won't care if he doesn't know.' 'Wait—so you reckon I'm *not* going to tell him?' said Marg. 'And what if I tell him about all the strangers you're fucking in the middle of the night?' Marg kneed her, gruffly, in the crotch. Ginny staggered across the room and the suitcase tipped, unveiling Marg's Nepalese panties stuffed inside her Ugg boots, and the two Lady Liberties clattered against the door. 'You think it's Dad I don't want them to see?' said Marg. 'Gee, open your eyes for once, you downer cunt.' 'I'll see you in a month,' said Ginny, reaching her hand over the mementos and gasping. She limped to the suitcase, grabbed her clothes and crammed them in two tote bags. 'You're going to freeze out there,' said Marg. 'All alone.'

Thirty minutes later, she arrived at Klein's apartment, tears frozen on her face, her bags overflowing with scarves, gloves and woollen beanies. 'You been schlepping that stuff all on your own?' he said, carrying the totes up the stairs, his button-down untucked from his black slacks, his bow tie dangling off his collar. 'But what have you been up to?' she said. 'Oy vey,' he said, 'I swear the handsomest man was eating at Thirteen Madison Park. I couldn't believe my eyes when I saw him again.' She huffed, trying to exhale her separation from her sister, trying not to acknowledge that they had always shared one roof, had lived together for every day of Ginny's life. 'He's rich,' continued Klein, 'and he's smart. He has that London–New England accent, like you can't quite place him. And he's an entrepreneur.' 'He must be so happy with himself,' she said. 'But happiness is a monochromatic feeling,' said Klein, balancing her tote bags by the couch. 'Is this the beautiful Black Knight again?' said Shelly. 'We've heard a lot about him. He's bigger than Obama, no?' Shelly rubbed the blood back into Ginny's fingers, one by one, dispelling the cold. 'But what happened, Sister Genevieve?' 'It's nothing,' she said. 'But you're nervous, no?' said Shelly. 'Nothing is ever nothing.' Anxiety flooded her chest, faster than she had ever felt in her life, and she tumbled onto the couch, horrified that, with all her strangeness, she had at last burdened these people she hoped to call friends. 'Marg freaked out,' she said, 'that I was having fun without her. So she left for Niagara Falls by herself.' She told them about the hotel, the tussle, the return flight to Melbourne dangling at the end of February like a noose. Klein slid onto the couch beside her, enfolding her knuckles with his palm. 'If life teaches us anything,' he said, 'it's that families always unravel. Friends, though, they stick around. Friends are the family you create.' He was a bastard-child,

120

he explained, raised by his upstairs neighbour, herself an orphan of two ex-Swamp Angels, that secret gang of Jews and Irishmen who once plundered the docks on Cherry Street and lived throughout the sewers. 'We don't have a choice in being born,' he said, 'but we have a choice in how we live. Ever upward?' She hugged him, inhaling the aroma of his cologne. 'Ever upward,' she said, and stole into the bathroom to change into her flannel pyjamas, buttoning the sleeves around her wrists and smoothing the trousers down to her ankles. She strode to the couch and curled beside the corduroy cushion. 'Good news,' said Klein, loading the website of a restaurant on the Upper West Side. 'I've spoken to an old friend, Yuval. He co-owns this place in Manhattan. Set your alarm. Chef wants to meet over breakfast. You want to stay here, right? You want to make a life in New York?'

The next morning, outside Bistro Sognare on Amsterdam and Seventy-Third, Ginny huddled in a ski jacket and peered through the frosted windows at a waiter crushing a sachet of Splenda in his fist. She walked between the tables, past the bottoms of wine bottles leering like glassy eyes, and stood by the bar, unpeeling her gloves. 'We're closed,' said a woman in the corner. 'Service starts at eleven.' The woman crossed her legs, brushed the dust off her leather pants and adjusted her studded wristwatch. She wore a Lululemon tank top, a ribbed Moncler jacket with a fox-fur lining and matted concealer on her hairy top lip. 'I'm looking for Mr Saltsman,' said Ginny. 'He's not here,' said the woman. 'It's his day off. He has culinary school. He teaches.' 'I'm a friend of Yuval's. He knows I'm coming.' 'Yuval? How's that madman doing these days? I hear his name uptown-downtown but I haven't seen him in weeks. Saltsman is in the walk-in. You tell him Arabella sent you.' Ginny edged between the stacks of upended black chairs, the undersides pockmarked with bubblegum and wet tissues, and through the kitchen, past the clanking dishwashers, to find a man standing inside the enormous refrigerator, his pressed shirt pulled tautly over his corded torso, his apron folded over one shoulder and a silver hotel pan balanced on the other, squeezing the deadbolt in his sinewy fist. 'You're Mr Saltsman, aren't you?' she said. 'I'm busy,' he said, 'with this inventory.' 'Sorry, Mr Saltsman.' '*Chef* Saltsman,' he said. 'Now, who is this?' 'I'm Ginny. I'm a friend of Arabella's. And Yuval's. And Klein's. They think you might need some extra hands.' 'So, you're the Aussie ginger, huh? How's that working out for you these days?' He raised his hand and snapped at the icy air. A boy skittered into the walk-in and piled the hotel pan with turnips and puréed beetroot. Chef Saltsman led her to the kitchen, where he fished

122

a rag from the sink and filled a sani-bucket with water. 'Let's see how you clean up,' he said. 'We'll yak-yak after your trial.' The work was methodical, elementary, but essential: wiping stains off the tables and sinks, funnelling spilled salt back into the shakers, unloading cloudy glasses from the dishwasher, cleaning up after customers who spilled in from the snow and wiped ice off their boots. She racked the veined coffee cups upside down, lined the demitasse and bouillon bowls along the polyester napkins, twirled the plastic stems of the poppies to loosen the mould from the inside of the vases. Chef Saltsman summoned her to the kitchen at six p.m. He rolled his sleeves and shook her hand. 'Tomorrow morning, tchotchke,' he said, 'come for Round Two.' She burst onto Amsterdam, ran to Broadway for the downtown express and shot across Manhattan on the L. Maybe, she thought, there was a life here after all. Her feverish jive lasted until the apartment, where she met Gordon in the stairwell and jumped him in a bear hug. 'So how does he split his tips?' he said. 'What do you mean?' 'You should check that. They say minimum wage is going up. For everyone, even busboys. Better you know how you'll be paid.' On her second day, Ginny shimmied between the tourists and the front of house, mopping around the urinals and sinks, darting between regulars and Arabella's friends: bedazzled women with plump upper lips, all squeezed into Lycra leggings and designer crop tops, who giggled when Ginny mopped their spilled drinks, patting her neck and shoulders, cheering their Cinderella from Down Under. 'No seriously, just listen to me,' said Gordon, washing his Speedos in the kitchen sink. 'You going in again tomorrow? You have to pin him down and get him to sign something. How's he going to pay you?' The next shift was another snowswept afternoon and she became the centre of Bistro Sognare. She loved spreading tides of blue degreaser across the restaurant and becoming a spectre in the steam, astonishing her audience of French dogs, child tourists with fidget spinners and widescreen tablets, middlemen executives in heavy grey suits, mob wives from Staten Island in their red petticoats, new-money Chinese families in Canada Goose jackets. 'For God's sake, Ginny,' said Gordon that night over a bowl of ramen, 'if you don't get a contract off Saltsman, I'll go in there and pull it out of him.' 'S'il vous plaît?' said Shelly. 'Not once,' said Gordon. 'Your visa, no?' said Shelly. 'I bet your Chef Saltsman's never heard of an I-9 status,' said Gordon, 'I bet the government lets Israelis in for free.' 'Maybe he can pay her under the table. Cash,' said Shelly. 'It's fine,' said Ginny, calmly raising her palms above the table. 'I'll ask Chef tomorrow. Promise.' The next day was Chef's class at culinary school, so she tailed the full-time dishwasher, DeMarcus, and badgered him with questions about her wage, her documents, her hours. 'Baby girl, listen to me,' he said. 'I just clean the plates. I'm no oracle. You think I got all the answers?' Saturday was the Sabbath, so on Sunday, at last, in the midafternoon lull, while a snowstorm blanketed the street and the restaurant regulars were stuck inside their Soul Cycle studio, she cornered Saltsman in the fridge. 'Of course!' he said. 'She is some patient, this girl. You've confirmed already with Yuval, no? What's your social security number?' 'Yuval hasn't given me anything.' 'Where are your papers?' 'I'll bring my passport,' she said. 'Passport-shmassport—you got a visa? Or a Green Card?' 'Can Yuval just pay me cash?' 'Can Yuval just pay you cash? You're telling me you just showed up, unannounced, to scrounge a job without papers? That's your brilliant idea? It's not the nineties no more. Yuval pays you under the table and he'll have every auditor from here to Secaucus on his tochis. It's high pressure running the city's best kosher Italian restaurant—one no-good slip-up and they'll take us to the baths!' The colour drained from her face. She paced out of the walk-in and shut the deadbolt. Chef Saltsman hollered in the cold, banging on the steel

124

door. She raced out of Bistro Sognare, sprinting to the subway with her eyes smarting, terrified that he had severed her one tie to the city, that she was fated to spend her days tumbling, further and further, until she woke up at the bottom of the world in those woeful suburbs she knew all too well.

'Forget Yuval,' said Klein. 'Let us extend the search.' The next day, she trekked to Wall Street and met a manager at the Irish Thorn. 'I love your accent,' the woman said. 'You getting a visa soon? Then we'll talk.' She walked up to SoHo, to the Mercer Kitchen, and shared a negroni with the manager at the bar. 'No papers?' he said. 'Then as passionate as you are for New York, honey, I'm afraid I can't help you.' 'I'm walking around out here with a stench,' she texted Klein. 'I thought I'd left Melbourne behind.' Back in Greenpoint, she loaded a picture on the family WhatsApp chat: a selfie of Marg under a jet of water, hair wicked across her forehead, the arms of her plastic green poncho flailing in the wind. 'Doing Vegas next,' she wrote. 'Having the time of our lives xo.' 'This is what I need to get me up and about,' wrote Betty, with a smile emoji. A hot flush spread through Ginny's hair, down her back and across her abdomen, but she didn't care anymore. She yanked off her shirt, airing the pockmarked flesh on her arms and belly, and lay on the couch, fanning her face with a crumpled résumé. She split a vial of manza, gouging the penknife up her fingernails. Her hundreds of inch-long scars were sickly pink under the living room lamplight. Shelly ran their fingers up her arms, playing her blemishes like the keys on a piano. Gordon stroked his fingernails down her back and massaged her knots. Klein knelt on the cushions, pressing his lips over her scars. They gleamed under his kisses. 'But the origins of this fuck-up are decades old,' said Ginny. 'Y'all have never heard of Betty Anton this side of the Pacific.' She recounted her mother's final beauty pageant, when Betty clomped into the powder room in platform heels and a gold string bikini, yanked the pins from her dyed brunette curls, wiped the concealer off her alabaster cheeks, beat her fists into the stretchmarks on her thighs and smudged foundation all over her belly to hide her C-section scar. And all the while, in a playpen surrounded by nail-filers, hair-straighteners and eyelash-curlers, Ginny clapped her infant hands to the resounding applause from the convention centre: for Miss Geelong, in second place, and Miss Toorak, the debut champion with the flawless figure. 'So you think they're worth the hype or what?' said Betty, hissing under her mane of hair. With a mother's precision, she found the nail-filer, clutched Ginny to her bikini top and sliced open her freckles, one after the other. 'She did *what* to you?' said Gordon. 'She called it "cosmetic surgery." And then she wanted to get rid of me, but who in their right mind would want a daughter like this? It's funny, really, when you see how cartoonish it all is.' 'Honey,' said Klein, holding her hand. 'You know why we love you? You're not sentimental. You don't wallow. You want to remake yourself, no matter what. It's more than we could say for half the normies who move here and think they're real New Yorkers.' Ginny's frown softened with a simple truth: there was clarity in anger. Her sister and her father were antiquated, barbaric compared to her family in New York. But it was Betty, the queen of that mansion in Carnegie, the symbol of that second-rate city, who had botched her ambition and taught Ginny to deny her own. Her mothering was a rotten web, stinking of suburbia, woven with shame, and would be overcome at all costs.

She slept deeply, waking at midday to an empty apartment. Tiny mice scratched in the walls, rustling until she stepped off the couch and creaked up the corridor. An arctic February front had swept over the city, freezing the puddles on the road, icing the sidewalk and frosting the windows of the living room. A siren wailed and the apartment glowed blue and red. Muffled voices shouted in the street. A gunshot. Scrambling feet and shattering glass. She wrenched the window open and crisp air scalded her arms, then her hips, freezing the tips of her hair. A police car hummed at the corner of Leonard. She leaned out the window and saw a ring of officers around Chase. A heist. She leapt onto the fire escape as the arctic air drenched her thin pyjamas and, just as she saw a woman, handcuffed, hunch-backed, being hauled out of the bank, the iron railing cracked under Ginny's weight and she slipped, smashing her face on the bricks. She clutched the window for balance and scurried back inside. Her front tooth had split in half, like a ticket ripped from the stub, and her mouth had filled with blood. She googled a nearby dentist, but the closest was shut for the storm. She called one in Williamsburg and the secretary quoted a replacement tooth at ten thousand dollars. 'But no problem, Miss Antonopoulos,' she said. 'You got insurance, don't you?' 'But come on, honey,' said Klein, when he found her sprawled on the couch, her hair matted on her face. 'You don't need a fix-up so urgently. You're in the greatest city in the world. You have three days left. Let's just have a good time.'

He reserved her a seat by the bar at Thirteen Madison Park from ten to eleven-thirty each day. She sipped a single martini, forcing a smile, and although reservations ran into March, Klein wouldn't accept her thanks. 'I want you to see my world,' he said, 'in all its sublimity.' He scampered between the tables, lit by the baroque chandelier, snapping at the wait staff to prepare the morning decanters and linens. She rationed her martini in cautious sips, wincing as the Austrian crystal skimmed her broken front tooth, trying to distract herself with the morning rituals: linens draped over the tables, cutlery polished and placed, wine glasses aligned, tulips cut and rearranged. The guests arrived at quarter to eleven, bankers, mostly, pale old men with their bellies corseted in black suits, or old-money families assembling for brunch at four hundred dollars a head. The waiters decanted the Bordeaux by the light of a candle and a chanteuse sang, 'Non, je ne regrette rien,' from the elevated stage. At ten to eleven Klein pinched her swollen cheeks and said, 'He's here, the Black Knight.' And yes, there was the handsomest man in the city after all, tightening his collar while reaching for a menu, rolling his sleeves up his forearms. At eleven-thirty, Ginny stumbled from the bar, rubbing her aching mouth, as the wind whipped around the Flatiron Building and circled in Madison Square Park. 'You have *got* to see a dentist,' said Gordon, letting her into the apartment on her last afternoon. 'You look like a chipmunk.' 'It's too expensive,' she said, wiping her pink spit off her lips. 'I don't have that kind of money.' 'Fam, it's your health,' said Gordon, and he called Klein, who hurried home from the restaurant and crouched beside her on the couch. 'Ginny, honey,' he said, 'when did you start swelling?' 'But I'm going home.' 'But I have an idea,' he said. He called an uncle, then a father-in-law, then a godfather and a sister's boyfriend's niece, and ordered an Uber to the Upper East Side. 'He's the best in the business,' he said, holding her tightly in the car. 'You'll be okay.' 'So what you want is a serious sterilisation,' said the dentist, a bald man with bulldog cartoons framed on his office walls, 'and a root-canal and then a ceramic filler. I'll make it super-sharp, okay? Michelin star in time for your flight tomorrow. Now, Klein explained your situation to me. I can work for no charge, no problem, but you won't have anaesthetic. No laughing gas. You see what I am saying?' 'I'll see whatever I want,' she said, and pulled Klein into the bathroom, knifed each of her nails with manza and tipped the last drops into her eyes. As she lay in the dentist's chair, she floated along Fifth Avenue, past the halal vendors with cardboard prayer mats, past the marching band headed to Union Square, past the waving mannequins in Kate Spade and Zara, past the Con Edison trucks upending the blacktop. Digging and cutting. Grinding and gluing. Klein stroked her hand as the dentist bored into her gums. Three hours of excavations to repair her tooth. She floated into the Box, flying with her friends around the electric saws and jackhammers onstage—and she awoke on an airplane. 'Klein?' she said, shrinking into her seat. The first return flight. JFK to LAX. She clawed her hands up her neck. Her face was soft, smooth. She slid her tongue over her gums. The new tooth was indistinguishable from the rest. Marg yapped on about the Sands Hotel. The Sapphire Club. The Stratosphere Casino. Ginny chewed her emerald nails as Manhattan shrank beneath the plane, an island of snowcapped towers and underground spectres. She had relinquished her divinity. She had become a lone cadaver, a corpse in a Qantas coffin, shipped out for burial.

Jim yelped across the arrivals barrier, his rubbery face turned the colour of a tomato in the February heat. Betty sat shotgun in the car, her shoulders caved, her eyes glazed. 'My girls have come home,' said Jim, skipping through the parking lot. 'Back where they belong.' They drove down a long arterial highway, past discount factory warehouses, golf courses, fields of spare grass and telephone towers. 'We just want you to know, girls,' he said, patting Betty's thigh, 'there'll be no drinking or drug-taking in this house. Is that understood?' Ginny stiffened. She buried her fingernails under her jeans. Finally, Jim pulled the car into their driveway. The lawn was buried under new concrete slabs and the roof covered in garish pink tiles, the colour of a dog's erection. Ginny hefted her luggage out of the car and limped into the house. The living room stank of lemon detergent. The late-summer air whisked through the windows, swirling the citrus tang. The couches had been rearranged to face the walkway to the kitchen, where the fridge stared her down with a brooding hum. She climbed the stairs and collapsed on her pillows as the last drops of New York water pooled in her bladder. Her cell filled with messages: pictures of Shelly's new latex corset, lines from Gordon's thesis on *The Will to Power*, screenshots of Bitcoin's rising value. 'Text us if you ever need a thing, honey,' wrote Klein. 'We miss you already.' She created a WhatsApp group called 'Excelsior' and sent them a selfie in the sun. She woke in the middle of the night, her brow furrowed as her curtains and bookshelves refocused, radiating in the green glow from the zipper of her unpacked suitcase. She crawled out of bed, yanked the suitcase open and held the last vial of manza. The presence of the green glow helped her grow a second skin, a shield to carry as she trudged through Chadstone the next day, past the boys in frumpy Superman costumes and the geriatrics on walking frames. She walked into Reynolds and Püd chuckled. 'My, my, Miss American Pie,' he said. 'Welcome home.' Nadine huffed, clunked into the store on her platform heels and said, 'Home already? You didn't have to rush back or anything, you know.' Ginny paced through the mall to the emergency balcony, returning to her old perch, rolling a cigarette as she tongued her porcelain tooth. The Red Plains flickered on the edge of all those roads she knew so well. She wondered what her friends would think if they could share this view. 'It seems the Melburnians are a people undisturbed in their little town,' Gordon would say. 'They carry a carcinogenic complacency, willing nothing, devolving through humanity into their mid-brain ancestors. Working menial jobs. Pining for the next public holiday. To take it easy. To kickback.' 'How will she and her brilliant mind survive?' Shelly would say. At Reynolds, Ginny tore the acknowledgements pages from the bestsellers and folded them into paper planes, suspending Mighty Mites and Nakamura Locks from the ceiling. They hovered, four feet above their heads, close enough to read the acknowledgements of friends, agents and editors, but high enough to always float above a customer's hands. After dusting the untouched register and tallying the unsold books, she closed the store and sat in her car, her head on the dashboard, groaning in the gloom. At Jim's house, she unwrapped a set of noise-cancelling headphones and took the box to the recycling bin. Discarded in the trash were bottles of nail polish remover, hand sanitiser, Listerine. Any trace of alcohol, abandoned by the roadside. They were really trying it all, she thought, grimacing in the dark. She clunked the yellow lid shut, limped upstairs and registered on CoinSpot, making her first Bitcoin trades.

That Sunday, at the support brunch, Jim opened a letter from Betty's homeopath in the dining room. 'May the First. The mind has started to heal. The poison has been drained from the body for four months. Four, in East Asia, to symbolise death. Oftentimes, withdrawal leads to psychic inversions, as the old ego withers. Keep persisting. Relapse will set you back one week at a time. In another four months, recovery will be complete, and you will be reborn into your best self yet.' He started clapping, Marg joined, then Jason, who promised to take Betty cruising in his Nissan to celebrate her news. Ginny clenched her fork against her plate. 'But hey,' said Jason, after the applause, 'I never asked for your thoughts on Vegas, Ginny.' 'My thoughts?' she said. 'I'm planning my best mate's bachelor party,' he said, 'and I want to suss the place. Marg has her own special way of thinking. I could do with a second opinion.' A slice of sausage caught in her throat. 'Come on, love,' said Jim. 'Tell Jason about your time at the casinos.' She mumbled about musical theatre, losing some money at blackjack. 'Show us a picture, Miss United States of America,' said Jim. 'We only got to see Marg's photos, but not yours.' 'Sorry, y'all,' she said, 'I guess I must have deleted them.' 'You deleted them?' said Jim. 'She's lying,' said Betty, tapping her glass of boiled kudzu. 'A mother can always tell.' Then Ginny tried to take her cell from the table and a stream of notifications filled the screen. Klein's pictures of the frozen fountain in Madison Square Park. The letter of recommendation from Gordon's philosophy professor. Shelly playing a saxophone, nude, between their legs. 'I stayed in New York,' said Ginny. 'I stayed with my friends.' Betty swished her kudzu between her teeth and Jim burrowed into his tea towel. 'You know this isn't my fault, right?' said Marg. 'I told her to come with me. To stick to our plan. I swear, she could've been

134

shot or something. It's Brooklyn, Dad. A-me-ri-ca. I've seen how they live.' 'But it was our secret,' said Ginny, and she was grounded, immediately, ordered to repay Jim for the trip. 'You know what the homeopath would say about secrets?' he said. 'They're very toxic.' 'No toxins,' said Betty. 'We all need a clean house,' he said. 'The cleanest there can be.'

Though Ginny had never cared about her bank balance, now she had to draft a schedule to cover her debt to Jim: twelve hundred dollars on the first day of the month, six months in total, with a hundred-dollar fee for tardiness. 'You can put it in the family account,' said Jim, 'to help cover the homeopath's fees. The nutritionist's, too.' Minutes at Reynolds blurred into hours. She tilted her paper planes towards the Pacific and they rippled under the air conditioners like a flock of greying seagulls. Her fingernails faded back to regular old pink. The scar above her tooth sealed over. One morning, just when the linoleum floor seemed to be melding over her legs, pinning her for all eternity beside the bookshelves, a boy ran into the store, panting, and said, 'I'm on a break from uni and I'm wondering if you might need some extra help.' His grey eyes glinted above his hollow cheeks. He clutched a crumpled résumé. She avoided his stare and edged away, towards the backroom, but he wouldn't leave. His palms left prints on the dust jackets of the bestsellers. 'Do you even read?' she said. 'I like Russian books, yeah,' he said. 'Tolstoy. Dostoyevsky. Franz Kafka.' He extended his hand and a laugh escaped her lips. 'You don't even know why that's funny, do you?' she said. He folded his résumé on the counter and left the store, leaving the dust to envelop her again. But by the afternoon a group of schoolkids swept through the doorway, yelling through the aisles, dumping their schoolbags over the unboxed books, yapping on their phones, demanding her attention. She couldn't bear to deal with these banal people, to take seriously this store that was only her means of missing New York. Before closing, she retrieved the boy's résumé and called head office. 'We need to grow the team,' she said. 'The customers need a fresh face, more attention. I have an applicant who volunteered at St Vincent de Paul.

And he's worked in retail for years. He could be a positive influence. His name's Titch Antoine Clement.' 'I don't know, darling,' said the regional manager, his voice hammering down the line. 'What if I told you we had a very long conversation?' she said. 'He thinks this place could be more than books or shelves. It could be a community.' 'You'd have another schedule to manage. You got new Lamy fountain pens coming in.' 'Well, they'll be perfect Christmas-in-July gifts.' 'Three sales staff under one manager? Big responsibility. But you're confident, aren't you? Let him be your first hire. Fuck it. My congratulations.' She ended the call and stayed in the backroom, scrolling through Klein's photos of falling sakura petals while the customers rang the bell at the register and banged on the counter. The next day, the regional manager emailed through the Reynolds newsletter with the news of Ginny's first hire, and that night Marg shared the notice at the dinner table. Betty nodded slowly, twirling her straw inside her tumbler of milk-thistle tea, and Jim smothered Ginny in a reconciliatory hug. Marg snapped a photo and posted it on Instagram. 'Little sis is a big-time manager,' she wrote. 'I'm astounded,' said Jim. 'They should get Dusty Martin off the telly and put you there instead.' 'You know, Ginny deserves a friend for all her hard work,' said Marg. 'And Jason's brother runs a farm in Lysterfield. The hamsters need homes or they'll become sausages.' They went on yapping as Ginny poured a cup of lemon tea, sucking her porcelain tooth behind her pursed lips. When Marg finished her hoopla, climaxing with an order of a titanium cage off the Pet World website, Ginny crept upstairs to her bedroom. She put on Kerouac's *American Haikus* and opened CoinSpot, joining her tribe of crypto traders to forge a borderless future, one without visas, or national identity, or the melancholy of home.

Cryptos

FINALLY, TITCH HAD A PLACE TO BE. He was scheduled at Reynolds from ten to six, with a forty-five-minute smoko—paid—in the middle, and they sent his pay to his bank every fortnight. He'd never felt so sure of himself. He was a 'casual part-timer', but they always needed his help, sometimes seven days in a row. He manned the Self-Help, Memoir and Philosophy bookshelves. It was his job to alphabetise the books, place the bestsellers face out and glue handwritten reviews on the shelves. He never read the books, so he rehashed the blurbs and added the right internet zingers: 'intergenerational', 'intersectional' and so on. When the shelves were sorted, he'd re-order the Lamy fountain pens at the register and double-check the stock in the backroom. One Lamy cost a hundred and fifty bucks, yeah, just sniffing the ink made him smile. Only rarely did someone stray in from the Chaddy crowd, their eyes flicking around in the dark, confused by all the hush-hush and low lighting. If they spent even two minutes in the aisles, peeping through the pop psychology, then Titch had a chance to shine. 'You looking for a gift, hun? That's generous of you. This writer's disrupting the scene. Award-winning. I'm surprised you haven't heard of her yet.' Or, if he really had to convince: 'They're making this one into a TV show.' Sometimes he chatted to the schoolkids, but his favourite customers were all the old peeps who took their time, who bussed to Chaddy from their nursing homes on Tuesday and Thursday mornings, who wore bifocal specs that made them tilt their heads whenever Titch recited the arty-farty reviews he concocted on the loo. There was one old woman with dyed blue hair who was always keen on Titch's help. She would sit in the vintage section, curled on the leather armchair, reading this or that forgotten classic, umm-ing and ah-ing to herself as she read, as if she were discovering secrets long forgotten by society. He would amble over, offer a cup of mint tea and make her feel like she was at the Ritz Carlton. In return for his weekly chirpiness, she slid two fifty-dollar bills onto the counter before leaving to Hairhouse Warehouse. 'When you get older,' she said, 'the world thinks you're invisible. I didn't think you'd even notice me.' On his lunchbreak, he always bought a sweet potato from Coles and left it by the dumpsters for the bloke who helped him get the job. Every day, when he went back, the spud was gone—just the paper bag left, yeah, sometimes with a note scrawled in Sharpie. 'You're a champ.' 'Good lad.' 'Thought our only listener was up on Degraves.' The days never changed. Titch could bank on this routine. True, Ginny was a little stiff at first, but she wasn't as weird as the others made her out to be. 'Definitely a lesbian,' he overheard Nadine say to Püd. 'She's such a headcase, Nads,' said Püd. 'I reckon she should've stayed on holidays.' But Titch had reasons to like Ginny. She was the one who put him on the payroll and calculated his weekend penalty rates. Time and a half on Saturdays. Double on Sundays. Double and a half on public holidays. She even sorted the shifts six months in advance, so he could plan his pay all the way until Chrissy time. While ordering the books, he tallied up how much he made. Two and half hours into a Saturday shift? Seventy-five bucks. Three hours into a Sunday? One hundred and twenty. The mental maths kept him on his toes and the hours passed without him noticing. So, yeah, there was plenty to love about Reynolds. Swiping his ID at ten to ten. Chatting to strangers without spooking them. Adding paper planes to the overhead fleet. There was no need to think about the past anymore. He loved waking up with something to do, a place to be, peeps who expected to see his face, yeah, who were counting on him to play his role.

The best shifts were Monday mornings, when Püd shared his stories with Nadine. Once he went on a bender in Frankston and woke up with a starfish down his jocks. One night, when his mum visited from Western Australia, he stiffed her dachshund using peanut butter for lube. Püd had grown up in Perth, played soccer for fifteen years, and won a scholarship to go to uni in America. 'At this place called Albany, you know it?' 'Nope,' said Nadine. 'It's in New York.' The scholarship would cover Püd's classes, food and flights, and all he had to do was play soccer. But right before leaving, his mates took him to Indonesia for a farewell trip. 'We thought we could do Bali in a couple of days,' he said. 'It was a bit over the top.' On the return leg, as they boarded the plane, the boys realised they still had twenty bucks' worth of magic mushrooms, so they offered them to Püd as a gift. 'Don't ever do this, Nads,' he said. 'If your mate ever offers you shrooms before a Tiger Air flight, just take a raincheck.' Püd left the plane covered in munt and went home to prepare to leave Perth. But after a month his guts still hurt. He couldn't eat. Couldn't shit. His fingertips turned brown. His toes, too. He kept putting off going to the hospital until one day he couldn't walk. The doc said his pancreas was infected. He had gangrene. It cracked off the top of his littlest toe. 'She reckoned it was the shrooms combined with the aeroplane pressure.' He contracted diabetes and couldn't walk. He explained the situation to the coach in Albany but he couldn't understand. Uni never came together, so Püd moved to Melbourne to play in the B-leagues and find a job in retail. 'Hindsight's always twenty-twenty,' he said. 'I might have pulled plenty of poon, but fuck America, we don't need it. Everything we need is right here,' and he pinched Nadine on the bum as Titch peeked through the shelves of Classic Aussie Fiction.

But one morning Püd arrived with his trousers streaked with oil, his face dusty, his eyes sunk in dark rings. 'I got to tell you guys something,' he said, panting, as he tumbled into the bookshelves. Titch fished a spare tee from his backpack and Nadine put her phone away. 'You smell like shit,' she said. 'This is really grim,' said Püd, his voice breaking, his shoulders shaking, clenching his fists until they turned white beneath the grime. 'Me and the boys drove down to Dandy,' he said. 'Rob was supposed to know the way to a hot house. But he cooked it and got lost. We ended up in the Red Plains.' 'You out of your mind?' said Nadine. 'We didn't plan on it,' said Püd. 'Our wheels break down. And it's so dark out there without any lights. There's nothing around. No houses yet. Absolutely doughnuts of anything. So I get out and start running for a few ks. After maybe twenty minutes, I find this one motel. I go in but there's no one. I'm up on the desk, looking for anyone, but the phones won't work and the computer is kaput. And then I start freaking out, thinking I hear someone in one of the rooms, someone yelling, real mad, thudding against the walls. And all I want is a phone to buzz someone to help us with the car. By that point I've lost the boys, so I have to go through the rooms alone. And I start at the top, thinking I'll work my way down. The first five are all locked but the windows are open and I see people sleeping inside. A family in one. An old fella in the next. Two old birds with their dentures out in big vases of water in another. I knock on the doors but they're lying very still, like mannequins. I get downstairs and all of a sudden I hear the screaming again. I open a door and there's this girlie on the bed, her legs spread, heaps of blood on the sheets, and she's howling her throat out.' Nadine clutched her fist over her mouth. 'I try to help her, but I don't know what to do, and she keeps yelling with her eyes shut, and I'm trying to calm her down, and then at last she stops screaming and she pops out a kid. A little baby. But it has no face, no eyes, just a shiny metal head. And all I see in the reflection is me.' 'Oh my fucking God,' said Nadine. 'Why would you even tell us that?' Titch rubbed the goosebumps out of his forearms, afraid the Reynolds stories would be over forever. 'I saw my worst nightmare,' said Püd, 'and my worst nightmare saw me.'

Titch spent his downtime in bed, tapping the floor with his toes, researching his ants on the internet. They would drag blowflies and beetle husks across the flat, jamming them in the plasterboard, orbiting the nest by sharing their vibrations in the tiles. They peeled resin off the eucalypts on the nature strip and lugged it back upstairs to the queen. Her warmth was enough for a thousand workers. Then Titch's payslip came and he loaded his CommBank app. He earned six-fifty most weeks. Seven-fifty if he covered one of Püd's shifts. He paid his rent for the rest of the year. He bought a Dell laptop. A Bluetooth speaker. A new iPhone. He updated his Facebook profile. 'Rig Burns,' it read. 'Bookseller at Reynolds.' He downloaded Instagram and saw the stories from the high-school lads. Gilly in his bathroom shaving his snail-trail. Danny Abdi crying into the camera after he broke up with his boyfriend. He followed World Famous Cats and cycled between their albums and his CommBank page, tracing his finger over the HD photo shoot with the Siberian lynx and refreshing his bank balance. Two grand this week. Two point six the next. Instead of sticking with the air mattress situation, nah, he could save another three grand and one day buy a king-size bed with satin sheets. So Titch lived frugally, waiting for the day when he could live in style. He ate two-minute noodles for lunch, fried eggs for dinner and sometimes, if his pep was low, brought home a Subway meatball footlong, licking the marinara sauce from his fingers as he ate. He downed canned tuna on the loo because he didn't want to stink up Reynolds on his break. He squeezed the last slithers of toothpaste from the tube and fixed his beaten-up Volleys with electrical tape. Quickly and surely, his money piled up. The savings weren't going away. No need to feel so alone, nah, enough of that. The money was his shield, thicker and sturdier with each week.

'Now maybe we got some excess dosh,' said Titch a few weeks later as he hunched over the ants. 'What should we do?' He lined up the notes and the ants crawled along his air mattress, trailing down the stitches in a single file, under the money and over the doona. He counted along with them. Four hundred bucks on this corner. Three on the next. In a glass jar were some coins for his Myki, maybe fifteen dollars in total. He could pump the lot into his bank account. Four thousand bucks all up. The ants crawled up his fingers and tickled his palms and he giggled. He had never seen so much money. He leaned his head on the bills and crinkled the laminate edges. He watched the rainbow refractions of the holographs and the grainy faces of the jackaroos printed on the notes. 'So I should live a little?' he said. 'We sure about that?' The ants parted around his busted shoes and crawled between his sheets. 'Get a new look? Really?' he said. 'You're right, yeah.' The next day, Titch booked it to Myer in his black tee and torn jeans, wandering through the rows of collared shirts, counting the styles and brands as he went. Sixty? Seventy? If he wanted the right fit, yeah, he couldn't skimp on the patience. He'd need to try them all. Slim fit. Button-less. Wrinkle-free. Italian brands. French brands. UK street style. Shirts for broad shoulders. Shirts for narrow waists. Linen. Cotton. Satin. *Seersucker.* Standing between the valleys of knitted jumpers and plaid trousers, Titch felt at the advent of something newer, nek-level, a chance to become someone else. What a rush. Walk in wearing a ratty T-shirt and jeans, dump them in the fitting rooms, slip into a new kit, and the old Titch would be gone. A proper Titch would return to Reynolds after his smoko, swaddled in satin shirts and tailored trousers. Maybe Ginny would think he also had a private-school backstory and well-off folks. That he ate at Toorak restaurants and holidayed at

Byron Bay. That he had done Paris, New York and Hong Kong. The story was ridiculous, but it was there to be written. He was as legit as any doctor or lawyer in the whole of Chaddy, and he had the money in his account to back him up. It was all fair dinkum. The dosh did not discriminate. 'Might I give you a hand with anything?' said a girl at the Ralph Lauren counter, rapping her lanyard with glossy white fingernails. 'Just having a look, yeah,' he said. 'Cheers.' The shirts were balanced on brass coat hangers and hung off marble shelves. 'Has anything caught your eye?' 'I want a new me,' he said. 'Why don't you come this way?' she said. 'I can take care of you.' Her name was Sophie, according to the badge pinned under her collar. She had strawberry-blonde hair tied in a ponytail with a red clip. Titch followed her to the fitting rooms, by a porcelain statue of a stallion. 'Take a moment to model these,' she said, thumbing through the bundles of shirts. 'You'll look dashing.' So he tried them on. Unbuttoning and buttoning. Smoothing and creasing. Tucking in and leaving out. He slid open the curtain to show Sophie, who popped a wad of chewing gum, diabolically, when he donned the red linen Ralph, the collar flared over his neck, two buttons undone. 'It's confident, Ralphy,' she said. 'Even assertive.' And he nodded as if he cared, because what really mattered was having the gold polo player front-and-centre on his chest for everyone to see. 'But try these,' she said. 'You'll be turning heads, a modern-day dandy.' She burst the gum between her lips and piled another bundle of shirts in the fitting room. 'Right-o,' he said, but what was the time? He'd left his mobile on the counter and didn't want to walk around with his ribs out, so he tried each of the new shirts, parading down the mirrored corridor. He had only come for one, but he ended up buying three *and* a brown leather belt—but the Ralphs were *confident*, and *assertive*, weren't they?—and only after leaving did he hear the distant burst of Sophie's bubble-gum and wonder if she was expecting a proper goodbye, a thank-you, too. Come on mate, don't be rude. He jogged between the gangs of Myer mannequins, with the shopping bags thwacking against his thighs, and when he arrived at Reynolds he apologised to Ginny for being late and fixed his hair in the backroom. 'Right-o,' he said, still chewing the inside of his cheek, swivelling his mobile in his hands, and after work he sprinted to the bus, jogged down Springvale Road, locked the flyscreen and lay on the air mattress, his breath warming the mobile as he loaded Facebook. 'Sophie. Ralph Lauren. Chadstone,' he searched. And there she was, first on the list, one arm around a redheaded girl outside some school gates, two blue-and-white plaid dresses shining among the emerald fronds. Animal Volunteer at the RSPCA. He friended her and wrote, 'Hey, cheers for the help today. Really nice of you.' And waited. Took a shower. Hung his new Ralphs off the curtain rod. 'You really left me wanting, Rig,' she wrote. He vaulted off his bed, over his audience of ants, and whooped and laughed and clapped his hands. 'What are you up to?' he wrote. 'Waiting for you to take me out,' she wrote. 'Out? You want to chill on Saturday?' 'Oh,' she wrote, 'I have too much energy to do anything chill. Maybe we can come up with something else?'

'I think I'm having a date this weekend,' he wrote to Püd. 'You wouldn't believe it, but there's someone at Myer...TBD.' He laid a piece of plywood under his sheets and ironed his new shirts, down the sleeves, around the buttons, up under the collars, working diligently while the ants climbed over his toes. He had never needed to go on a date before, but he liked making the iron hiss and filling his room with steam. He hung his shirts back on the curtain rod, thinking it was about time he bought himself a wardrobe, and that same night he ordered one online, a desk and a wheelie chair too, and the next day, midday, it all arrived. The bed could wait, yeah. He broke open the cardboard box and hammered the shelves with the bony ridge of his palm. Soon he had a place to keep his new kit, away from the dust and the ants, and somewhere to hide   's wallet. 'To be determined?' said Püd, the next day at work. 'What are you talking about, mate? Just bring a box of dingers. The ol' Durex six-pack.' 'Oh, nah, I don't know about that.' 'We all worried you were gay,' said Nadine, 'and if you don't put one through her she'll think you're a pipsqueak.' 'Look at this little madman,' said Püd, 'finally adding some balls to that cock.' So Titch wrote to Sophie at every chance possible. On the bus. On the loo. Walking through Chaddy before his shift. He looked through all her photos on Facebook—one from Christmas with her folks, another at the zoo with a little cousin, another on a volunteer trip in Papua New Guinea. She had gone to Lauriston Girls Grammar, the private school in the posh end of Armadale. He copied her full name from Facebook and found her on Instagram. Public profile. Seven thousand followers. Eight hundred and ten photos. She'd posted a throwback to summer, leaning back on an inflatable doughnut in a backyard pool, sunnies on, big wide smile, busting out of a red-and-yellow Triangl bikini. He played her story and there she was, standing by a white wall in a blue tee with 'Done with Slut-Shamers' stencilled on the front, her nipples pressing through the fabric like two-dollar coins. She'd made a video at the Rainbow Serpent Festival, wearing only three gold stars and a crown, her legs and arms flying in different directions. After work, Titch went for a haircut at Trim Tidings. The owner, Faz, was from Kuala Lumpur. He wore rings in his nose and circled the chop-chair like a field hawk. Mostly, Titch liked the way Faz massaged his scalp, those warm, wet fingers working in his hair, and the woody scent of aftershave in the towels. That alone was worth the sixty bucks. 'Your lady will have no trouble falling in love with you,' said Faz, dusting Titch's neck. 'She'll not hesitate to give you her heart.' He dropped the day's sweet potato at the dumpster, stopped at the florist, bought a red rose and kept it in his sink, and finally, yeah, it was the weekend. He woke up early on Saturday to a stream of texts. 'Going to have a blinder this Friday, Rig.' 'You want to rendezvous at three on Sat.' 'Get a wriggle on to the pizza parlour on Swan Street.' 'I might still be peaking.' 'That's in-du-bitable.' 'Haha.' 'Lucky you, Rig.' He hurried to the shower, lathered his neck and face and arms, humming as the water ran down his collarbones and pooled in the ridges of his ribs. He slicked his hair back with Suavecito pomade. Rubbed Old Spice in his armpits. Stuck a wad of Wrigley's Chewy in his mouth. He picked the red linen shirt, buttoned up before the mirror and grabbed his phone. He sent a snap to the Reynolds WhatsApp chat. 'Titch! Yum!' wrote Nadine. 'This boy,' wrote Püd, 'better have a hectic tale to tell.'

It was still raining at midday, so he brought his backpack to keep the rose dry. He caught the 900 to Huntingdale Station and stood behind the turnstiles, pacing by the platform edge. First time on the rails in a fair while, yeah. On the train he sat by a girl in a headdress who held a footy between her knees. It was Saturday, yeah, Richmond was playing at the G. He cracked his knuckles, munched on his gum and leaned into his reflection in the carriage window, sitting very still in case the rose thorns pricked the inside of his backpack. The train screeched by the cafes in Caulfield, through the muddy embankments at Toorak, under the bridge to South Yarra and through the warehouses into Richmond Station. A few Hawks fans pushed past as he ran to the southern end of the station, away from the G. The crowd petered out on Swan Street and he bounced down the footpath, looking for the pizza shop. It was two-fifteen. He walked inside Domino's and bundled into a booth as the waiter changed the telly to the footy warm-ups. He ordered a ginger beer and sipped it down, burping under his breath, then pulled the chewy out of his mouth and stuck it underneath the table. At five to four his phone was still blank. He left Domino's and walked across the road to Lucky Slice, holding his hands over his face to peer inside, but the place was shut, and then onwards to You Want a Piece of Me, but the only people inside were a girl holding her boy's hand, a slice of margherita pizza between them. How many pizza joints could you open on a single street? He went back to Domino's and fingered his chewy under the table. He texted Sophie and she texted straight back. 'This is a mare,' she wrote. 'I got caught up in something, Rig. Let's meet at my place before we go.' 'I'm all the way at the Domino's on Swan Street near the G,' he wrote. 'Okay, you're super close.' 'Yeah?' 'Townhouse at the corner of Swan and Stanley. Take your time, no rush, okay?' He found the waiter at the counter. 'I'll be back in just a sec, yeah,' said Titch. 'Can you reserve that table for us?' 'No one's here, kid,' said the waiter. 'Just calm your tits.' Titch tramped onto the footpath, his shirt fluttering out from his pants, his heels jamming on the bitumen, his gut gurgling. Got nothing to do, yeah, day off anyway. He jogged up the hill to settle his nerves. The townhouse was two storeys, weatherboard, with a cracked cement path running to the front fence. He nudged the gate, releasing the latch, and crept to the veranda, the wooden slats creaking underfoot as he reached the flyscreen door. He slipped a hand through his fringe, slid his belt around the buckle. Refreshed the messages on his mobile. Still nothing, yeah. Doughnuts. Titch opened the door and found himself in a sitting room. There was a table in the corner, covered in beer bottles, ciggie packs and a coconut husk freckled with ash. Pairs of shoes lined the entryway. Mid-heels. Uggs. Thongs. Runners. Stilettos. Ballet flats. Steel Blue workboots. 'Are you the next appointment?' said a woman leaning back in a La-Z-Boy recliner, staring at him from across the room. She had a pixie cut and a pierced lip. She patted a hairless kitten in her lap. A sphinx. 'I'm Titch.' 'Really?' she said, lolling her head along the backrest. 'What's a name like that doing on a boy like you?' 'I'm here to pick up Sophie.' 'But do you want some?' She tipped her head to the coffee table. There was a bowl of weed beside a shoebox. He stepped closer. Inside the shoebox was a Polystyrene cup and a pile of pills. There was a duckling in the cup. Its tawny feathers were all wet. 'Nah,' said Titch, 'I don't really do drugs.' Then a bloke padded down the stairs, pulling a T-shirt over his head, his meaty neck covered in scratches. He was enormous, maybe two metres tall. He stretched his fingers over his scalp and tied his long black hair in a man-bun with a red clip. 'Alright, you lovebirds,' he said, thrusting his toes into the Steel Blues. 'You better not go smoking up all the bud. No such thing as an open society. Or do I got to remind you again, Tayla?' 'See you, mate,' said the woman on the La-Z-Boy. 'Bye,' said Titch, but the man was already gone, thudding away over the veranda. 'Don't mind Damo,' said the woman. 'He can get a bit toxic. A bit possessive.' Titch fingered the fade in his haircut and took his backpack off his shoulders. 'You brought a toy, did you, maestro?' she said. 'It's for Sophie,' said Titch, holding up the rose. The woman rocked out of her chair, clenching a fist to her mouth. 'Mr Romantic,' she said, her face turning red, 'this is the gayest thing I've ever seen. I'm dead. Want me to go get her?' 'Okay,' he said, and she skipped up the stairs. The backpack dropped between his feet. His knuckles brushed his belt buckle and it was cold, like a fish's eye. He sat on the couch. Turned on the telly. The Tigers were up by five goals in the last quarter. The Hawks had lost their pep, slipping over the turf while the Tigers kept their footing, darting through tackles and carving up the G with long, loping kicks. There was a muffled quack inside the shoebox and Titch opened the lid to see the duckling tipped sideways, half-flapping its wings, its down streaked with Polystyrene, its rubbery beak burrowed beneath the pills. MDMA. Or benzodiazepines. Maybe fifty. The cup was leaking. Ochre water washed across the corners of the box, stinking of shit. There was a shriek from upstairs and Titch sat upright. Another voice, and the shrieking turned to raucous laughter that resonated through the townhouse. 'Rig?' Sophie called down the stairs. 'I'm just on my way into the shower, okay, cutey? Someone came a bit early.' The laughter faded and footsteps padded overhead. 'Give me un momento!' she said. He closed the lid of the shoebox. His gut felt uneasy, twisted, and his hands started to shake. Something slunk between Titch's legs and he stiffened. It was the sphinx kitten, massaging its slender, hairless spine against his ankles. 'Hey, you,' he said, but it didn't say hello, eyeing instead the quacking shoebox. He nudged the lid and the MDMA scattered across the coffee table and over his taped-up Volleys. Upstairs, the shower started and the pipes creaked in the walls. Then the duck ate the pills and Titch's gut started to ache. Poor thing, yeah. 'Almost there, Rig!' yelled Sophie. 'You all relaxed, my little guy?' Damo, yeah, now he could see it all. The huge dirty boots. The cheap T-shirt. The man-bun in Sophie's red clip. The kitten pawed at the coffee table. He picked up the shoebox and drained the shitwater on the La-Z-Boy. The lid came off. The duck wheezed, shivering, its feathers flecked with powder from the pills, its eyes turned to black buttons. Help him out, yeah. Another little guy wanting to be free. Titch put the shoebox under the table and the kitten lunged. As he knelt on the carpet, he saw, behind the shoebox, a brick of weed wrapped in thick plastic. The rain hissed through the windows and over the coffee table. 'When we're behind you'll never mind,' sang the Tigers' fans, 'we'll fight—and fight—and win!' The kitten finished playing, twisted over his laces and scampered away. Titch fixed the lid over the ball of bloody feathers and, lifting the box, his hands brushed the brick of weed. There was heaps. A pound, maybe. How much was that worth? Three grand? Four? Spring was coming. A lot of kids wanted to smoke up in the sun. Deakin students on the lawn, yeah. Private schoolers outside Coles in South Yarra. He pulled the weed out from under the table. Stuffed it down his backpack. He scaled the telly, pounced through the window and sprinted into the August rain.

On Monday, Titch found Püd snoring by the lockers, a paperback tented over his nose, his cheeks stubbled and flecked with bread-crumbs. 'Ginny's coming,' said Titch. 'But it came out of her snatch,' said Püd, exhaling twice, his chest sinking, before leaving a stream of green spit on the book. Titch ran a hand down the nubs of Püd's spine and over his frayed shirt. 'I haven't been good since the Red Plains,' Püd said. 'Guess I saw what I never wanted to admit. Now I'm crook. Don't sleep right.' Titch opened the window and fanned in some air with the page of a newspaper, then he draped Püd over his shoulder and dragged him out of the store. 'But how'd that root-and-boot go, mate?' said Püd. 'I need me a laugh.' They shuffled down the emer-gency hallway, the halogens blazing over their heads, and emerged by the dumpsters, the wind cool on their faces. As Püd's hand clung to Titch's hip, he felt a splinter of envy for this bloke who lived without keeping count, saving his dosh to get plastered on the weekend, rinsing his payslip on beers and amphetamines. 'So did you give it to her?' said Püd. 'How was her rig?' 'I don't want to talk about it.' 'Oh, right, he thinks he's Ca-sa-no-va.' The pound of weed was sitting around on his air mattress at home, stinking up his flat. It should be out on the street, yeah. That afternoon, while Ginny played with her stocks on the com-puter, Titch texted Püd saying he had found a lot of weed, enough to last months, and that he didn't want it. 'So can you sell it?' 'Fuck off. A pound? Really?' wrote Püd. 'I think so.' 'We're in for a stellar pay day then.' Come Titch's off-day, he knelt on his air mattress and lined up the bills on his bed, counting aloud for the ants. 'One grand.' 'Fifteen hundred.' 'Two grand.' 'Three gs, oh boy.' 'And we're at thirty-five hundred bucks. Get around me, fellas.'

Titch brought out the leather chair, dusted the crevices along the seat, brushed the dirt from the curved mahogany legs and put the teakettle on the burner. He waited for an hour, but the old woman didn't show, her blue hair nowhere to be seen, so Titch had to make some new chitchat. He offered the cup of milky tea to Ginny and said, 'You're okay, yeah?' She grabbed the tea and grimaced. 'You had a late night? You playing with your stocks again, or nah?' 'They're not stocks. They're antithetical to stocks,' she said. 'This is a new currency that will make trading firms obsolete.' Titch pressed himself on the counter, squinting over the screen at the graphic, not unlike the one on his CommBank app. Only these gains were hectic, bigger and better than anything a bank could offer. 'Is that how much it's worth?' he said. 'We're the avant-garde, Titch,' she said, and hurried off into the backroom to file her reports. He refreshed her MacBook and found another graph: twenty-five per cent in ten hours. Titch leaned closer to the screen. The coins were appreciating before his eyes, the trend lines rising like mountains. In forty days, there wasn't a single decline. As the shift went on, Titch kept circling back to the register to refresh Ginny's crypto page. It was outrageous. The growth was stellar. And for so many weeks he'd been watching his money dawdle in his CommBank while he worked like mad to pump up the balance. He did some mental maths and scrolled back to the graph from when he started at Reynolds: if he'd put his dosh on Bitcoin on his first pay-day…If he'd put even *half* his dosh…After clocking off, Titch ran to the bus bays, caught the 900, hurtled upstairs to his flat and opened his laptop. He loaded CoinSpot, sent a picture of his learner's permit and his payslip to the admins, and within an hour he was transferring his money from CommBank onto the cryptos. He took a whiz and when he sat back at his laptop, the cryptos were already up and about. Seven grand to seven and a half in thirty seconds. His hands twitched. And now eight grand. His mobile rang, startling him, and he put it to his ear without checking the caller ID. 'So, Ralphy,' said Sophie. 'We're having an inquisition over here. Why are you suddenly avoiding my calls?' 'Hey, yeah,' he said, 'I'm a little flat-out at the moment, but—' 'Shut your gob and listen to me,' she said. 'Tayla thinks you ran away with our bud. You know anything about this?' He threw his mobile on the pillow and hopped off the bed. But chill, yeah, not like she had any proof. Not like she knew anything about him. No one did, yeah, and he refreshed the exchange. The graph lit every corner of his pining eyes. 'Eighty-two hundred,' he said, and the ants trickled behind the laptop and over the ridges of the desk. 'Get around me, boys,' he said. 'Get up and about.'

'It would be wise to diversify your portfolio,' said Ginny, who patted his back when she saw his crypto exchange, 'in case something
calamitous happens.' She propped her wallet between their laptops.
Little digital polaroids filled her desktop background. The New York
City skyline. Ginny in a gown at uni graduation. Hugging a girl who
looked like her sister, only with blonde hair and sausage lips. He
refreshed his browser and stroked the edge of the crypto graph. Then
he asked if she had a family around and she said, 'Of course. But
they're not the most stable people.' She said they were violent, known
for a tussle. Problems with booze, too. 'I know what you mean,' he
said. 'Legit.' Leaning closer, he smelled the coffee on her breath. They
were standing side by side. Had been how-long since he'd hung out
with someone one on one. Maybe he could do the maths, tally up all
the lonely months. But he didn't have to dwell on it, yeah, that was the
point of being with other people. So he said, 'Thanks for taking me
on. This whole gig has really helped me out.' Ginny laughed, closed
her wallet and said, 'Well, it's no sweat off my back.' Then she went
to the bathroom, leaving Titch licking the tops of his teeth. Alright,
then. He unclasped the wallet, pressing an old photo of her sister
beneath the plastic film, those plucked brows and that terracotta tan
staring him down. Then he sussed through the compartments to see
what else Ginny carried around. A State Library pass. A Melbourne
Uni ID. A Boost Juice loyalty card. A photo of the Brooklyn Bridge.
And there, in the last pouch, a clean white envelope, unsealed, thick
with wads of dosh. He shut the wallet and dumped it on the laptop.
His heart went rat-a-tat. He slipped from the register and inspected
the books on the Non-Fiction shelves, chewing his dry lips. But how
much was in there? Were those hundy-dollar bills? Later that evening,

after they closed the store, Titch slunk through Chaddy with his teeth grinding. 'I'll see you tomorrow, Titch,' said Ginny. 'You're asking the right questions.' But all he could see were the mint-green bills jammed in the envelope. Four grand? Nah, more. The wad was as thick as his middle finger. Let's say five grand, yeah. And if that went onto the Bit-coins it was, by the time he reached the bus bay, already at fifty-three hundred bucks. 'Right-o,' he said, but Ginny was gone to her car.

It wasn't his fault, nah: over the next shift, he found himself spending more time with Ginny, tracking his cryptos as she tracked hers. 'You gunning for assistant manager?' said Nadine. 'Always thought you were a bit of an arse-kisser.' That arvo Ginny took him out for a smoothie. 'I'm in a good mood, Titch,' she said. 'What do you do outside this godforsaken store?' 'It's just me and the ants,' he said. She pulled the straw through the lid, unclasped the plastic and stirred around the sides. 'But yeah, I like shopping too, I guess. I've always liked a bit of dressing up.' Mostly she stared at her ballet flats as she walked, but then she raised her eyes and fixed him with a placid stare. 'Do you always unmask so easily?' she said. 'I guess,' he said, holding up her wallet as she pulled a napkin from the counter. The wallet was so heavy. So prime. And then they were walking back to Reynolds, Ginny sucking the dregs of her smoothie, flecks of juice dripping down her straw. A Mango-Tango Crush. She didn't touch the cash to pay for it. She used her debit card instead. Back in the store, he held her wallet over the register and said, 'Don't forget this.' And then, at the end of the day, after the routine bag check, she said: 'But what are you doing tonight, Titch?' 'Nothing,' he said. 'Do you really live all alone?' she said. 'You want to see the ants?' he said. Things seemed to move real fast, yeah, out of Reynolds and into the rain, and he didn't know what she wanted, nah, but he liked her company. 'Usually I get the bus,' he said. 'I'll let you take the lead,' she said, so instead he led her into a taxi, his fingers freezing, his plaid Ralph soaking, maybe ruined, and the pomade leaking out of his hair onto the back seat beside her bag. Maybe it wasn't so far away after all: twenty grand, yeah, enough to donate a squat rack. He could call up Niki and see if she had room in the gym, listen to her voice break as he told her a delivery was on the way. 'How you been holding up?' Niki'd say. 'Really good, yeah,' he'd say. Finally, the cab reached Springy and he took Ginny up to his flat. She stretched across his air mattress, her feet on his pillow, her hands buried in his sheets. As he squeezed the rainwater from his shirt, staring at her bag hanging off his wheelie chair, weighed down by the wallet inside, he felt his stiffy nudging the elastic of his undies. She trawled through his Spotify and refreshed the crypto exchange. The light from the road glowed against the frosted window. He remembered Sophie's sharehouse, her flatmate running his rose upstairs, the sets of shrill laughter on the landing. Here was a girl at the other end of kindness, a manager after all, older and switched on. Ginny sighed, pressing her hands against his pillow. 'I should shower. Do you have a towel?' 'Use mine,' he said. 'Is it clean?' 'Sure.' She jumped from the bed, her hair tumbling over her face, her feet thumping over the army of ants, and unpeeled her shirt outside the bathroom. She closed the door. Alone at last, he hurried to the tote, yanked the zip open and rummaged through her things. A novel. Some Wrigley's chewy. Two doctor's needles. Glass bottles of gym juice. And, wrapped in a cardigan, her wallet. He ignored the needles and the grog and unclasped the flap, riffled between the IDs and the discount cards, and there it was, the envelope, unsealed after all. He thumbed the notes, twice, guessing there were at least fifty hundred-dollar bills, all lined up, with that fresh-pressed ATM smell. He grabbed the envelope, slid the paper into his wallet and buried the steal in his desk drawer. He rearranged her things, one inside the other, wrapped the cardigan around the wallet, leaving the druggy gear in its place, and zipped the bag shut. Titch breathed slowly through his nose, his teeth grinding. 'Guess you never know someone,' he said to the ants, his stiffy softening. 'Don't say a word, yeah? Be cool.' The water shut off. He heard Ginny sliding the screen door open. Her feet splatting on the tiles. She gurgled some

water and spat in the basin. He took   's wallet from the new
wardrobe and propped it on his pillow. She opened the bedroom door,
holding her shirt to her chest, and instinctively he looked away, not out
of politeness but out of shame. He couldn't believe that she was here
after all, that she had let him take the lead. As she sat by her tote bag
and unfurled her hair, his willy went limp. She didn't even see the ants.
'Careful,' he said, reaching for a Kleenex to wipe up her wet footprints.
'Okay,' she said. 'Guess I should shower too, yeah,' he said, 'to warm
me up.' 'Okay,' she said, but it wasn't okay, nah, taking his towel from
her. She had no clue, the poor girl. He unclasped his belt, thwacking
the buckle against the floor, and hurried from the bedroom to stand
under the steel slit of the shower head, his cock drooping against his
thigh. Maybe he could tumble down the drain. Maybe he could evap-
orate in the ceiling fan. He slicked his palm with the Coles shampoo
and lathered himself. 'Up and about,' he said, picturing that silhouette
shimmering over his bed in the Melbourne High boarding house, the
chalky residue mixing with the sweat in the air, the sunlight shining
off their shirts and the scraps of their wet blisters, and with a gasp he
felt his stiffy pulsing in his hand. 'Right-o,' he said, hobbling from the
shower. He combed his hair and waltzed into the bedroom. But Ginny
was gone. The front door was open and her footsteps echoed down the
stairwell. The blood pulsed in his stiffy and his gut ached. He was out
of sorts, yeah. Untimely.

That night, he curled on his pillow, watching Püd's story on Instagram. One mate sat with his legs outstretched beneath a wattle tree, staring into a campfire. Another bloke strummed the wiry strings of a wooden guitar, playing a song that Titch had heard but couldn't remember. A third guy stumbled out of the tent holding a snapper on a fishing line. 'Thanks for watching us real men rejuvenate,' said Püd, and he ended the stream. Titch scrolled through Facebook and saw an ad for a crypto exchange. 'Buy in now,' said the flashing green letters, 'and don't be the boy who misses out.' He scrolled through the Iron Edge website and saw a squat rack for nineteen grand. Room for two barbells. Free delivery and installation. Finally, it was morning and he awoke with his sheets twisted around his feet, his hands clasped on his belly. The sun streaked across his mattress and the shining silver laptop. He checked the cryptos. No severe overnight changes. Today he could load the new dosh into his account. Maybe he would 'diversify,' maybe move into the next step of crypto-investing. In case of calamity, yeah, and he pulled his pants from under the bed. His laugh stuck in his gullet. The lining of his pants was spotted with black husks, each no bigger than a freckle, buried in the stitching, the seams, the casing of the pockets. Ants, yeah. All dead. He ran a hand down his legs. His skin was smooth. He thwacked his pants against the doorway and the bodies tumbled free. He fluffed up his pillow and folded the sheets over the air-mattress protector. They stank of sweat and stale shower water. Getting a little gross. Need to do a wash, yeah, but he was late for work. It was already ten to ten. He bundled out of his room, keys jangling in his pocket, and ran to the bus stop, his face flushed red in the spring air. His phone rang, an unknown number. 'Hello?' 'Ralphy, mate, we know what you've done.' A gruff voice. The guy from the townhouse. Damo. 'You actually think you can move a whole pound without the heavies noticing? You walking around with a fake name, too?' It was ten, Titch's shift had already started, and the bus was nowhere in sight. 'Oh, nah,' said Titch, and he hung up, hailed a taxi, counted the exact change as they rolled up the ramps to Chaddy's southern wing and sprinted through the smokers' yard by the dumpsters. He was famished. Hopefully Püd had left his salt-and-vinegar chips lying around, or Nadine her tub of whey. He pulled out his keys, rolled open the gate and fumbled in the dark for the security alarm. It chimed, shrill and hawkish, following his every step, as if he himself had become the siren. He punched in the security code and checked the roster. Püd and Nadine were starting around lunchtime. Ginny to close, well after he'd be home. Easy, yeah. No dramas. And now he had time to grab a feed. He sauntered down to the food court. Sumo Salad had a quinoa harvest with chicken breast and avocado. Indochine had a ramen special with beef or chicken or pork or tofu and a big cup of pearl milk tea. And Schnitz had their classic: pan-friend chicken breast, lightly seasoned with lemon, lime and sea salt. He paced from one shopfront to another before deciding to treat himself to all three. Parking himself at a table, he stuffed a napkin down his collar and crushed each meal as if he had just returned from the bush. 'Yeah, that'll do,' he said, leaning back in the curved wooden chair. A good, clean feed. He sipped some more tea, shaking the ice in the cup, burping the bubbles of beef broth up his throat. Time to get on with it, yeah, strolling back to Reynolds. A couple of paperbacks had tumbled off their shelves. He went to pick them up and found their pages torn in half. Thick scratches ran up the glass cabinet. The fancy Lamy fountain pens were gone. 'Hey?' he said. 'Anyone here?' He checked the alarm, but it was off. Forfuckssake. He leaned on the backroom lockers, his palms sweating. The window was open and the tangy smell of pollen covered the shelves. Thick-headed, yeah. Dumb dill. He shut the window, locked it and huffed. The halogens glared down on the lockers and in the heavy silence of the store, he rubbed his hands over his face, his back to the water cooler. They'd stolen at least twelve pens. More than eighteen hundred dollars down the drain. On *his* shift. He dialled the police from the Reynolds landline and that afternoon a cop inspected the store, said he could maybe have a look at the CCTV, and lectured Titch about hiring a security guard for the shop. 'I'm the new guy here,' he said. 'That's no excuse,' said the officer. 'Grow up.' Püd swept his hands in circles over the cabinet, polishing the glass. 'So you weren't here when the robbers came in?' said Nadine. 'Where were you then?' 'Just chill, Nads,' said Püd. 'The boy's in a state of shock.' Titch camped in the backroom with a Biro between his legs, eyeing the papers the cop left him, thinking how best to explain it. Maybe he had rocked up a little late, unlocked the shop, but his stomach had gone iffy, he'd hurried off to the loo without locking—and in that time they pounced? But what was he doing on the loo for twenty minutes? The Biro spattered and squirted ink down his pants. Forfuckssake, yeah, crumpling the cop's papers in his lap. It was three-forty. His shift was wrapping up. He would deal with this tomorrow.

'Titchmeister,' the Facebook message began. 'How you doing? We've still got that spare membership. Want to watch the Tigers this Friday? First qualifying final in sixteen seasons. Let me know ASAP. The missus would love to check in, too.' He read Bruce's message as he climbed the stairs. So now they wanted to chat, yeah, after all these months. 'Active Now,' it said beside the little green dot. He dropped his mobile and opened his laptop. The exchange refreshed, casting an orange glow across his hands as he squeezed the sides of his desk. Ten grand, he read. Ten and a half. 'Do you see what I see, boys?' he said, switching on his lamp. 'We happy or what?' He swivelled on the chair. The floor was coated with ants. Their bodies covered the floorboards, their abdomens crooked, their legs bent into their husks. They covered the bedsheets. The windowsill. The AC vent. The door handle. Their remains made one thick black lattice, so dark in places that he couldn't see the floor. He swept the ants with his laptop case, yanked off his bedsheets and piled them on the air mattress. He dumped them in the wastebasket, handful after handful, until they spilled over the rim, catching on his palms and the fine hair on his arms. Must be sick, yeah, troubled, and he was supposed to take care of them. But in the gaudy glow from the crypto exchange, there was no telling where the ants ended and he began. He carried the basket to the loo and poured them into the bowl, flushing until the toilet rattled and the pipes groaned with the clods of muck. He picked at the webbing in the mattress with the end of his coat hanger, but his grip slipped and he pierced the seam. A low whine filled the room. The mattress started sinking. He yanked open the windows, scattering pollen over the sill and across his new shirts, and with every cloying breath, the air stuck in his nose, and he sneezed, monstrously, losing his footing and collapsing on his laptop. His mobile rang. The message went to voice-mail and the phone stopped buzzing. He pressed play. 'Hi, Titch? Pick up. It's Ginny.' His fingers plucked at his calves, over his pubes, prying off the ants like flakes of dried skin. So many, yeah. More than could be counted. His nails nipped something under the flattened mattress. A folded purple flyer. In his ruined room, Titch held the paper to the moonlit window. 'Mother Pulse,' he read. 'Your Lifelong Listener & Subterranean Storyteller.'

Stalking under the streetlights, Titch walked parallel to the tracks, tracing the tremors of the citybound train in his shoes. The sleepers were slick with rainwater. His head rang with the messages from Ginny, Sophie and endless unknown blokes, a single stream of questions and curses. He was sick, yeah, didn't they get it? He was off-centre. Hollowed out. And now his ants were dead. Felt them with his own hands. Lost his mind. His mother's son, yeah, kneeling at the platform edge. But no way could he end up like her, all diagnosed, therapised, locked up and out of sight. 'Mother Pulse,' he said. If she was underground after all, he could tell her the truth, get it all off his chest, and not worry about the cops getting involved. Ginny must've brought the flyer for him, must've sensed he needed hearing out, must've known he had no one else around. That's why she wanted to hang. A little act of care before she realised what he had done. A train raced through the underpass, headlights flaring over the concrete pillars of the carpark, and ground to a halt at the platform. A Flinders Street Express. Passengers filled the aisles of the carriage, hunched over the seats, clasping the rubber handholds from the ceiling. Kids crouched on their parents' legs, pinching at rain-flecked overalls, their teeny faces inside plastic ponchos. Richmond fans. Heading to the G. More than he'd ever seen. He nudged through the doorway to a handhold beside an old fella, his face covered in wrinkles and an auburn beard, his yellow-and-black blazer lined with badges of the players. Dusty. Cotch. Rancey. The supporters bristled, their mangy hair streaked with rain, their voices crusty and hoarse. This was how the poor fools strived, yeah, like   would say. Spurred on by the hope that this year would be different. Three hours later and they'd be back, sitting in stiff silence, a lump in their throats after another four-point loss, or six-goal last-quarter fadeout, or hundy-point shellacking. They had seen every decimation, but they were still here by the hundreds. 'Reckon we're built for finals,' said the old bloke. 'The Cats don't know what's coming. And then we're only one game from the granny.' Titch's mobile buzzed. Ginny. Asking about his absence, maybe, or her unreturned calls, or the missing envelope of dosh, or now, surely, the police report waiting in her email. Did she think he stole the Lamy fountain pens? Did she think he'd eyed them since starting at Reynolds, fawning over the glass case, begging for the opening shift so he could have the store all to himself? Make an extra grand before running off? Titch pressed his head against the window and plunged his fingers in his ears. The tremors from the glass coursed up his forehead and he pictured his skull, like a beer can, shaking so much it exploded. He forced his eyes open. The express raced towards South Yarra, freezing the passengers on the Toorak platform in screenshots as the train swept by. Then a chill crept up his neck: a line of ants crawled out from his trackpants, down his Volleys and across the wet floor. They trailed by a pair of pink gumboots, through a picnic basket and over to the door between the carriages. He wrung his pants, scratching his calves. The ants scattered. 'You okay, champ?' said the old fella. 'Can you help?' said Titch. 'Bit wet, are you?' 'But they're coming out of me.' 'Well, you'll dry off in here, mate. Go Tiges.' Titch turned to the window, his face flickering in the concave glass, his heart hammering. The train whipped up the bridge to Richmond, along the steel trusses glistening with drizzle, past the shining light-towers above the G, and towards Degraves Street, where his subterranean storyteller awaited.

Aurora

'YOU'RE SOAKED,' she said, drying his face in her shawl. As her terror passed, and the pressure in her ankles started to fade, Maha felt a greater curiosity than she had ever known. The boy slowly followed her into the basement, where she burned some old receipts in a barrel, filling the chop shop with a tangerine glow. Crimson scratches spread up his fingers and under his rolled shirtsleeves. The ligaments bulged in his wrists as he squeezed his shirt dry. Then she limped to a work-bench, snapped the limbs off a stool and added them to the barrel, fanning spirals of smoke across his body. 'Why don't you change out of your clothes?' she said. 'There are overalls in the wardrobe.' Titch crept through the gloom and rifled through the unhooked uniforms, disturbing all the dust that had gathered over the decades. 'Luke,' he said, 'Angus. Christos. And Somnath?' 'Please do take whatever you need.' He unbuckled the last set and slipped himself into the trousers. As he slung the straps across his shoulders, Somnath's nametag shone in the firelight and Maha smiled, wondering at all the new forms her father had taken. She closed her eyes, listening for her breath. Here, gone. She listened to the boy's rhythms, heard the currents of smoke over his overalls and down his limbs. 'Where have you come from?' she said, reaching for her notebook. 'Southeast, yeah,' he said, 'out near Springy.' 'Can you tell me your story?' 'I can, yeah. I should, yeah. But I'm not sure you've got the patience for a lad like me.' 'You can trust me.' 'But I've fucked up bad. You sure you want to waste your time on some tryhard?' She closed the notebook and nestled her fingers between the pages. The lines of ink formed ridges on the paper; her father's story coated her nails, making her heart race. 'You have noth-ing to fear,' she said. 'I'm not here to judge you. All I want is to listen.' She told Titch about the many miles she had wandered in her life, the

175

endless hours spent watching human lives, seeing them from within. 'So you don't have anyone around?' said Titch. 'I have the whole city,' she said. 'I got your name,' he said, 'from a flyer. First I thought it came from my manager. But really I think it came from a mate of mine.' 'He couldn't come with you?' 'Not right now.' 'Maybe next time he'll join.' 'Nah,' he said, 'he's done.' 'What was his name?' 'Skeater,' said Titch, and he told her about the wake, the swimming lessons, the power-lifting, the long summer days in the boarding house, the alcohol. His story ran and retreated between his memories and his living grief. No one knew his history, not his wayward father, not his broken mother, not a single schoolmate who thought they had the story straight. Maha stopped writing and folded the notebook over her pen. So Skeater was gone, stealing death with his own two hands, emerged elsewhere in his next form, and here was Titch, the remainder, the boy left behind. 'When your soulmate dies,' she said, 'you lose a part of yourself. You go looking for him everywhere in this life, up and down, east and west. But you don't fear what you'll find, no. You fear that you'll be looking endlessly, on and on, with no end.' Titch flinched. His hair dripped down his haggard cheeks. 'Since his death,' she said, 'what has become of you?' 'I've fucked up, okay? I'm losing my mind. Just like Mum. But my eyes go wandering, my hands too. I shouldn't have done it, but I did.' He told her about the bookstore, his manager and all the money he had stolen. 'My head's coming off. I keep seeing things I shouldn't, and I've hurt her, hurt Ginny, real bad. All I wanted was to be on the way up.' 'Listen to me, Titch. There is one rule above all else. And only once we accept this rule can we take the steps towards liberation. All energy tends to zero. Here, gone. A motorcycle, when drained of petrol, slows to a halt and stops. A man's fortune, at the end of his life, passes from hand to hand and dwindles away. Bones are brittle. The blood cools. We insist that life is about accumulation, yet the path always leads to zero. Growth is an illusion,' she said. 'We've arrived in degenerate times.' She reached towards him, her fingers trembling, and brushed his arm. 'And if you can see this, if you understand the course of our lives, then we can begin to find—' He leapt backwards, toppled a bucket and knocked a titanium pipe off the bench. 'Alright, yeah,' he said, 'so I get rid of it?' 'Stop,' she said, 'there's no need to rush.' 'I return it? That's what you're saying?' He scrambled to the door, grimacing as he unlatched the lock. 'Where are you going?' she said. 'I'll give it all back, you're right,' he said. 'Liberation, easy. I'll go back to Chaddy, head into the store, take it like a man. Six gs by tomorrow, I got you. It's easy. I won't need any of it much longer.' She loped around the barrel and grabbed his overalls, but he sidestepped her, squeaking in his rubber shoes. 'Zero, yeah? I got it. That's all you have to tell me.' His voice cracked and she saw his eyes widen as he beheld the menace of the chop shop, the cavernous den illuminated in all its squalor, and her, of course, Mother Pulse, the centrepiece of this decay. In a certain light, all divinity was really a measure of monstrosity. He ran through the garage and slid beneath a workbench. She reached for his ankles but he yelped, knocked the wooden frame, and the bench toppled, pinning her to the floor. 'I'm fixing up my act,' he said. 'You're right, Mother Pulse. I'm out. I'm done, yeah. I know where to find Skeater.' The weight of the bench shuddered on her bosom, the wooden legs dug into her ribs, and the shadows of the chop shop loomed above the fire, devouring the pages of her notebook. She groaned, catching the wind in her throat, and crumpled under the bench, losing sight of her closest degenerate yet.

When she woke, her knees knocked on the singed underside of the workbench. The fire in the barrel had burned down. Her notebook was charred. She rolled onto her side and moaned as her blood coursed in her body. The roller door was open and rainwater streamed over the asphalt and the gutter. Sunlight streaked across the laneway, revealing the bowels of the chop shop. She staggered to the roller door and wrenched it shut. A heavy sadness settled on her shoulders at the thought of Titch and all the terror she had provoked in him. There was no one else to hear him. He would go for months without meeting anyone's eyes. She wondered how she could even begin to write his story. How, if at all, could she leave the shelter of her life and step inside his suffering? She had presumed there was an answer to this question in the city, some wisdom to help write another human life, but it was impossible to find here, in Melbourne, in the same old streets she had always known. There was no stillness to be found in the city. There was no room for silence. In Titch, she saw her father, his years of hidden suffering, the ruptured heart that took him in the end. She found the story her father had clutched as he died, rereading the tale of the jackaroo from *Man's Tales from Near and Far*. He had always longed for elsewhere. And maybe, she thought, holding the paper in trembling hands, he had wanted her to leave the trappings of the city, to follow the horizon until she found that unheeded red vista. For whatever a god desires to create, she must start with nothing, a single abyss, true and happy emptiness. The Red Plains. She shuffled to the doormat and found the most recent letters, unread for weeks. 'Hi Mama Pulse,' wrote Vicki. 'I'm not sure where you've been—You okay?—She comes in the mornings now and they do it downstairs when I'm asleep—So long as he's satisfied?—I've tried everything for him—Every wig—Every toy—Started watching videos—But I'm not going to try chemo this time, if ya still wondering—I'm going out this way—I'm done.' 'Joanne took my father's side,' wrote Taz. 'I didn't know there were sides until today. When my workmate sent her a link to my Reddit she didn't cry or say a word. Just packed her shit. Ubered to Mum and Dad with her laptop and scrolled through it all. The photos. Videos. Gifs. I came home from a conference the next day and they had Pastor Trevor around. First step in conversion therapy is an ice plunge. They stripped me. Dunked me in ice water. Tore my piercings out.' Tears speckled Maha's shawl. Her body ached from her laboured breathing. She had neglected them, these people who needed to be heard. She tore a sheet from a new notebook and held it to the lamplight. 'Dear degenerates,' she wrote. 'I am insufficient. I am ill-equipped. I am leaving, forever, to the Red Plains.' She pinned the page beside the roller door and gathered what few belongings she had: a wad of cash, a single notebook, a bundle of ballpoint pens. She telephoned the train company and told the operator her plan. 'You sure about that, darl?' he said. 'I'm certain,' she said. 'Well, just get the Dandenong train from Flinders,' he said, 'and stay on until the end of the line. You won't even need a ticket. And you'll probably have the carriage all to yourself. But you didn't hear this from me, okay?'

In the dark, as the night passed, she saw that her natural life had only offered her solitude. She realised all gods were irrevocably alone, that in the Red Plains she could live in the vast oblivion, that she could continue the work begun before she was born. As the sun rose, she was happy, and on her last morning in the chop shop, Maha stood at the window and listened to a magpie swooping down the laneway. She closed her eyes and hovered above a shopping centre along a highway to the southeast, above a child chasing a Frisbee down the muddy hill of a primary school, and above a fruit bat, a crumple of wings outside a milk bar, fried by the electric wires hung between the wattle trees. She gasped. A jolt raced up her ankles. She opened her eyes and retreated from the window. Her belly ached. Her hands felt clammy. She was filled with a sudden unease. The skin on her feet was cracked and her toes were blue. Her toenails peeled off and dropped onto the floor. She pinched the ridges of her bunions, where the calcite bulged against the flesh, and flakes of skin fell away, revealing the glinting tips of her bones. The pain crept, second by second, up into her calves. She had never seen her legs like this before, had not seen what had become of her own two feet, but in truth she'd had no reason to look. Remembering the Dandenong train, she wobbled to standing, grabbed the pneumatic lift and scrambled to the workbenches. Her shrivelled feet were as black as charcoal, brittle from the skin to the bone. She bent and pinched her little toe. It snapped into her palm: an offcut, a by-product, an old draft.

Maha pocketed the notebook and hauled herself up the stairwell, wheezing with every step. She had lost all sensation. Numbness, she learned, was worse than any pain. She clenched her eyes shut, slowed her breathing and whispered mantras in the dark, but her mind had short-circuited. Her words were useless. She climbed over the final step, opened the suspension lock and at last, with a sunken sigh, crawled onto Degraves Street, risen from her hovel at a quarter past one on a Thursday afternoon. Huge brick buildings lined the laneway. Garbage bins crowded the concourse, their red lids banging in the spring wind. Pigeons cooed in the exhaust vents and mice skittered beneath flattened boxes. A cyclist whizzed down the laneway, her tail-light flashing red, and a truckie unloaded trays of polished glass schooners to the back of a restaurant. Shafts of sunlight pierced the clouds and refracted off the whitewashed plaster buildings, the techni-colour graffiti, the glinting cutlery along tables and bar tops. The searing light hurt her eyes. From the window of the restaurant, a woman polishing a schooner yelled across the laneway, 'We don't got no cash. Or no drugs. We don't got nothing on the premises.' Maha crawled past a drain, towards a dumpster. She rummaged through the bulging garbage bags, wetting her shawl as she dug. She found a pair of sunglasses, electric blue with a titanium finish, and clamped them on her face. Alongside the dumpster was an aluminium trolley, about four-feet wide, with crooked wheels and a rickety frame. She lowered herself onto the tray, pressed her hands into the road and rolled past Andiamo Cafe and the Christian Science Reading Room. She turned onto Swanston Street by the Krispy Kreme, where a gaggle of school-boys were hunched over shiny, glazed doughnuts, and she passed Gong Cha, where the line of customers parted as she approached, pointing

181

their mobile phones in her wake. A young man from the Greenhouse Backpacker extended his hand, but he was speaking a language she had never heard. She puffed her cheeks and pushed herself up the hill, past the Duty Free and the Korean Fried Chicken shop. Enormous screens flashed on the sides of the buildings: men guzzling bottles of beer in slow-motion, a dancer in beige underwear filmed by her friends on their iPhones. A tram thundered by on screeching steel wheels. The street was lined with football flags, clashing shades of red and blue and yellow and black, flapping against the granite walls of a bank. Bald men in orange robes beat wooden drums, stamping their feet in arcs, chanting, 'Hare Krishna, Hare Krishna.' A girl at the kerb thudded on a bongo, her cap spun backwards, keeping time with her bare feet. The cacophony propelled Maha uphill, away from the only street she had ever known. Melbourne Town Hall loomed on her right, and the bluestone balconies, backlit by the westerly sun, cast a cold aura across the people who left apartments and shops and slipped into the streets, swallowed in the flow of the other Melburnians, becoming both the food and the flesh of this beastly city. She reached Bourke Street and found a policeman standing with his back to the Hare Krishna dancers, wearing that welcome blue garb, with badges on his shoulders and a collar stiff against his neck. She fingered the cuffs of his trousers. 'Easy does it,' he said, grabbing his holster. 'I need to make it to the Red Plains,' she said. 'You must be in a sorry state, hey, darl? Been shooting up again?' 'I need to go. Can you help me?' 'Run out of room for your jabs?' 'I need a doctor,' she said. 'I won't take you to the station, so don't get all uppity. There's a clinic not far from here and they're experts in addiction. They'll sort you out.' 'Addiction?' she said. 'I'll get you there, darl.' 'Where?' He stepped behind the cart, leaning one shoulder into the handle, and pushed her up the road. 'Gee whiz,' he said. 'Big girl. What are they cutting it with these days? Brown sugar?' Trembling, she lay back in the cart. Her eyes wouldn't close. The undersides of the cafe awnings were splattered with mould, wreathed in cobwebs and dead moths, and the trunks of the plane trees were sprayed with orange paint. The gutter was clogged with purple flyers, darkened from the rain, congealed on the concrete like a river of dried blood. The footpath turned to cobblestones and the wheels bounced in their sockets. Tremors spread up her calves and into her heart. They entered a set of gates lined with barbed wire and hooded cameras. A picket sign by the walkway read, 'Open Seven Days, Sobriety Never Shuts.' The policeman rolled her through a set of automatic doors. A woman with tinted glasses leaned over the counter and beckoned them forward. 'I picked up this one further south than usual, around Degraves Street,' said the policeman. 'She's in a sorry state. Her feet are pretty bung. Might still be high, hun, so be careful.' 'Cheers, Shauny. We'll send a note to your station to let them know how helpful you've been.' 'Nurse Maureen will sort you out,' the policeman said to Maha. 'She knows all the doctors in this joint. Most important thing is that you stop using. Stop the cravings. Break the habit.' Then the policeman readjusted his hat, wiped his forehead with his hairy wrist and left through the automatic doors. 'Right this way,' said Maureen, who smiled without moving her face. She heaved the trolley through a set of double doors and into the bowels of the building. Halogen tubes buzzed on the ceiling. Voices crackled from radios and monitors. They rolled by a stencil print on the wall of the corridor. 'Melbourne City Drug and Alcohol Rehabilitation Centre. For a Better Tomorrow.' A man in a mobility scooter sat by a payphone. His cheeks were slick and jaundiced and his red hair was tied in a bun. He leaned into the receiver and said, 'Harry's not coming back from his trip. They put him in the oven. So we need to commiserate. We need to salute him. So slip me a hundy and I'll get Stickers and you get Lu-Lu and together we'll cross the Styx.' 'What's your name, love?' said Maureen, leaning over the trolley. 'Mother Pulse.' 'Why, that's very lovely,' said Maureen. 'You'll never believe it, Pen,' whispered the man, clutching the phone to his ear, 'but Mama P is here.' 'That's enough now, Marty,' said Maureen, slamming the receiver into the socket. 'Go back to your bed.' She wheeled Maha into a room hemmed by green felt curtains. 'I'm Doctor Morton,' said a man with his shirtsleeves rolled up his snowy forearms. 'You can remove your sunglasses.' 'Please,' said Maha. 'I need to go.' Maureen slipped her hand down Maha's face and unclasped the sunglasses. The glare from the lamps burned her eyes. 'Let me have a look,' said the doctor, clawing her face into position. Her vision clouded. A chill crept up her neck. 'These pupils are badly dilated. She might still have something in her system. Get her sedated and bring her into the operating theatre. The infection could spread up to her brain. Has she been injecting through her ankles? When was the last time she used?' 'You won't get a response,' said Maureen. 'She's dissociative.' 'Run a blood test while we're operating,' said the doctor. 'What's going on in Melbourne town these days?'

She dreamed of swimming across the sandy floor of a prehistoric sea. The ocean was a blue membrane freckled with quartz. Protozoa burrowed into the sand and molluscs shimmered on the rocks. The currents turned her limbs to jelly. She was a leaf, a lamina, an untouchable sheath in an ancient shoal. Perhaps this was a previous draft, millennia before she was written into a human form. She swam with the trilobites, their trembling antennae nipping at the puffs of glowing algae in their plates. 'That's great,' said a trilobite, only it was Maureen looming over the bed. 'Bring your head up just a tad, alright.' Maha shivered. Her saliva tasted of battery acid. Her eyelids were granite. 'We'll get some water into you,' said Maureen, tipping a paper cup to her lips. 'That's a good girl, have a sip,' she said. 'We tried looking you up, but there's no profile in Medicare. You have an ID?' 'An identity?' 'Just to confirm who you are. We'll figure it out, sweetie. It's okay,' she said. 'Now, Doc Morton was pleased with how the op turned out. But we did get your blood tests back and wanted some help to interpret the results. Can you remember the last time you injected crystal meth?' Maha shook her head. 'But your insulin levels were horribly low. We don't usually get readings like that here. And your blood sugar is quite high, I might add. We'll take another test to see if it drops.' Maha grunted, sweeping the bedsheets off her body. Her legs were wrapped in gauze from her knees to her ankles. The bandages were stained yellow. They stank of sanitiser. Formaldehyde. She unwrapped the gauze. Her feet were gone. 'I know it's a shock and all,' said Maureen, 'but you're on the mend now. We'll give you a nice big bath tomorrow.' 'They were gangrenous,' said the doctor, slipping through the curtains. 'You had a severe lack of circulation. This isn't how it works with most of the cases here. You're diabetic, aren't you?

Too much sugar in your diet. We didn't know. You should have told us when you checked in.' Maha clutched her knees and hauled herself over the bed railings, but her eyes throbbed, her head pounded and she sank into the pillow. 'But the gangrene could have spread, you know,' said the doctor. 'There's a chance of infection from gangrenous digits. It very well could have migrated up to your spine and into your brain.' The doctor pressed a hand on her shoulder, but the weight of the gesture only pushed her deeper into the pillow. 'Rest up, please,' he said. 'Tomorrow we'll have a serious talk about your health and wellbeing.'

Marty snored in the opposite bed, one arm draped over his mobility scooter, the other wrapped in bandages from his shoulder to his wrist. His red hair shone in the gloom. His chest was crisscrossed with tubes. 'Painkillers,' the nurse had said. 'Fentanyl. Morphine.' At eight o'clock, a new nurse drew the curtains on the windows, turned off the halogens and locked the doors. A fluorescent exit sign buzzed above the doorway, casting a green glow across their bodies. They had left a torch plant beside her bed. Its branches draped across the floor, glowing silver and emerald. Medical equipment lined the walls: dialysis machines, defibrillators, oxygen canisters, syringes in sterilised pumps. From all the intermittent beeping, she could tell they were talking to one another, endlessly surveying. She unscrewed the tube of fentanyl from her arm and squirted the drip into her pillow. She reached over the torch plant and yanked the electric cables from the socket. The machines went silent. Lying in the dark, she shifted her attention up the points of each finger, the back of her palms, the rolling lumps of her shoulders, the bones of her knees and down the splintered flesh at the end of her ankles. She had stepped over the margins, only to return without her feet, abandoning them in the otherworld. Since her childhood, she had seen death as a hungry hound, a malevolent white void at the end of a page. She had imagined nothingness as the point of a whirlpool inside a drain—and yet nothingness was, after all, just nothing. A monster would need a presence, and bodies would need to be sketched, a form carved from matter and size. But that was not nothing, not as she was experiencing now, for nothing had no within or without. It could not devour or destroy. She swept her mind down her body and dwelled at the tips of her legs, this new limit to the extent of her being, the edge of all sensation. Maybe, in fact, there were ways of being she could never record, infinite moments that escaped articulation. Maybe words had their limits. But to write until the end of language, over and over, broaching the border of nothingness, was the only reason to write at all.

She opened her eyes and unclenched her fists; there was a train waiting, a pilgrimage to the Red Plains. She pulled the sheets from her
waist and dangled her stumps over the bed. Marty stirred in his sleep,
gnawing the tip of his thumb. 'Who's that?' he said. 'They given me a
cellmate?' 'Marty,' she said. 'Is it Mum Pulse, really? I couldn't believe
my ears earlier. Call me Carrots. Pleasure to make your acquaintance.'
He crossed one arm over his chest and twirled his bandages along
the metal railing by his bed. 'Bloody good fortune on my part,' he
said. 'They've been talking about you for decades. I remember the
rumours. A deity on Degraves. Blokes been wandering out of the
Flinders Mission hoping they'd meet you and be heard. And me, too,
I'm one for the yearning, you know?' 'I'm going to the Red Plains,'
she said. 'Are you coping okay, Mama? Seems they've squandered our
silver juice.' 'I'm leaving now.' 'They'd better get it back soon, if you
hear me, Mama,' he said, jangling the tubes in his arms. 'I'm pulling
a mad sweat here. But not you, Mama? You'd rather speak directly
to Mr Agony? Open the flyscreen? Offer him a biscuit and a cuppa?
You're not one to leave him lonely in the yard. Kudos to you, Mama:
you're the real healer we need. A lot of docs think a man is his matter.
Take some out. Pump some in. Shake him all about. But all they do is
weld us to another drug. They want to heal us, but they won't hear us.
They want to mend us, but they can't see how far we've sunk beneath
their silver juice.' 'Would you like to come with me?' she said. 'Here
I am having a chinwag with a god. I've been hankering for this my
whole life.' 'We can leave together,' she said. 'But you got a ride out
there?' 'I have a train to catch.' 'You'll need more than that, Mama,' he
said, searching through his jeans. 'You won't forget me, will you?' he
said, tossing a bunch of keys into her lap. They were rusted, pinned to

acrylic dog tags and a shark tooth. 'Miss Aurora runs on good vibes,' he said. 'Her four wheels won't ever fail you, nah, not for a second.' 'There's room enough for two,' she said. 'No, no, Mama. I'm only a man of the streets. I've paid all my love to the silver juice,' he said, stabbing the cable back into the socket behind the torch plant. The pneumatic pumps wheezed into life. The fentanyl spurted down the catheter and watered her sheets. '"Hosanna, hosanna," they'll be yelling along the Yarra,' he said. 'Mama, Mama.' She hauled herself out of the bed and onto the scooter. The engine hummed beneath her thighs as she read the label on the seat: Aurora Mobility. 'Ma-ma, Ma-ma,' whispered Carrots, nestling under his sheets. Inching her fingers along the handlebars, she sped through the double doors, her sunglasses crooked over her eyes, the gauze on her ankles leaking pus on the seat, and raced onto Degraves Street.

Partygoers mobbed the laneway. They milled in the bars, lounged out of apartment balconies, hugging and swaying on the footpath, gyrating to electro music as a disc jockey whooped behind a turntable. On a projector screen in Andiamo Cafe, an Adelaide footy player gasped for air. 'Eddie Betts,' said the interviewer. 'You're going to an AFL Grand Final.' 'I'm speechless, man. Thirteen years. Thirteen years and all you want to do is play in a Grand Final. We're finally there.' Maha rolled past the revellers and up the laneway, but when she reached the garage, the Aurora jammed in the stairwell. She nudged the roller door. It wouldn't budge. She had to go elsewhere. She reversed through the revellers, past the telecast of the prelim final celebrations, and back to the street, flickering now with the red-blue, red-blue of a police wagon. 'Get your hooves off me,' said a man, pinned in the gutter by the officers, 'and get a real job.' Maha whirred along Centre Place, by the ramen and fried-chicken shops, where a girl in a cocktail dress knelt in the gutter, vomiting as she swiped through her phone. The pressure on the street was becoming palpable. When the people woke up to their suffering, when they learned the true nature of their pain, all the unrest in this glittering city would overflow. Their dull comforts would erode, leaving them wondering how to be and what to do. Maha headed down Swanston Street and over the Yarra River, driving in the middle of the road, her body trembling above the shock absorbers and the cracks in the tar, speeding to six kilometres an hour, then fifteen. She rounded onto the Monash Freeway as a semitrailer blared from the overtaking lane, but she lowered her head and kept driving, her neck bent over the handlebars, the motorway breeze sweeping the antiseptic from her hair. She hit eighteen kilometres and her fingers turned white with the force inside her wrists. 'Oi, lady,' yelled a man in a Toyota hatchback, 'you lost the fucking plot?' The gauze unravelled around Maha's ankles and fishtailed in her slipstream, beating the windshield of a van as she slipped by Wellington Road, under the unblinking moon above the Dandenong Ranges, and then the bandages ripped, fluttered through the traffic and settled on an emergency telephone. The cars cleared off the highway. The Aurora's four tyres rumbled over the dividers. Forty years, said the road. Forty years and she had reached the end of language. The engine sizzled and the scooter trundled to a standstill. The seismic mountains loomed along the highway with the contours of a prehistoric order. Northwards, the clouds above Melbourne flickered crimson with her escape, and southwards, where the road dissolved into the horizon, the sky spun a whirling, magnetic purple. An inhalation. An ellipsis. And there, fifteen metres down the road, a tin sign trembled in the scrub. 'Wrong Way,' it read. 'Warning. The Red Plains. Turn Back Now.'

Heist

'WOAH, WOAH, HOLD YOUR HORSES, HONEY,' wrote Klein, more than two months earlier, at the end of July. 'You ain't given up on your NYC dream, have you?' He sent a screenshot of Marg's Instagram post announcing Titch, Ginny's newest hire at Reynolds. 'It's a gimmick,' Ginny wrote, as quickly as she could. 'I just can't be bothered talking to the customers and needed someone to do it for me.' 'You know, I spoke to the Black Knight at brunch today,' he wrote. 'His name is Harvey Jones. He's a big dog in the blockchain space. He's building a company from a WeWork on Twenty-Third. Already passed Series-A funding. So all the schmucks he brings to Thirteen Madison Park? They're his *candidates*, Ginny. And he can't *stand* them.' 'Why's he interviewing them?' 'He wants engineers. Full-stack developers. Front-end. Back-end. Data engineers. Dev-Ops. He thinks he's being too ambitious. I think he needs someone to do the work for him.' 'What's his company?' 'I've got to go—the four is here. Look him up and I'll text you later.' She buried her phone in her pocket and tramped onto the sales floor. Since hiring the new guy, Ginny had been ordered by the regional manager to clean up the store and start hitting their sales targets. 'The bosses are being tight,' she said during yesterday's staff meeting with Nadine and Püd, 'and they have a new zero-drugs policy. Nothing recreational. No alcohol, either.' Püd pulled his T-shirt over his chin and sighed into the collar. 'Is this for real or what?' said Nadine. Ginny shut the backroom door, held the master key aloft and swung Nadine's locker open. She unzipped her duffel bag. Vials of HGH and stacks of syringes. 'But that's for gym,' said Nadine. 'It's confiscated,' said Ginny. 'Get your shit together.' She opened Püd's locker and a no-name, malt-brown bottle rolled between his bags of Doritos. 'No more,' she said, wrapping the syringes in her tote bag and pouring the booze down the sink. Today, leaning against the register as Titch waited for the customers, blowing at the bottoms of the paper planes, she felt the dreariness of the mall settling on her shoulders. She googled 'Harvey Jones NYC' and found his website: a clean-pressed shirt, the stone steps of Columbia's Butler Library rising behind him. 'CEO and Founder,' it said. 'Nuevo Crypto.' Eton Boarding School. Philosophy at Yale. MBA from Columbia. Nuevo Crypto was building the first lending platform for cryptocurrencies, where the billions of stagnant dollars in Bitcoin could be loaned, with interest, to other parties who needed the funds. 'Jones is using the approach of traditional banks,' wrote the *Yale Alumni Magazine*, 'by parcelling client money into loans, increasing growth for cryptocurrency investors. By harnessing all the stagnant value, the average Bitcoin trader will reap longer returns. And Jones is adding much-needed legitimacy to the space.' She closed the tab, but her mind kept racing. Titch sat cross-legged at the roller door, worming his hands into the cleft of his knees, watching her with all the pep of a new hire. It was a quarter past five. She shooed him out of Reynolds, logged zero sales on the POS and ran to her car.

'I'm a cryptocurrency trader from Australia,' she wrote, drumming her fingers on the touchpad. She refreshed his website, traced her mouse over his by-line and settled on the 'Contact Me' button. The company was hiring. Yes, you are, she thought. 'I've been following Nuevo Crypto for many months,' she wrote. Something creaked in the hallway and she snapped her MacBook shut. She tiptoed to her bedroom door and held it ajar. Betty swayed on the landing, stroking the elastic waistband of her sweatpants, plucking at the scar tissue on her navel. 'Dad?' said Ginny, and Jim bounded down the corridor, wrapping Betty in a hug. 'Only one month left,' he said. 'Let's keep persisting. You'll be fully clean. Renewed. Ready for the world. Ready to be a mum again.' He guided her back to their bedroom, turning to Ginny at the threshold. 'The homeopath said we could expect some nightmares, even sleepwalking. The last of her cravings are getting flushed out of her body. It's all part of the plan.' Wordlessly, with her skin gone cold, Ginny locked her door and reopened her MacBook. 'I have experience with team management and sales,' she wrote. 'I heard you're hiring at the moment. When can we set up a call?' She emailed the address on his website, breathing heavily through her nose, and then she slid her suitcase out from under her bed, held up the manza and swivelled her feet in arcs. She paced down the corridor to her parents' bathroom. Her mother's contact lenses lay curled in their shells. She unscrewed the lid of the cleaning solution and tipped a drop of manza down the nozzle. The dash of green swam into the saline, resting around the rim. She sniffed the lid. Clean. Synthetic. No, thought Ginny, no need to suffer through Betty's return. She would delay this rebirth as long as she could. Wiping her fingers on her wrist, she slunk back to her bedroom as the crescent moon slipped between the rooftops and the mist.

But at seven a.m., there was still no reply to her email. She loaded LinkedIn, copied her note and sent him an InMail. Her shift started: eight dragged to eight-thirty, nine staggered to ten, and when Reynolds opened, she cradled a flask of chai, swaying with fatigue. A woman lugged to the counter a history of global sterilisation. Ginny fled to the stockroom, wincing at the stink of vodka and tortilla chips wafting from the lockers. Püd had come in drunk. She played his latest Instagram story and watched him mumbling some nonsense about a road trip, an unplanned pregnancy, a waking nightmare. She wrenched open the window: the parking lot was blanketed in fog. She ran to Coles for a can of Lynx and sprayed down the lockers, shielding her nose from the deodorant with her hand. Titch knocked on the door, folding one foot behind the other, avoiding her eyes. 'Püd's crook,' he said. 'Been poisoned. It's real grim. It could be salmonella. I sent him home. He wanted to come back in, but I said maybe he shouldn't. He was so crook, yeah, I could just relay the memo to you.' She reloaded CoinSpot. Bitcoin had dived. Ten per cent in ten minutes. 'He'll be right by tomorrow,' said Titch. 'Had something bad to eat. Ramen, yeah, with the salmon swimming around in it. If you ever go to the Japanese joint, you should avoid the waiter with the turtle-shell glasses.' 'You mean tortoiseshell,' she said, refreshing her email. Still nothing. Her cell buzzed. 'Did you bring any booze into the house?' wrote Jim. 'Your mum's acting off. Having visions. Spouting all this dribble about muses and heroes. Can't let this set us back!' 'You got a lot of emails today?' said Titch, peering at her laptop. 'What you doing?' 'I'm on a cryptocurrency exchange.' 'What's that?' 'Have you been living in a cave?' 'So it's like stocks, or nah?' She shut her laptop and jabbed his chest. 'Don't stress yourself out, kid,' she said. 'Don't you have shelves to organise?'

A week later, Ginny drove northbound on the Monash Freeway, past lanes of outbound traffic. The overture of Stravinsky's *The Firebird* rumbled from the Fiat's speakers, muting the concrete mixers beside the overpass, those machines that churned away, endlessly renewing these god-awful streets. Betty, too, would soon be renewed; her recovery was almost upon them. Ginny veered into the emergency lane, slowed the car and rested her head on the dashboard. The rear-view mirror reflected her fiery hair and the cabin filled with the stink of gas from the running engine. She reached for her phone and checked her LinkedIn. No InMails. A police car flashed its lights outside her window and Ginny waved her fist at it, swerving along the off-ramp towards Waverley Road. She remembered the woman being led from the Chase bank in Greenpoint, her windbreaker splattered with blood, her wrists in handcuffs, the antagonist of her own tale, ever upward until she could fly no higher. There's always a means of escape, thought Ginny. A plot. A heist. Ever upward. She raced down Waverley Road, nipped through the traffic signal and skidded into the driveway. She tossed Jim the last sixteen hundred dollars and climbed the stairs, unravelling her headphones, and called her friends in Brooklyn. Two a.m. in the apartment. Squat white candles lit the dining table, which was stacked with paperbacks. *Human, All Too Human. Beyond Good and Evil.* Her friends appeared in the half-light, roused from their rooms to the couch, settling into the lower half of the screen. 'I'm going to need your help with something,' she said. Shelly and Gordon leaned towards the webcam. The loft darkened. Their anticipation was electric. 'Let me map this out for you,' said Ginny. 'You got a notepad, Klein?'

Just as she ended the call, exhaling all the air from her lungs, a smile creeping up her cheeks, Ginny heard a murmur outside her door. She slipped from the covers, wrapping her pyjamas over her chest, and crept into the hallway. It was Betty, again: she crawled on her hands and knees, her ear to the door, her satin nightie sliding up her back, the tail of a tampon stuck to her clammy ass. 'Dad?' said Ginny. 'Darling daughter,' said Betty, 'you never told us you were opening a restaurant.' 'Dad, are you awake?' 'He's asleep. He can't hear a single thing. But I can.' Ginny stepped into her bedroom and Betty grabbed the door-frame, her scrawny fingers gleaming on the wood. 'You don't want to stay at the bookstore, Gin? You tired of reading? You done with your stories and plots?' 'Go away.' 'You know I always wanted to keep you, all those years ago. I never wanted to palm you off. He didn't think I was right for a second child.' Betty's eyes were shining. 'Now I'm going to be your mummy again. I'll make you happy. I'll be your guide, Gin. When I was your age, I had to learn it all from the telly.' 'I'm trying to sleep.' 'Let's talk, darling. Why not?' Ginny gripped the knob and went to slam the door. Betty whimpered and scuttled down the hall, into the ululating snores from Jim's den. Ginny set her alarm and lay on her back for three hours, pressing her pillow over her face. At five-forty, she slithered out of bed and pulled Nadine's syringes from the tote bag. She unwrapped the vial and sucked some manza up the needle, then teetered down the hall and into her parents' bathroom. The box of Carefree tampons waited under the sink. She took one and nipped the syringe between the plastic wrapping, through the applicator and into the cotton. The plunger lowered, stiff under her thumb, and then she nestled the tampon back in the rainbow box. She rubbed her eyes, lit now by the quotidian dawn of another Melbourne morning.

The heating vent hummed above the shelves like a nest of wasps. The dust in the books made Ginny's sinuses swell. Wads of phlegm clogged her throat, her nose, the cavities under her eyes. Her temperature ran to a hundred and ten degrees Fahrenheit. 'Have you been running yourself down again, Gin?' said the doctor. 'We all need to learn to listen to our bodies, especially *you*.' Her history of infections could be linked to her C-section birth; without the full slather of her mother's vaginal fluid, she was born with a depleted microbiome. 'A dodgy shield,' said the doctor. 'But I've been telling you this since you were a toddler. Are you sleeping properly? What's got into you?' 'I just can't slow down, not now,' she said, as her WhatsApp filled with notifications. Later, she swayed between the aisles at Reynolds, coughing mucus into a floral handkerchief. She swallowed an antibiotic and held a yawn for ten seconds. Titch sidled up with a flask of foaming chai and said, 'You're okay, yeah?' She took the cup, clenching her jaw, mumbling her thanks. 'You had a late night?' he said. 'You playing with your stocks again, or nah?' She pulled him over to her laptop and loaded CoinSpot. 'They're not stocks. They're antithetical to stocks. This is a new currency that will make trading firms obsolete.' Titch fingered the graph on the screen and said, 'Is that how much it's worth?' 'We're the avant-garde, Titch,' she said, before her phone chimed with a call from Klein. She left Titch to explore CoinSpot and she snuck into the backroom to check her WhatsApp. 'Résumé printed,' said Klein. 'Gordon's Yale connection reformatted everything. I've set the reservation for next Thursday. No Wednesday openings, unfortunately, but the Black Knight will be there anyway. One day later, bueno no bueno? We're still waiting on confirmation for Shelly's sound check. I'll write you once it's final. You're still sure you want to try this?' 'It's going to work,' said Ginny. 'I just know. Ever upward, right?' The next day, after another sleepless night discussing contingencies and hacking phlegm into a bucket, Ginny napped over the register, dreaming of the walk from Twenty-Third to Thirteen Madison Park. Titch clunked his Dell on the counter, flipped up the screen and shook her awake, unveiling the coins he'd bought overnight. Bitcoin. Ethereum. Ripple, too. Even Paxos. 'Look at the gains, yeah,' he said. His ambition radiated through the store, energising her, a reminder that a life could progress to a higher realm. 'Shelly's confirmed for Thursday,' wrote Klein. 'We all want you back here so badly. Laissez-nous danser.' She clucked her tongue, locked her phone and patted Titch's cowlick. She pressed his collar across his neck and smoothed the creases in his linen shirt. She told him to register on another exchange so he could profit off arbitrage. 'We call it high-frequency trading,' she said. 'Cheers,' said Titch. 'Good on you for all your help.'

'I'm at my wit's end with this,' said Jim, grabbing Betty by the hair and lolling her head to the sunlight at the kitchen window. 'I've checked every nook and cranny for her booze. How long do you want to set yourself back?' Betty groaned and pulled her knees up to her chest, holding a foetal position at the kitchen table. 'What do we really want?' she said. 'What are we all missing?' Her eyes shone blankly at the skylight. 'C'mon, Dad,' said Marg. 'She's on her rags. It's just a heavy period. Leave her be, alright?' 'But she's hallucinating, saying she's seeing the future,' said Jim. Ginny reached between them for the box of Corn Flakes and filled her bowl with almond milk. She wiggled her headphones into place over her ears and glided to the car, munching her cereal in time with the piano chords of *Rhapsody in Blue*. Tonight was the night of her heist—and, given her mother's impending regeneration, not a night too late. After work, she set the alarm at Reynolds, saluted Titch as he waited at the bus station and stopped at the Telstra store. She bought a new data plan. She couldn't risk the wi-fi lagging; if Marg's episodes of *The Bachelor* were interrupted, she'd throw a tantrum at any hour of the night. Ginny left her dirty dishes with Jim at the dinner table, tiptoed past Betty muttering beside the hamster cage and plugged the new ethernet cable behind the television. She connected her cell phone and MacBook. She snuck upstairs and disentangled her headphones, winding the wires around her fingers, and burrowed under her comforter with her heart racing. 'It's time,' wrote Klein, two hours later, after he'd hidden a webcam behind the TMP bar. 'We're actually doing this.' She lowered the volume on her MacBook, muting the shrill opening of *Swanee*. Crossing her arms over her chest, she nestled her microphone to her jaw and said, 'Never a better time. You're on, S.' At ten fifty-five in New York,

207

Shelly marched into TMP, through the marble tables, wearing a black suede romper, their sinewy arms swinging between the guests as they unhooked their saxophone and climbed onstage, fluttering over the ivory piano like a raven in a mound of snow. Applause followed, led raucously by the man at the second table from the stage, who ate alone, a copy of *The Gay Science* tented over his vichyssoise. 'Settle a little, G,' said Ginny. The hoopla faded and the performance began. By eleven a.m., after Shelly's first song, a sultry number with the saxophone snug between their legs, Klein guided Harvey Jones to his regular table beside the stage, one chair for himself and another for a jetlagged Java developer. 'They're here, S,' said Ginny. 'Get ready to break that fourth wall.' Harvey draped his jacket over the chair. He slid his wristwatch across the tablecloth, opened his dossier, fingered the engineer's résumé, and asked, 'So you've only ever worked in JavaScript? Do you have any experience with microservices?' At eleven thirty-three, Shelly slipped offstage and said, 'Qui va danser avec moi?' And Harvey flinched, crumpling the engineer's messy résumé in his hands, as Shelly squeezed his shoulder, his forehead freckled with beads of sweat. 'Laissez-nous danser,' said Shelly, pulling him from his foie gras and onto the stage, then wrapping his tie around his eyes. Gordon yelled, 'Laissez-nous danser!' and the inebriated bankers chanted along, filling the restaurant with their ruckus. 'Money talks, K,' said Ginny, and Klein strode to Harvey's guest and said, 'Will you be covering the cheque?' The guest stiffened, verging on a dire professional faux pas, and flipped through his wallet for his MasterCard—no, his Visa Debit—no, his American Express for tax deductibles—as Gordon unfolded a sheet of paper out of *The Gay Science*, snaked an arm across the table and slipped the résumé inside Harvey's dossier. Top of the pile. Front-facing. At eleven forty-five, the climax of Shelly's performance, they grazed their bustier down Harvey's head, imprinting his sweaty face on their chest. And thousands of miles away, in the back pocket of the globe, Ginny sighed and smiled under her sheets. The heist had worked. She had never felt so certain. The sun reddened the horizon, making her bedroom glow as the house below creaked in darkness. She sent a screenshot from the webcam to their WhatsApp group: a lone, blurry frame showing Harvey spread-eagled under Shelly's saxophone, the software engineer fumbling for his wallet, her résumé slipped into the leather dossier. Ginny was enveloped with joy. She felt a deep, hard-won satisfaction. 'It has taken me a while to remember,' she said, 'that New York is not indifferent.'

'Ginny has already crossed the tightrope,' said Gordon, 'between man and overman. To think this gonzo plan actually worked.' 'And to shake his hand,' said Klein, 'and to feel how spooked he was. His closeted little heart couldn't handle the song.' Shelly drummed their fingers on the kitchen table, building a percussion solo, silver rings on pinewood on ceramic mugs. Melbourne and New York melded together as four plastic flutes of champagne clinked against the screen. 'I won't need to imagine his handshake much longer,' she said. Three days later, while helping Nadine unbox more Lamy fountain pens, her inbox chimed with an email. 'This might be unexpected,' wrote Harvey Jones. 'I stumbled upon your CV in a back pile and didn't know what to make of it. Could we arrange a Skype call? I have some questions for you.' Early Friday morning, after patting clods of Marg's concealer on the rings under her eyes, she opened Skype and called him. He cuddled his computer to his chest as he headed into a private room, flooding her screen with the indents of his seersucker shirt, his keyboard swishing against his navy trousers. 'I want a sense of how your mind works,' he said, opening the blinds across the window. 'How would you describe the internet to a kindergarten class?' 'It's like having everyone you want in the same room at the same time, no matter where in the world they were born.' 'And how would you describe the blockchain?' 'As if everyone in that room has a list of what they've eaten at recess, so if you trade tickets you know what's been eaten, and by whom, even if you haven't seen those meals with your own eyes.' 'Do you trade on an exchange yourself?' 'I do. Every night.' 'Good,' he said, cracking his neck as Midtown glowed over his shoulder. 'You shouldn't trust a skinny chef. I'm going to explain my company for a moment.' Dusk descended over the skyline as the streetlights on

Lexington began to luminesce. The spire of the Chrysler Building flickered in the distance, an amber totem, a talisman in the dark sky. 'But isn't a money market against the ethos of cryptocurrencies?' she said. 'Isn't it ideologically at odds with an unregulated future?' 'To an extent, yes, but if we really want a strong base for cryptocurrencies, then we need to welcome some kind of financial establishment. The big banks will only be interested if the ground is stable underfoot.' 'I have a hundred questions,' she said, 'but I can't ask them all on a call.' Harvey spread his hands on the desk. 'Well, looking at your CV,' he said, 'I'm impressed that a woman your age holds a senior management position in a company. It says a lot about your leadership capacity. Right now, Nuevo Crypto has reached a juncture: I've built the product, and I have the funding, now I just need to scale it. And to scale requires more support, more engineers to code, test for reliability and start engaging clients, but I'll admit that I don't have the patience to hire them myself. So, the long and the short is that I'm looking for someone to lead the Talent Acquisition team. She'll need a strong grasp of cryptocurrencies and the concepts of full-stack web and server development. And, I'll be honest with you, tech startups can turn into frat houses, so you would be a good candidate for the sake of diversity.' She fixed the headset under her chin as her chest swelled with warmth. 'I'd be very grateful for the opportunity,' she said. 'It sounds like the role for me.' 'First, I'd like to meet in person. It's essential for trust,' he said. 'How long do you want me to stay?' 'Maybe you can meet my team and trial for four months.' 'I'll book my flight as soon as I can,' she said. 'Remarkable,' he said. 'Can you get here next week?'

She stretched her feet down the comforter and cracked her smallest toes, moving upward to her largest. An hour passed, then another. She opened her window and let the easterly sun douse her face with its rays. 'So, how'd it go?' wrote Klein. She sent a selfie from the Friday morning glow. 'Homecoming,' she captioned the photo, and began searching for flights online, comparing the earliest one-ways to JFK. When she checked her ESTA waiver, she realised it was only valid for ninety days. Harvey wanted her to stay for four months. She would need a B-1 visa, and for that she needed to schedule a formal interview and pass the consulate interrogation. She ran downstairs, raced to her car and sped along the highway to Chadstone. She sprinted past Reynolds, Specsavers and the Reject Shop, and on to the travel agent. 'In a rush, possum?' he said. 'Where you headed?' 'New York.' 'Going to do the Big Apple?' 'I need to fly after this weekend. Monday at latest.' 'That's a bit early, possum. Most folks plan months in advance. Don't you got to book long-service leave?' 'I'm the boss.' 'Don't know if our discount will cover it, but let me have a squizz at the rates.' Looking at his computer, he scratched his bald head, which was covered in moles from his nose to his nape, like drops of congealed Coca-Cola. 'I need a B-1 visa too,' she said. 'Do you have those? I need to stay for four months.' 'Well, that's a sticky wicket,' he said, pursing his lips. 'But no dramas. I got a friend at the embassy who can expedite those. She's nailed a couple already, for some models and DJs.' 'Laissez-nous danser,' she said. 'It'll take forty-eight hours and I'll need the money upfront,' he said, folding some pamphlets in a briefcase and rubbing Vaseline on his scalp. 'The process isn't cheap. He asks for twenty-seven hundred all up. Add your one-way flight and we're at five grand. I'll only take cash for this. You in, possum?'

On Saturday, Ginny strode through the weekend shoppers to the ATM outside Baker's Delight. With a silent sigh, she sold the Bitcoin she had been saving for so many months. She withdrew five thousand dollars in reams of fifty-dollar bills, jammed in an envelope as thick as her finger. The fiat was a potent antivenom, her poison and her cure, but she felt certain, for the first time in months, that she would make it back to her friends in Brooklyn. She stuffed the cash in her wallet and returned to Reynolds, where she found Titch at the register opening his laptop. She leaned over his computer and smiled. He had added Ripple and Neo to his roster and his opening balance had tripled. How long had he been trading? Two weeks? An old man ambled into the shop, peering down his bifocals at the Non-Fiction books, so Ginny nudged Titch to attention and stole into the backroom to text the Excelsior group a photo of her thick wallet. 'It's really happening: I'll see y'all next week.' When the old man left, Ginny strode back to the register and clapped Titch on the shoulder. 'Would you like a smoothie?' she said. 'I'll buy you one.' They walked together to Boost Juice, the first time she had stepped foot outside Reynolds with a co-worker. 'Is this my quarterly review?' he said. 'I'm in a good mood, Titch. What do you do outside this godforsaken store?' He told her about his ant collection, about how organised they were, how there were more than he could count. 'But yeah, I like shopping too, I guess,' he said. 'I've always liked a bit of dressing up.' At least the kid couldn't be faulted for not trying. He was seventeen years old and already paid his own way. Suddenly his meagre lunches and his faux-preppy fashion made sense. He wanted to craft something of himself. She had never met an orphan before—but was 'orphan' even the right word nowadays? 'You remind me of my friends,' she said. 'They're not like anyone here. They're ambitious. I'm leaving to go back to them, Titch,' she said, recounting her month in New York, her growing cryptocurrency expertise and the invitation from Harvey. 'That's wicked,' he said, after she finished telling her story. 'Sounds like a movie or something. My mum was in England, yeah, before I was in the picture. She did Philosophy at Oxford and wanted to stay so badly that when she came back to Melbourne she didn't leave the house for years. She just stayed at home, taking care of me and her old friends. She wasn't an English girl anymore, nah. Maybe she never was.' Back at Reynolds, they walked shoulder to shoulder between the shelves and he said, 'Not sure if overseas is for me, nah. Don't know how I'd handle all the glitz and glam. But good on you. Good luck with it.' He slurped the dregs of his mango-tango smoothie, holding her wallet at his hip, and she patted down his collar. She offered him a smile. He lived a life worth admiring, but he was bound to his 'yeahs' and his 'nahs', stuck with yet another simple suburban script.

'Today calls for celebration,' texted Jim. 'Our mummy has made it through the wilderness. I'm inviting the family over to celebrate. See you girls at seven-thirty! Love, love, love, Dad.' Ginny gnawed the inside of her lip. The day had come; no way would she bear witness to the whole damn charade. She would do anything to avoid that house. 'But what are you doing tonight, Titch?' she said, arming the security alarm at the front door. 'Nothing,' he said. 'Do you really live all alone?' she said, looking up from her cell and into his eyes. 'You want to see the ants?' he said. They walked under the dripping awnings by San Churro, past the stunted palm trees howling in the wind, and waited for a cab. She could've offered to drive, but she liked this freedom of letting someone else worry about the road. Raindrops wet her lips and cheeks and she smiled into her sleeve. When the taxi arrived, they tumbled inside, her bag jolting in her lap. Titch fumbled with the buttons around his wrists and rolled up his wet sleeves. 'Where are you two strays headed?' said the driver. 'We're going to Springy,' said Titch. He lay back in the seat, drying his sopping hair between his fingers, shivering like a discontented dog. A public bus thundered down the transit lane, spraying rainwater over the hedges and fences along Princes Highway. 'Might've drowned outside,' said the driver, reaching for his radio. 'Lucky I found you when I did.' The radio squawked from the dashboard and a football talkback show resumed. '...Played them earlier this season at Etihad and got sphinctered. Now we have a spot in the top four up for grabs. Do you know how many decades I've waited for this? Fair dinkum, guys, me and my stepmum have seen our fair share of pain. She was there in Bali when the bombs went off. I lost my job down at Holden a couple of years ago. But this year...Should I trust true Richmond happiness or get my heart ripped out again?' 'Yeah, sorry,' said Titch. 'You mind offing that?' His face drained of colour. She reached for his hand in his lap. The taxi slowed on Springvale Road by a landscaping warehouse and an Indian grocer. His apartment block looked like a penitentiary: whitewashed, concrete facade, bars on the balconies, a rickety gate over the driveway. 'Not a palace or anything, nah,' he said, pressing the button for the eighth floor on the elevator panel. When the doors closed, he tried to comb his hair with his fingers and she chuckled again, dripping rainwater down her collarbones. They left the elevator and stood outside Titch's apartment as he jimmied his keys in the lock. Inside, the walls were bare, the lights fluorescent; the place seemed hardly lived-in, as if he were only passing through. He kept a folded card table and an air mattress on his bedroom floor. On the table was a laptop charger and a silver coat hanger. Minimalism, sure, she thought. Her waterlogged sneakers slurped as she stepped through the living room. 'I should shower,' she said, sniffing the working day's sweat over her shoulders as she lay on his air mattress. 'Do you have a towel?' 'Use mine,' he said, tiptoeing across the bare tiles, as if there were tripwires under his feet, and pulling a towel from a pile of clothes in the corner. 'Is it clean?' 'Sure,' he said. He opened his laptop on the desk and reloaded his crypto exchange. Inside the bathroom, she shook out the towel, leaving the door ajar as she paused before the cracked mirror. She waited for steam to smother the vanity and draped her blouse over the tiles, crumpled her trousers on the bathmat and slid off her underwear. She crept into the shower. The water gurgled from the faucet and down her chest. The steam kneaded her back, opened her pores. A strand of hair slid from her scalp, slithered down her legs and floated on the tiles. The drain gurgled and the strand slipped into the spiral, sucked in revolutions, devoured by the whirlpool. She flicked the hair with her toe, breaking the spiral, but the current resumed, down and down, sucking the strand through the grimy grill. 'Jesus,' she said, suddenly dizzy. She cut the water, plunged her head into the towel and padded into the bedroom. Striding past his desk, she dropped her clothes on the floor, but he was muttering, maybe giving himself a pep talk. Her teeth chattered and her fingers were pale prunes. 'Careful,' he said, finding a tissue to dry the floor. 'Okay,' she said, as he dabbed the water, his eyes darting over the tiles. 'Guess I should shower too, yeah,' he said, 'to warm me up.' 'Okay,' she said, stretching her body over the bed. Titch thudded the door closed and scampered to the bathroom. She spread her hair over the sheets and hid inside the pile of clothes. She smirked, wondering where all his ants were hiding, and then her hands grazed a leather wallet on the pillow. She pulled it open. An old photo of two white adults and a little boy, his chubby face painted in yellow and black. A photo of the family at Healesville Sanctuary, an eagle perched on the mother's wrist, the toddler holding a worm in his fat pink fingers. And, folded in a cellophane pouch, a photo of the parents alone underneath the light towers around a football stadium. 'Richmond FC Members, 2017.' A tremor went up her hands. He'd implied he was an orphan. That he was emancipated, independent, self-made. She flicked through the wallet and found a flyer. 'Mother Pulse,' read the title in cursive print. 'Your Lifelong Listener & Subterranean Storyteller.' So his mother was some shyster in a city office. Scamming tourists out of their Euros and Yuan. Paying for his apartment in bi-weekly doses of fiat. In the bathroom, the greywater spun down the cavernous drain, and the gurgling turned to laughter in her ears. She threw the flyer on his pillow, huffing, shaking her head. She pulled on her jeans and buttoned her blouse. 'She is destined to flee Australia,' Klein would say. 'Not to fuck it.'

A kebab truck sat in the driveway, billowing clouds of chicken fat over the yard, and streamers hung from the awnings, noosed the lion statues and fluttered into the puddles. Cars lined the driveway, the embankment, three-sixty degrees around the cul-de-sac. She parked at the end of the street and walked between the balloons. Music blared from the hallway, the windows rattling with the base. American pop. Miley Cyrus. 'It's a party in the U-S-A,' she sang. An uncle from Nunawading hooked his arms around Ginny and thrust a kebab at her forehead. 'She's back to her best,' said the uncle. 'Gee, you've got to be proud of her.' Betty wore a floral gown, a wreath of geraniums snuggled in her hair, and perched on the couch as Jim clacked his nails against a flute of apple juice, calling for attention. 'Can I get my girls up here?' he said. Marg lassoed Ginny and skipped between the guests to the centre of the living room. They sat on the carpet at Betty's feet. 'This is family,' said Jim. 'We pick each other up. We light up the dark. I'd like us all to sing "Happy Birthday" because she's been born again.' A cousin recorded the song on Snapchat and swivelled her phone to Ginny's face. 'So what do you think?' said the cousin. 'Should she start modelling again? Pretty inspiring, yeah?' Ginny hid behind her hand and climbed the stairs. She dried her socks and shoes on the portable heater beside her bookshelf and tumbled into bed at eight-thirty, her earliest night's sleep in three months. She imagined sprinting through Manhattan, north up Riverside along the Hudson, ten then twenty then thirty blocks north, where the frost clung to the chain-link gate of the Amtrak line, following the burning red pupil of Klein's Marlboro. They squeezed through the battered fence, she first, Klein second, Shelly and Gordon to follow, and skipped down the tracks. Klein said, 'Freedom Tunnel, come and take us.' They crept up the defunct shantytown, past corrugated iron upended on the gravel, past walls caked with graffiti and 'GET OUT' posters, and Klein flicked his cigarette into an icy puddle and steam rose off the surface like a kiss. They split a vial of manza and sat inside the tracks, cloaked by night so thick it hid her alabaster breath and luminous fingertips. They lay back, bracing for the Amtrak. Then came the tremors in the tracks, the steel shrieking up from Midtown, the headlights swooping over their folded bodies, flaring behind their clenched eyelids. Whitegrey, it said. Whitegrey. And it swept over her face, an inch from her nose, the thunderous clank of the steel pistons like a hundred hands drumming either side of a coffin: one breath, then two, three, and then it passed, en route to Hudson, and Syracuse, and Niagara Falls. Klein giggled raucously, clutching her wrist, and she grabbed Gordon and Shelly in an exhilarated embrace. 'Come and take us,' Ginny said, fanning her face, and at her station in Melbourne, the phantom Amtrak roared over her bed as she nestled into her hard-won dreams.

'Mugged?' said Jim, piling the paper plates in the living room. 'So my baby girl has been mugged? Right under my nose. On the first day of the rest of our lives.' 'Jesus, Dad, this wasn't a mugging,' said Marg. 'It's plain old theft.' She yanked Ginny's face into position. 'Now,' said Marg, 'what's this rat's name?' Betty inched across the kitchen, running her fingers through the scrunched beer cans and mounds of multi-coloured confetti, clutching her gown across her shoulders. Her wreath of geraniums wobbled on her head. 'Just tell me his full name,' said Marg. 'Titch Antoine Clement,' said Ginny. She had woken that morning, rolled from her bed, slipped into her plaid trousers and opened her wallet. The bank envelope was gone. She unbuckled each flap, unzipped each pocket. She rummaged through her tote bag, shaking, the Reynolds paperwork and the syringes and the booze jostling in her grasp, but she couldn't find the money. She fainted on the bookcase. Cracked her head on a shelf. Marg yelled for Jim to inspect the commotion and when he opened the door, clutching the inner tube of a BMX tyre, he found Ginny unconscious in a pool of blood. The morning was groggy, subdued. 'I think she should take a sickie,' said Betty. 'She could be concussed.' Marg tramped through the pizza boxes and souvlaki wrappers from the party, clutching her cell in one hand and a pink stress ball in the other. 'I could have left it at Reynolds,' said Ginny, and in the afternoon her phone chimed with a slew of texts. 'Emergency at Reynolds,' came the message from head office. 'Reported robbery. Police on site.' 'We were supposed to open,' she said. 'Titch and I.' 'He's on a spree,' said Jim. 'Did you know he was a junkie when you hired him?' 'You got a pic of this rat?' said Marg. Ginny scrolled through the store WhatsApp group until she found his selfie from three weeks ago, standing by the mirror in a red linen shirt, his pale skull glowing beneath the shaved sides of his head. 'I'll get the sting on him, don't stress,' said Marg. 'You can always trust a girl to find a boy's dirt.' 'But, Gin,' said Jim, 'you've already cleared your debt. Why were you walking around with so much dosh?' 'She's planning to run away,' said Betty. 'She wants to open a restaurant in America.' 'You don't know shit,' said Ginny, and, with the blood pounding in her eardrums, she told them the real story. The late nights trading Bitcoin. The heist at TMP. Harvey Jones. The travel agent. 'But it doesn't matter now,' said Ginny. 'It's all gone up in smoke.' 'But you just have to tell Harvey Jones,' said Marg. 'Put your ego aside and tell him you were robbed. He's a rich bloke. A big dog. He'll get it.' 'It's time for Ginny to lie down,' said Betty. 'She's had a long day.' Jim hauled Ginny over his shoulder and carried her upstairs. The chandelier made her eyes water and the tinsel on the bannister scratched her cold toes. Jim tucked her into bed and locked the door from the outside. She opened her laptop. The sentences in her email blurred into a single, motionless worm. 'There's been a robbery,' she wrote. 'I no longer have the money for my flight and my visa. Can we postpone our meeting?' She hit send. Four p.m. in New York. Five. Five-thirty. She copied the text from her email and sent it to the Excelsior chat. She rummaged through her bag for the vial, but the manza was finished. No, duh. 'Don't you worry, sis,' texted Marg, 'I'm searching thru the grapevine to suss this Titch kid. I'll get to the bottom of this fiasco. Don't you fret about a thing. K?'

Jim unlocked the bedroom door and stood over her bed. 'We shouldn't let you back into work without knowing how badly you've been hurt,' he said. 'Your mum wants to start driving again. She'll take you to the doctor.' Betty drove with her chest over the steering wheel, balanced on the edge of her seat, swaying as she swerved up the streets and parked outside Glen Waverley Medical Centre. As if hypnotised, she watched a man unloading a lawnmower onto Springvale Road, and in the waiting room, she scrolled intently through Instagram, enlarging each post with two fingers until it filled her entire iPhone screen. 'All I'm seeing is anxiety,' she said. 'You young people need better role models. You won't believe what I saw during my detox, Gin. I saw hope. Real hope. Someone with a smile on their face, who can give young people the right advice for joy.' Ginny crumpled in her chair, tracing her fingers over the bulge in her head. In the consultation room, the doctor eased his stumpy fingers over her skull, tracing her eyes left and right with a rubber pen. 'This is a severe concussion,' he said. 'Her cerebellum has really copped it.' 'I'd like her to have a doctor's certificate,' said Betty. 'For the week, thanks.' 'I'll arrange that, no dramas,' he said, sliding a needle through the corner of the wound. 'She hasn't been taking it easy, has she? I've seen her at least once a month for twenty-five years and, as nice as her visits are, I think it's time she learned the limits of her body.' 'How do I fix this?' said Ginny. 'With a knock this severe, it'll be hard to sleep and focus. You'll get irritable and confused. You can't drink or smoke or do any physical exercise. If you exert yourself, even in the slightest, it'll only get worse.' 'But after all that,' said Betty, 'it would be good for her to start working out with me, right? Get her weight down. I'm thinking Bikram yoga and Pilates?' 'A lot of people don't know this,' he said, 'but happiness is actually the best pill.' Ginny

223

lost the next ten days upended on the couch, her pupils magnetised by the plastic chandelier, her family slowly orbiting around her. Jim's meaty hands on her neck. Marg kneading her calves with the sharp bones of her elbow. Betty humming from the ottoman, legs crossed, her pale, lunar belly gleaming under her sports bra, scrolling down and down her Instagram feed, blowing her bangs off her forehead in curt puffs. 'I need to go back,' said Ginny, and Jim hefted her upstairs, lay her under the sheets and locked her in the room again. She tried refreshing her inbox but the light from her laptop made her head pound. She thumped the computer closed and groped for her phone, trawling through Harvey's emails to find his number. 'This is Harvey Jones. Sorry I missed your call. You can forward your message through my personal email.' 'It's been an awful week,' said Ginny. 'Let me know when we can reschedule my visit. You can't understand how fucked up this is.' One night, two weeks later, Marg sidled into Ginny's room, switched on the bedside lamp and unveiled a ream of A4 papers. 'Have a squizz,' she said. 'I've printed them so they're easier on your eyes. I've found the scoop. Seems this kid has an alias or two. "Ralphy." "Rig Burns." You remember Jason's brother from Lysterfield? Damo? Turns out his Tinderella might have had her own run-in with him.' There was a line of texts from a Facebook group chat titled 'Gurls Rule The Wurld' with a fist emoji and a rainbow. Ralphy had snuck into Sophie McCleary's sharehouse, perved on her in the shower and run away with her marijuana. The roommate, Tayla Brown, saw him going through their stash. 'He even ripped apart Quackie Chan,' read the message. 'What the fuck makes this kind of monster?' She folded the page and returned it to Marg. 'Ralphy?' 'Rig Burns?' The Excelsior group was filled with messages: question marks, emoticons, an offer of a loan. Leaning over Marg's lap, she rubbed her head on her sister's jeans, tasting bile at the back of her throat. 'Give me your mobile, Gin,' said Marg. 'Why?' 'We have to reach him.' 'I'll just give you his number.' 'No,' said Marg. 'He needs to think it's from you.' 'What do you want to do?' 'Get your dosh back. Teach him a lesson.' 'This is crazy.' 'Almost as crazy as running away to America? Come on, Gin, seriously, I'm doing this for you.' 'I need to sleep,' said Ginny, sitting up, fending her sister away. 'Goodnight.' Marg picked up the discarded printouts and shut the door. Ginny sniffled into the dank folds of her pillow, then spread her hands on the bedspread and sat up. No. She would not spiral into some suburban vendetta. She would continue as manager at Reynolds, start saving again, reschedule with Harvey and come home the legitimate way. If he really wanted her, he could wait a few months. She would brave the deadening drone of Reynolds and climb out of this cave relying on no one but herself.

At eleven p.m., her phone chimed between her legs, once and again, but Ginny was burrowed under her covers. The next morning, she saw a barrage of calls and couldn't believe she'd overslept. 'I told you to use my fucking email,' she wrote to Harvey, fingering the wound on her scalp. 'That's how you're supposed to contact me.' She would reply to him properly at Reynolds, away from Jim's endless interrogations, in the calm hours of her return shift, which, on that rainy September morning, was thankfully quiet. Not a single customer entered the shop. She scrolled through her cell, looking for the late-night speaker, but the calls were all from Titch. 'You can't be serious,' she said, dropping her phone in the metal tray of the register, cushioned by the piles of untouched bills. And, like a taunt, her cell rang again, a hidden number. 'Ginny Antonopoulos?' 'Yes,' she said. 'This is the regional manager calling. I wanted to check in after the theft and touch base on sales, which are looking lowly, to be totally frank. Do you have a moment?' She stumbled to the ramen shop, dodging a shopping cart and a service dog, pressing the phone to her ear. 'Money matters,' he said. 'We're not some arty-farty inner-city independent. We're a successful brand. Maybe I didn't make this clear before giving you a crack at hiring someone.' He said he was going to call her every day to read the budgets off the POS and make sure she was running a bag check. 'Check everything,' he said. 'Backpacks. Pockets. Handbags. Even inside their shoes, you'd be surprised.' The nature of the theft warranted a rigorous investigation. 'Weren't you supposed to open that morning?' he said. 'I was injured,' she said. 'I have a medical certificate.' Püd arrived at Reynolds with a limp, lumbering down the aisles with a drunken gait, and the regional manager ended the call. She pressed her fingers on the glass shopfront, retying her ponytail, the blood from her stitches irrigating her hair. 'You alright?' said Püd. 'You seem a little gacked.' At the house, Jim explained the app he had downloaded to monitor her whereabouts. It would track the GPS in her car and follow her trip to work. It was linked to her credit card to block extraneous expenses. If she drove off her regular route to work, the app would alert Jim and he could shut off the engine. If she spent her money too quickly, he would have an hour to freeze her account. 'You're in a gnarly state of mind right now,' said Jim. 'You can't be trusted. These are the happiest days of our family. Didn't you get the memo? Let's not jeopardise the rest of our lives.'

The next morning, Ginny woke to find a Holden Commodore by the Hills Hoist in the front yard. Its tyres had minced the azaleas in the garden bed. After her shower, as Ginny ambled to her Fiat, Marg smuggled a very tall man in a grey hoodie downstairs and into the yard. 'This is the famous Damo,' she said. His outline stretched ten feet across the ground in the dawn glow. 'Just give us your mobile, sis,' she said. 'And we'll find him.' 'He's a ratbag,' said Damo. 'Lot of people need to get a hold of him, you know.' Ginny pushed between them, through the sunlight streaking off the tin patio of the house opposite. She buckled her seatbelt and skidded down the driveway, swerving onto Waverley Road towards Chadstone. When the traffic stalled behind a dump truck, she levered her seat flat and lay under the parabolic ceiling of the cabin. She imagined Gordon sitting on the steps of the New York Public Library. Klein pedalling around the Flatiron Building on his slim black single-speed. Shelly reclining on the rooftop playing their saxophone to the Chinatown water tanks. She drove to Chadstone on her back, swerving through the talismanic triptych of her Manhattan, clicking her fingernails on the steering wheel. Surely failure, she thought, was the most pathetic hallucinogen. The parking lot was overrun with mothers and strollers, children and footballs, boyfriends and girlfriends, grandmothers and their baskets of baguettes, blue cheese and puffs of cilantro. It was a public holiday. The eve of the football grand final. Inside Reynolds, the aisles were as dusty and empty as ever, and the register sat stolidly with its untouched supplies of cash. Nothing to report. When Nadine left to buy a tub of whey protein from GNC, Ginny climbed over the register and lay face down on the counter. She closed her eyes and tried to sleep, begging for oblivion. Her phone buzzed. An email. Harvey Jones. 'I apologise for being out of the loop,' it read. 'I had a conference in Washington DC and another in Copenhagen. I've tried calling you over the last few days but haven't been able to get through. I've reviewed your last emails and thought seriously about the costs and benefits of having you fly all the way out here. There are so many fantastic candidates, exceptional even, and competition for this role is remarkably high. I need to find someone I can trust, but I gather as of late you have some erratic perspectives. I've been in tech long enough to know that any hesitation this early into a process is usually a sign to part ways.' The heaters filled the store with a howl and she dug her chin into the counter. 'The costs,' she said, pushing her hands in her hair. 'The benefits.' She clamped her face into the linoleum and pressed until her mouth filled with blood. 'What's going on, girl?' said Nadine, hugging a barrel of powder to her chest. 'You looking extra-pale. You want some Nodoz? Zero calories.' Ginny reached for her mouth. A slice of her tongue slid onto the counter, like a glistening pink maggot. 'One moment,' she said, and staggered from Reynolds, past the deli, up the escalator and into her car, filled now with late-September heat. She drove home and stopped behind the Holden Commodore. Jim would have left for work. Betty would be at a body-sculpt class at Fitness First. 'You having second thoughts, yeah?' said Marg, rising from the couch. Ginny hunched over the kitchen sink. Her crimson spit spiralled down the plughole and clung to the teeth of the drain. She slowly handed over her phone. Damo skipped down the stairs, his fat feet thumping on the carpet. 'Cheers,' he said, unlocking the phone. 'We'll take care of this,' said Marg, scrolling through her text messages. 'When it's all said and done, you're doing Melbourne a favour,' said Damo. 'Now he won't ruin another girl's life the way he's ruined yours.'

Granny

ON THE LAST SATURDAY IN SEPTEMBER, the clouds broke above the Dandenong Ranges and rain sluiced over the southeastern suburbs. Swallows swooped in the spring humidity as the rain fizzled in the sky, stretched above the city like a carnival tent, hovering over the people pacing along footpaths, squatting at bus stops and stalled in their cars at traffic lights. Melburnians hurried from cars to houses and back again, arms laden with party pies, slabs of beer and loose coins for the afternoon's bets. Rain cut down the mountains and over the bedrock, draining northward into the Yarra Valley dams, where the water ran off the vineyard hills. Tributaries washed up trampled grapes and rabbit poo, trickling over rocks clad in winter's moss and down the valley to Lilydale Station. The creek dipped beneath the Metro overpass and widened at Mullum-Mullum Reserve, where the bike paths zigzagged through gum trees and green ovals, as yelps' from clubs and pubs severed the Saturday arvo peace. The river swept up dog leashes, fishing wires and lolly wrappers, muddying at the electric generators at South Yarra. At five p.m., a shadow fell over the condo balconies draped in yellow and black towels, sheets and bikini bottoms, and the light towers of the G rippled on the smiling brown face of the river. A rascal cannonballed into the water, swinging his Tigers jersey over his head, wetting Titch on the bridge and bellowing, 'We won the fucking granny!'

Titch was waiting on the footbridge to meet Ginny and return her dosh. He had not slept for the last two weeks. Each night he had replayed, over and over, the moment he had opened Ginny's wallet. The poor girl, yeah, his gut aching. The poor dreamer. How crook for her to be messed up with him. All through those nights, the ants had flaked off his sheets, twisting beneath the baby hairs all over his body, from his shoulders to his jocks and down to his toes. When the sun rose he'd sweep their hundreds of husks off his arms, whimpering as they crawled on his cheeks, twitching at his eardrums. He'd have a peek at his mobile. Calls from Sophie. A couple from the cops. Some from Ginny. In demand, yeah, and spread too thin. The days had dragged. Titch nestled in the yellow overalls from the chop shop, his arms folded over his chest, pinching the skin on his ribs to stop himself from snoozing. They were on their way, yeah. Just a matter of time. In the loo, the overalls slid down his wiry frame, so he spent an afternoon digging new holes in the belt, plunging the kitchen knife through the smudged yellow fabric. 'All energy tends to zero,' he said, remembering Mother Pulse's teaching, the last words he heard before running off, back to the calls, the texts, all the mess he'd made. He opened his bedroom window and clung to the frame, leaning into the spitting rain. All life did tend to zero, yeah. Didn't have to look so far. Zero on the road between the semis and the bus. Zero on the divots in the concrete. Zero on top of the electric wires. Zero and he wouldn't have to deal with this anymore. Zero and he wouldn't be around to shoulder the load. Zero and see you later, mate, done and dusted. A light buzzed in the window below him and he saw the top of some girl's head, her dyed silver hair still dripping from a shower, her hands clasping a silver necklace around her neck. Swarovski. The light split off the crystals and dazzled in the window. If he'd taken a dive that night, the girl would have to deal with the memory forever. He wouldn't have wished this curse on anyone else. He tramped back into his bedroom, drew the window back along its socket, and the heavy air flooded his mouth and weighed on his eyelids. He realised Mother Pulse was right after all. Ginny's dosh sat on his desk, stuffed inside the envelope. He jammed his fist in his eyes and made whiteouts on his lids. He had been so thick-headed. So greedy. What was the use of all that money, anyway? 'Here, gone,' he said, and if he really wanted zero, yeah, he could just disappear. He wouldn't dump the blame on anyone else. No need for any hoo-ha. No need to make a scene. He loaded a Google search. 'If you stop eating and drinking,' it said, 'death can occur as early as a few days, though for most people approximately two weeks is the norm.' Just another fortnight. One last diet. He'd have time to talk to   after all this idle silence. He took his mobile off the pillow and read the most recent text: 'If you keep ignoring me, i'll come over with my mates and bash you up. You really think i'd forget the shithole where you live?' 'I'm sorry, yeah,' he wrote. 'I made a mistake. I'll give it back.' 'Do you want to see me?' 'Yeah. To give it back.' 'All of it?' 'And more. For damages.' '6 g.' 'I can do seven.' 'Yeh. Where are we meeting?' 'Somewhere public.' 'The city. Next Sat. Bridge by the G.' The switcheroo didn't have to be so difficult. No need for her to freak out. He would give it back, plus a fair bit extra. He'd apologise, shake her hand and disappear. Day One of his diet, yeah, and his ribs yelled against his pasty skin. The air ballooned in his belly. The breath slithered out his lips. He'd stick it out until next Saturday, surely. Last until then. Play things on the front foot, yeah. Pay his dues. All life tends to zero. Get dosh, lose dosh. Here, gone.

Titch watched the rascal from the footbridge and gripped the barrier with his dry palms. He switched up the settings on his mobile. Speaker on. Ringer primed. Notifications to chime. He clutched the envelope inside the chop-shop overalls as the larrikin lumbered along the riverbank and the cops gave chase, thudding over the cobblestones in their black boots. The crowd surged out the MCG gates by the thousand. All these people, yeah, all come for one game. The concrete pylons of the bridge groaned as they ascended the stairs. 'You coming?' wrote Titch. 'Lots of peeps out here.' 'Yeh,' came the reply. 'We see you.' He reread the message. Searched across the bridge. Hid deeper in the overalls. Someone tossed a bottle of Carlton Draught off the bridge and it shattered on the train, spilling foam over the windows and the tracks. A giggling girl climbed the fence, tiptoed along the barrier, yanked her leggings to her knees and mooned the skyline. The waves of people swelled with a rhythm Titch had never heard. They trundled up the stairs in their hundreds, handballing footies in arcs over their heads. First came the kiddies, their faces painted yellow and black, waving Richmond pennants and unwinding scarves from their necks. The older folks wiped tears from their flushed faces. With a riotous scream they all began to sing, hundreds upon hundreds, the Tiger anthem shrieking out of every hoarse throat. 'Are you here?' wrote Titch. 'Yeh,' came the message. 'Where you?' A little boy ran to Titch and opened his hand for a high-five. 'Oh, we're from Ti-ger-land,' said the kid, rubbing Titch's overalls where the black oil smudged the yellow shine. 'It's history, mate. The end of history.' He skipped down the bridge, singing the last lines of the song, and Titch refreshed his phone, squinting into the crowd. Suddenly a bloke lunged through the supporters and wrung Titch by the neck. 'Here's the little ratbag', he said, snarling. It was Damo. He wore black soccer goalkeeper gloves. A snapback over his man-bun. Titch ran into the crowd, but Damo grabbed him. Tackled him at the hips. Smashed his cheek into the footpath. 'You think you can go around town nicking shit?' 'Nah, where's Ginny?' 'Shut the fuck up, twiggy ratbag, and listen to me—' 'Looks like we've got a hothead over here,' said a mum stopped in her tracks. 'Must be a Crows fan,' said a lad holding a ball pump. 'Go have a cry somewhere else,' said the mum. Titch squirmed in the headlock, his back cracking, his ribs bulging, blood drizzling where the bitumen had cracked the cartilage in his nose. The mum walloped Damo on the arse with her blow-up Richmond hand and the lad poked him with the pump. 'You guys go away,' said Damo. 'This one's between me and him.' 'This is the best day of our lives,' said the mum, pulling Titch up by the scarf. 'So don't you ruin it.' 'Get out of here,' said Damo, but the lad had enough and punched him in the jaw. A king hit. Damo's eyes rolled, his shoulders slumped, and he collapsed. The mum screamed, heaving Titch to his feet as he clutched his nose. 'Let's go fuck-ing mental,' said the lad. 'Let's go fuck-ing mental.'

Titch pushed into the throng, the blood dripping down his kit. He tore off his overalls and dropped them on the footpath. A decoy, yeah, something to get them off his tail. He booked it down the leafy fields wearing only his running shorts, looping by the G and past the Tigerland Superstore, where fans were taking pictures with the Jack Dyer statue. Two other blokes yelled out the door of a Holden Commodore, pumping the horn as Titch hurdled a bench. 'Mangy thief,' said the driver, as Titch ran to Richmond Station—but the turnstiles were shut. Clogged with fans. Totally fucked. He ran past the station as boys hurled clumps of flaming gum leaves off the curb. Two girls downed goon sacks in the gutter and another ripped a bong in the lane. Titch reached Swan Street as the Commodore revved in the foot traffic. The fans drummed the bonnet, the windshield, the boot. The car was stuck. 'Stop that shirtless psycho, alright?' yelled the driver. Titch ran down the tunnel to the tram tracks, now engulfed with more people than could be happy in one place and at one moment. Clinging to the tram. Smacking the driver's window. Pummelling the glass with their fists. Rocking side to side as the driver yelled from his tiny cabin, 'Bugger off or I'll call the police.' 'Fuck the pigs!' they chanted. 'Go the Tigs!' Two young ladies cartwheeled off the kerb. Little kids jeered and jived, reliving plays from the granny on a big-screen telly at the Corner Hotel. 'Goes wide—wants Martin—reasonable spot—Brown at the back—Martin won the footy—he willed his way through it—Little kick forward—Houli to kick a goal—He does!' One bloke, trapped up a gum tree, tossed cans from a bag and sprayed foamy beer over their heads. Titch sprinted on, gasping by the tram stop as a circle of five fellas used the plastic blockade as a trampoline, squirting water on the tracks. Another lad clutched a trumpet to his nose and said, 'Ladies and gentlemen, I have a song for you.' The mob at Botherambo Street circled the trumpeter, clambering on wheelie bins and makeshift ladders, on tin construction signs and steel kegs, as he honked out the first bars of the Richmond song. A woman rolled on a bench, her head full of crystal meth. 'Oh, we're from Ti-ger-land,' she wept. 'A fighting fury we're from Ti-ger-land...' The guys on the wheelie bins unbuckled their belts and yanked off their undies, spinning their stiffies left-right-left-right like windshield wipers. The skies exploded over the G and the revellers stopped, frozen in their dancing, mute amid their chaos, magnetised by the thunder in the sky. 'Fireworks!' shouted a kid in the Coles clock tower. 'Yellow and black,' yelled a girl scaling a light pole. 'It's fucking done!' With a thousand cheers, the amber crackers flashed against the black spring sky, and the people sang, awestruck at the truth of a Tiger premiership, before shimmying back to their apocalyptic party.

Titch found his way to Domino's, where fans sat on the counter with their bums on the pizza boxes, popping the yellow and black balloons in the doorway and tossing streamers over the countertop. The smell of baked dough and salty tomato sauce struck him in the gut and he felt lightheaded, indivisible. A woman leaped from her stool and grabbed his neck. 'Look at you!' It was Delta, her eyes red, her cheeks plump from smiling. 'You're here. I can't believe it. We did it, Titch. We're premiers!' Bruce appeared, a strand of mozzarella hanging off his chin, a piece of pineapple stuck between his teeth. Never seen him without a collared shirt, nah. And never seen him smile like this. 'He must be loving it today,' said Bruce. 'He must be so happy, wherever he is, watching all this unfolding.' Titch rolled his face on Bruce's chest. The carpet of hair warmed his nose and his jaw. He smelled Bruce's sweat, rolled in his untouched musk, and then the tears, yeah, all that had been won without his done-for son. Titch knew he and Delta were okay, had gone on living, had reasons to laugh and sing. But he wasn't the one they wanted, he'd never been quite right, not now or then, so he pulled himself from Bruce's grasp, turned to the shiny shop window and saw the ants trickling down his face, crawling out from his hair, over his bare shoulders, down his ribs. 'I've got to run,' said Titch. 'But where are you headed?' said Delta. 'Got to find someone,' said Titch. 'A lucky lady?' said Delta. 'Why don't you bring her over sometime? We'd love to meet her. And it looks like you could use a solid chicken parma.' Titch backed out of the pizza shop, running by Hunky Dory and up the hill, away from the cauldron of Tiger fanatics and clouds of capsicum spray. A car growled. A red Nissan. He ran by the bonnet, hiding his face from the hoons behind the tinted windshield, shivering with every footstep. The ants burrowed out of his skin like water sucked from stone. They crawled under the waistband of his running shorts. Through the mesh. Above his balls. He loosened the shorts, peeled them over his calves and dumped them on the road, sprinting ahead in his undies. He crossed the road by the bottle-o and saw a magpie scavenging under a Richmond scarf for a box of chips, and as Titch neared, the bird cawed and swept past the letterboxes and upturned tables, over the busted wheelie bins and slews of spilled garbage. If all life tended to zero, had   crossed the finish line first? 'Hang on, man,' said Titch. 'I'll be with you pretty soon.' The magpie shimmered at the traffic lights and faded down a side street into the melee of the riots. Titch turned towards South Yarra Station, the breath steaming out of his nose, his hands trembling. He shut his mouth, worried the ants would climb over his lips and down his tongue. There was the train station, at last, not a fan around. He wheezed through his nostrils, his legs burning, and jumped the turnstile, barrelling by the ticket inspector and sprinting down the ramp onto the Dandenong service. The train honked. Shuddered. He bound onto the final carriage, not a single person in sight. Curled his feet on a four-seater. Hooked his Volleys in the neck rest, so wrecked, so spent, that it took until Caulfield for him to see that he was sitting on a Crows jumper stuffed with shitturds.

'This service will terminate at Dandenong,' said the conductor on the overhead speaker. 'Alright, you lot. This train will terminate at Dandenong. Please avoid all foot traffic into the Red Plains.' The train trundled along the unfinished houses. The wooden frames were orange under the streetlights. Chain fences, rusty after months of winter rain, creaked above concrete slabs. Sandy plains swamped the estates. Black tar roads snaked up the mountainside. Titch had never been to the edge of the suburbs—or not alone, at least, remembering when he and
rode the after-school service playing Doodle-Jump on their mobiles, so intent on breaking a new high score that they missed their stops and travelled to the end of the line. They sat speechless, waiting for the conductor to turn the train back to Melbourne, their mobiles zapped of juice, their noses pressed against the window. Miles of dead grass. Abandoned cars. Shrivelled trees. Faded Mirvac billboards selling house-and-land packages. Tonight, Titch clambered to his feet, stumbling between the seats, gasping in the balmy air, his stomach growling against the elastic of his undies. 'Dandenong,' said the sign on the platform. Three boys in singlets skipped ahead and climbed the fence by the tracks, whooping, slapping each other on the back. 'Look onward to see the light,' said the shortest, who pulled a ciggie from his bumbag. Titch hurried out of the station, but when he hopped the barrier the boys were gone. The shrill screeching of crickets filled the evening air. The footpath led to a roundabout covered in dandelions and thorny stems. Fields of blackberry bushes stretched for acres on either side of the trail, lit in patches by the streetlights and the glimmer of foxes' eyes in the brush. When he walked by the first roundabout, the train honked at the station and headed back to the city. Laters, yeah. He strummed a hand over his ribs for warmth. He unlocked

243

his mobile but there was no reception. Not a single bar. Delta and Bruce deserved some congratulations, yeah. They'd been faithful for thirty-seven years. Titch held his mobile up to the sky, waving it on his tiptoes, but there was still no service. He climbed a sycamore tree and crawled along the branches, reaching his screen towards the telephone towers on the horizon. 'Sorry I've been away so long,' he typed. 'The granny, huh? Go Tiges. Must finally be sinking in. Send my congrats to your parents. TBD.' He hit send. The message stuck in his outbox. He walked down the highway, past another roundabout covered in rubbish bags and busted birds' nests. It was his chance to be alone with no one looking, yeah. No comparisons to be made anymore. No one sizing him up. No more scripts to rehearse. Zero was everything, yeah, and he giggled at the thought of it, so free now with his head clear and no one on his tail, not Damo, not Ginny, not even Püd. Just himself. After walking in the dark for a k, he reached a Shell servo with massive orange signs buzzing into the atmosphere. He snuck between the petrol pumps. The servo was vacated. He paused, remembering Püd's story, his waking nightmare. Then he walked past the Cokes in the fridge, the meat pies in the oven, the Mars Bars in the rack. He ran a hand along the bananas and mandarins. C'mon, yeah. Don't give in. He stalked through the homeware aisle. Buckets. Sponges. Detergent. Garbage bags. Mousetraps. And there: Mortein bug spray. Behind the counter sat a blow-up love doll, life-sized, wide-eyed, with a pleated school dress pulled up its hips and over its bulging tits. 'That's enough,' he said, rolling a can of Mortein before its plastic mouth. He slid a twenty onto the counter, avoiding its deadpan eyes. 'No food for me. I've got to tidy up,' he said, plunging the Mortein in a bag. 'Spring cleaning.' And he staggered from the servo and onto the road.

He walked around for hours. Cracks splintered the road. His heels made divots in the bitumen. The estates ended and a reedy brush spread by the highway, dotted with mattresses and shopping trolleys. After another few kilometres, the scrub faded and the ground was freckled with seeds from burnt-out gum trees. The rising sun melted over the sky and a cadaverous claret streaked through the clouds, announcing another day of his diet. Felt peaceful not taking up all that room, to drift along, as light as a page torn from a book, but after twenty minutes his neck bristled and his shoulders had turned pink. The sun was insufferable. He left the road and headed to an acacia, but when he peeked inside, searching for sap, the bark crumbled to dust. The tree was dry, stale, like a cardboard prop. The shade would do, yeah, nestling his head against his shoulders, clenching his nostrils against the deadfish-stink in his armpits. He held the tree, eyeing the roots for water. He couldn't see his shadow, he realised, spinning in circles as the sun brightened the dirt around his feet. A magpie swooped onto a branch, splintering the wood with its sharp talons, tilting its head, surveying the desiccated field. 'Hey man,' he said. 'Is it really you? Just tell me. TBD.' But this one didn't seem to know him. 'I gotta go,' he said. 'We'll talk?' Trembling, he shambled back to the highway and found a bicycle in a trench by the side of the road. It had pink tassels, a set of training wheels and a basket on the handlebars. It was a fab number, but cycling would ramp up his caloric deficit, yeah. He dropped the Mortein in the basket and rode onward, clutching one hand to his scalp in case the magpie flew after him. He had ridden a bike like this before, yeah, on a race around   's block in Year Nine.   had found the bike in the shrubs one autumn day, buried beneath orange oak leaves, and he had made Titch ride it.

had looped him, thrice, on their laps through the carports and over the grey-water drains. Now Titch shut his eyes, feeling the bumps with every pedal, the vibrations up the training wheels, the seat creaking under his bum. Almost like he was himself again, circling the concrete hills to the sound of   's laughter, bouncing up grill-faces and onto yellow lawns. The memory dripped down his burning cheeks, so close he could taste   's slipstream, when his tyres rolled across a sheet of paper. It was a cartoon. A rainforest, split by a riverbed. A giant crocodile with serrated teeth. A huge, clawed kangaroo, three metres tall. It was part of a poster, yeah. Victorian Palaeontology Society. Digs, fossils, prehistoric treasures. Soon, yeah, he'd be in the ground and they'd wonder how he'd gone extinct. No one would know. How could they? He stepped off the bike, trying to stop himself from shaking, from unearthing all the feelings he'd worked to forget. 'Sure, you cut his name,' he said, 'but you really thought you'd cut the pain?' His stomach gurgled. He hadn't touched a calorie in so long but his belly flopped over his jocks. And there, cheers, up ahead was an orange portaloo. Probably abandoned by the tradies, yeah. He dropped the poster and pumped the pedals, his guts ready to blow. He skidded the bike to a stop. Locked the door. Patted the knot in his belly. Tore off his jocks and pressed his palms to the portaloo walls. Then he squatted, lower and lower, only there wasn't a bowl, no seat in reach, and he rocked past his heels and took a tumble. His cries echoed up the metal walls. Help, yeah, nowhere to sit. Then there was a tingling stink. It eked off the metal and the concrete. That pool chemical. Chlorine. And then a whistle blew, a short, sharp blast, and he sprang out of the loo, dragging his jocks up his legs. The magpie cawed from the portaloo as he stumbled to the road, righted the bike and pedalled, the chain creaking, the brake pads grinding on the tyres.

Squinting in the sun, Titch rode with one hand over his eyes, bouncing from side to side on the rickety training wheels. He remembered   's face the first time Titch had sat on the bike, his goofy grin, his eyes filling with wonder, adoration, hooting as Titch pedalled up to the nature strip. 'I'll catch you,' Titch had said, amplifying his imbalance, his seesawing momentum. 'Just have a look at these Armstrong-legs of mine.' And   had laughed, keeling over on his side, hoots coursing through his muscle. 'It's the Pyrénées stage of the Tour de France!' yelled Titch, starting his climb up the concrete driveway. 'Where's my yellow jersey?' Titch had spat in his palm, run his glistening fingers through his fringe, teasing the strands until his hair stood on end.   had rolled over Delta's tulips, his hoos and hahs bouncing off the brickwork, sounding more than he was. And all of this, yeah, five years ago? The Red Plains loomed over Titch's shoulder, swelling with every slow pedal. How could Titch have been so full of plans? Without sensing what would happen if they parted ways? No matter how strong he was, how controlled his reps, how disciplined his sets, he and   were one unit, moulded together, that was his only true strength. Alone, Titch teetered along the cliff of manhood, yeah, one staggering freefall that dashed the measures he thought had made him strong. All those gains whittled away. All that power for nada. Titch rode into a pothole and the handlebars slipped out of his hands. Really, yeah, what had he been doing for these last months? Just buying and pining, buying and pining, like   knew from day dot. Titch had joined every other man, young and old, and he swayed, catching the bike, only to find, in the corner of his eye, a fluorescent yellow truck sitting on a pile of clay. He jumped off the pedals and ran across the road on his wiry legs. 'Oi,' he said. 'Dad?' It was a Caterpillar digger.

247

The metal trough buried in the clay. Flecks of dirt on the barrel. The pistons gleaming in the sun. The low hum of the engine. He climbed up the track pads and into the cab. The seat singed the wet blisters on his palms. The digger leaned over a deep pit and he couldn't see the bottom through the sun streaking over the windshield. He leaned his head out of the cab, gripping the rubber window lining, but he still couldn't see the bottom of the hole. He stretched further out the window, shoving his feet into the seat and clinging to the windshield for balance. How deep was it? Thirty metres? Fifty? The digger creaked forward, rocked over the mound, the back tread lifting off the soil, the trough tipping as the clay tumbled into the hole. Get over with it, yeah. Here, gone. The digger inched forward. The ground rushed up. And yet some impulse pushed him off the seat and out of the cab. The Caterpillar tumbled off the mound and into the black. He waited for the crash but there was only a rush of air from the pit, the stink of diesel and rusted iron. He unpeeled his hands from his head, waiting, hoping. But some things fall, yeah, and never land.

The road was sinking into the soil. The air turned stale and clammy and the bike rumbled over stones and broken twigs. With every bump, the handlebars drilled into his arms and his shoulders ached, his sweat drying on his chin. Then the strength left his legs and he rode aimlessly, without a single inkling. North or south? Who knew. Without the road, there was no way to retrace his steps. No map for his route. 'You wanted this, mate,' he said. He reached into his bag, hoping for some food, yeah, the Mars Bar, the meat pie. But there was just the can of bug spray. The bag fluttered in the basket. This was taking too long, yeah. Mortein. He unhooked the lid. Pressed the nozzle between his lips, over his tongue, down his throat, knocking against his tonsils. He inhaled once and exhaled as deeply as he could. He pressed the plunger. The can spluttered at first. A few dribbles. He groaned. Then a hiss, a scalding mist, and a burst of cold shot out of the can. He fell on the dirt, clawing at his windpipe, spitting the bug spray down his collarbones and ribs. The Mortein filled his lungs. His ears. His guts. He rolled over the clay and hid his eyes in the soil, cackling. For all these months, he'd thought he'd only made missteps. Denying Delta and Bruce. Stealing Sophie's weed. Munting Ginny's trust. But really these were all steps in the same direction, one way, yeah, towards dissolving. It was all in motion. An ending from the start. He was so close to the other side, closer to   than he'd been in months. 'Are you there?' he said, and then he felt something protruding from the clay. He swiped it with his Volley. A tennis racquet. He pulled the handle from the sand and smacked the dirt off the strings. The air filled with dust and nylon twangs. He bounced the racquet off his knobby knees and the points of his elbows. An old Dunlop that had seen better days. He walked to the bike and his foot caught another racquet. He plucked it from the clay and huffed. There was another one to his right. He hobbled across the ground, mining the racquets, one by one, from the red earth and piling them by the bike. Then he pulled up a vodka bottle, covered in clods of clay. He looked to his right and found another. And another. The soil was filled with bottles of booze, yeah, the grog sloshed inside the bottlenecks and made whirlpools when he held them to the sky. Smirnoff. Grey Goose. Johnny Walker. Belvedere. The rum. The mescal. The Spanish tequila with the gold flakes. Titch swung onto the bike and munted in the basket. Red. Lumpy. The back tyre burst. The seat snapped under him. The rubber grazed along the tar. He tried pedalling but the bike was fucked. He crouched, pressing the tread with his thumb. The tubing was popped. He felt for a puncture, some glass or nail or pointy pebble, but he couldn't find one. Weariness settled on his shoulders like a mantle of lead. He was draining into the dirt, sinking into the soil. About time, yeah. But something glimmered in the tyre. A tiny, black body. He knelt by the bike, clutching the pedals for balance. The ant crawled out of the tubing and onto his Volley. Its belly scratched over his sneakers. Its pincers clawed up the seams. He shivered, but there was nothing to munt. He lowered his hand and the ant stepped on his palm. His thumb twitched on its head. A shadow fell over him, one silhouette that swallowed his body, the bike, the trickle of munt. 'Titch.' A motor whirred in the breeze. He gripped the broken saddle, hid behind the handlebars. It was Mother Pulse. Her legs were yellow stumps. Her face was worn leather. 'Come calmly,' she said, swaying in an electric scooter. The ant left his laces, crawled over the spokes of the bike wheel, arced across the ground and faded, infinitesimal in the red. Then Titch lost his little idol and collapsed on the clay.

Keepsake

THREE DAYS AFTER THE GRAND FINAL, in her latest video, Ginny's mother twisted on a yoga mat and said, 'Today we're going to make a Feelings Ball. We're going to find ourselves a Sharpie and a big, soft exercise ball. Okay? Now I want youse to write whatever you been feeling today onto the ball, nice and big, that's it, don't hold nothing back.' Ginny paused the video and the car filled with the early-October heat. She had to park above-ground, with an uninterrupted line between her car and some satellite, so Jim's GPS could track her drive to Chadstone. '"I am depressed because I lost my job." "My winter weight gain gives me anxiety." "He stopped texting me back." Whatever feelings you might have felt today, I want you to write them in big black texta on your ball. Let them all flow out.' Ginny unlocked the car, tramped onto the smouldering parking lot and hunched over her phone to shade the last frames of Betty's video. 'Now take your Feelings Ball and give it a good bounce. Get it moving. Try turning this into a workout by adding a jump squat to each throw.' She hurled the exercise ball against the garage wall, twinkling in her sequined sports bra and leopard-print tights. The PVC walloped the plaster-board, bouncing back and forth. 'And before you know it,' she said, 'your feelings will have disappeared, and you'll feel so much lighter and more toned.' She spun the exercise ball, now covered in dusty, black bruises, and a pink watermark filled the screen. Betty Anton: Right Advice for Joy. The post made Ginny shudder. The inanity, the plastic therapy, the masquerade of care. Comment on comment. Like after like. Ginny's patience for life, with its waves of expectation and failure, was gone. She wondered how, as a child, she had decided to go on living when she first befriended death, all those years ago, sitting by the bath with her pills peeking out from their bottle. She thrust her phone in her pocket and passed a ring of tradesmen who had rigged a portaloo next to the escalators. One of the men pointed at the side of the mall, squawking into his walkie-talkie, and a second man pulled a sweet potato from a paper bag, tearing off chunks with his serrated teeth. She wiped a smear of saliva from her mouth and kept walking. The spring sun lit the windows and ceramic tiles, carving the entry to Reynolds between shafts of light. At the register, she asked the others if the tradesmen were building a parking lot. '*Parking lot*? You mean a carpark, Miss America,' said Nadine. 'Maybe Chaddy's getting a facelift.' 'They could be adding a Costco,' said Püd, fiddling with the bandages on his right bicep after he had scraped off his Kanji tattoo. 'Maybe they're putting in a hotel,' said Nadine. 'For who?' said Püd. 'The fobs,' said Nadine. 'They're out here like their lives depend on it.' Ginny hurried into the backroom, but hopelessness followed her as her steps reverberated in the barren bookstore. She was as much a consumer of this hopelessness as she was a creator. She was as much a Melburnian as anyone else. 'Ground Control to Major Ginny,' wrote Klein, sending an astronaut GIF to the Excelsior group. Ginny sat on the swivel chair in the backroom, spinning until the halogens flipped from vertical to horizontal to vertical again. Warm blood slid up her throat. Her stitches unwound with the pointless pressure. 'Where are you?' wrote Gordon. 'Come back to us, Sister Genevieve,' wrote Shelly. 'Now is no time for a vow of silence.'

Jim clapped the clay off his boots and padded to the kitchen in his fluffy socks, plunging his arms into the soapsuds to begin washing the dishes. 'Sixteen thousand followers,' he said, 'in three weeks. Can you believe her, Gin? She's a star. She's brand new. All the inspiration is right here. Don't need no America, do you? The Right Advice for Joy. Have you made your Feelings Ball today?' Ginny sat by the toaster, squeezing the edge of the dining table, collecting beads of blood in a saucer. 'What's happened now?' he said. 'You right, Gin?' 'Perfect,' she said, half-smiling, revealing her rows of pink teeth and bloody tongue. 'Gin, what the hell?' he said. 'Did your neck give out? You get your head banged up again?' 'I'm perfect,' she said, but Jim raised her by the armpits, lay her across his shoulder and carried her down the hallway, past the tripod on the stairs and the tanning bed in the study. He draped her across her bed, wiping his fingers along her swollen lips. 'Whiplash,' he said. 'You need a neck brace or you'll be wobbly forever.' He returned in forty minutes, unfolding the old hamster cage, untwisting and stiffening the titanium in place, locking the legs with a pair of pliers, crowning her forehead-to-temple-to-chin with the silver wires. 'And wa-la,' he said. The brace creaked around her neck. She angled to the mirror. Her head was stuck. Scaffolded. At Reynolds the following day, after another dervish stint in the stockroom, she leaned her brace on the desk. It was cluttered with reports from head office and the daily tabloids. The grand final had been four days ago, but collages from the football celebrations still plastered the back pages. A crowd of players in canary-yellow jerseys burst champagne bottles over a balcony. The club president wept in his wife's arms. A riot on Swan Street ended with orange flares and clouds of pepper spray. 'You yearn for something your whole life,' wrote a journalist, 'and then you finally get it, and then you have to ask yourself: what's next?' Ginny opened the newspaper, flicking past the football fanfare until she noticed a tiny article. 'One Sick Healer,' read the headline. 'The self-described "listener" was wrongly admitted to Melbourne City Drug and Alcohol Rehabilitation Centre with a crystal methamphetamine addiction,' she read. 'Sometime before dawn, she stole an electric mobility device (an Aurora) and assaulted a fellow inpatient. She is known to be at risk.' The report spilled to the centre pages of the newspaper. 'Police uncovered thousands of letters inside her illegal residence, an abandoned garage on Degraves Street. From the correspondence, investigators have reason to fear the disappearance of her followers from their families.' Ginny fingered the accompanying freeze-frame from the CCTV footage. A gargantuan woman hunched over the handlebars of a scooter, her hips sagging over the seat, her jowls wobbling under the streetlight. She wore a pair of cracked blue sunglasses. Her legs ended in stumps at her ankles. The backroom door opened and Ginny stopped reading. She left the newspaper on the lockers and turned to face Püd. 'People posting that she's a big old junkie,' he said, as he looked for his Tupperware, 'but I'd never think of hurting no one if I was high. The right stuff mellows you out. Maybe gets you keen at best. Probably she wasn't from here, you know?' 'I think she was born here,' said Nadine. 'That makes her even worse,' said Püd. 'That means she was radicalised.' The listener's blue sunglasses followed Ginny between the lockers, watching her rise, wince inside her brace and push onto the sales floor. She breathed from the bottom of her lungs and counted the day's money, gripping the register like the bow of a ship. The listener was mystifying, preposterous, an icon of monstrosity, another surreal hero for all of Melbourne to misconstrue.

The store was so silent without Titch. The next day, Ginny left her shift early, sat in her Fiat and drummed her fingers over the steering wheel. She retrieved her cell from her tote and left it on the seat. After taking the green Coles bag from the trunk, she walked to the ATM, withdrew a hundred dollars and found a taxi outside San Churro. It would take about an hour for Jim to call. The cab rolled towards Springvale Road, past the yellow hedges and oil slicks in the gutters. Outside the apartment block, she handed the driver a fifty-dollar note, and in the elevator to the eighth floor, she steadied her brace against the panel. The box groaned in the shaft. The doors jolted open. The corridor flooded with sunlight, a pastel hue of cream and white and summertime yellow. Diamond sandals and polished boots gleamed outside the apartments and down the corridor. She found his door and knocked. A breeze funnelled up the emergency stairs and billowed up her calves. She called through the door, wondering what, if anything, he would let her say. 'We got the message through to the little crook,' Marg had said, the night of the grand final, dropping a green Coles bag on Ginny's bed. 'Here's a keepsake. He won't fuck with you again.' Inside the bag was a set of yellow overalls, covered in oil and dried blood. Ginny banged on the apartment door and it opened. The place was unlocked. She found the air mattress flattened into a puddle and the window ajar. 'It's just me,' she said. The breeze caressed the bag against her hip. 'Titch?' Untying the bag, she spread the overalls on the desk. She slid her hands through the breast pocket and stopped. A page. Torn from a magazine. *Man's Tales from Near and Far.* She unfolded the paper and held the faded ink to the sunlight. 'THE NIRVAASIT,' she read. 'Submitted by S. S. Sonpate. Once there was a boy who felt very empty. He wandered to his maa and she said, "Why is my child so sad, when he has so much of talent and good looks?" He wandered to his father and he said, "Why is my child so quiet, when he has such smarts and ideas to share?" The boy left his village and wandered far away, over dirty rivers and across flooded fields, and he came to a city by the sea, where the women wore the finest of silk sarees, the men kept their coins inside the finest of cotton trousers and the children waved from balconies high above the street. "Such fullness a life can bear," thought the boy, who quickly found work to make himself some rupees and become a man. "One day," he said, as he polished the lawyer's shoes, "I will have for myself six sons." "Never have I heard of a nirvaasit with six sons," said the lawyer, who paid and went on his way. "One day," he said, as he polished the doctor's shoes, "I will have for myself six sons and thirty-six grandsons." "Never have I heard of a nirvaasit with thirty-six grandsons," said the doctor, who paid and went on his way. "One day," he said, as he polished the teacher's shoes, "I will have for myself six sons, thirty-six grandsons and two hundred sixteen great-grandsons." "Never have I heard of a nirvaasit with two hundred sixteen great-grandsons," said the teacher, who paid and went on her way. After many moons of hard work, the boy was summoned to the maharaja's court. "My whole city is afraid of the nirvaasit and his wretched empire," said the maharaja. "Have you forgotten your lowly place with the chickens and the dogs?" "No, please," said the boy. "These are but dreams inside my head." "Best to let them stay like that," said the maharaja, who cut off the boy's head and sent him from the court. Once more, the boy felt very empty, so he took his head, left the city and sailed to a dry, deserted island very far away. Every day and every night, the nirvaasit saw inside his head the smiles of all the sons he would never have and heard them laughing as all good boys do. "Such illusion a life can bear," thought the nirvaasit, who went off to nowhere and built himself a castle. "Finally, we are no longer wandering," thought the nirvaasit, who hid inside his castle, left his head outside and smiled a big smile. Not a soul could find him. He was at peace at last, for the walls were so thick and the rooms were so dark that his dangerous dreams would never trouble him again.' Ginny read the page once more and folded it between her fingers. The paper was dry and brittle and came from a time when people still cared for stories. In this unkempt room, amid these chance artifacts, she felt welcomed by an otherworldly order. She spun, uncertain that she was alone. The window, matted with dust, smudged with handprints, veiled the sprawling suburbs and washed the walls in an ethereal hue. Her hands trembled. The page twitched in her grip. She sensed someone watching. The sensation was overwhelming, undeniable. Maybe there was a design to this, a truth beyond everything she had ever seen. Melbourne had never offered her mystery, never given her a single reason to marvel. For all of Titch's simplicity, and in spite of what he had taken, her heart struck a sudden chord of awe.

The next morning, the Chadstone tradesmen leaned backwards off the building, their harnesses pulled taut, unveiling an unpainted bill-board on the roof. Ginny clasped her phone and reloaded Instagram. Betty had posed nude beside her old pageant photographs, clutching her breasts with one hand and holding a bouquet of poppies over her crotch. The scar across her navel was gone, airbrushed into the cleft of her abs. 'Real talk, friends,' she wrote. 'I used to drink a lot. I had a problem. All I ever wanted was something to fill me with joy. But in my cleanse, I had visions. They showed me what I had to do. And now I'm back, ready to let my followers know that the world is joy. Hug it! Marry it! Love it! Stir it into your soul. Betty Anton xx.' Eighteen thousand likes. Seven hundred comments. A blush rose from Ginny's collarbones to her cheeks. The story she knew so well had been cut and polished. It sat in her palm like a counterfeit diamond. Pocketing her phone, she held the titanium cage with both hands and hurried into the mall. Reynolds was still closed. It was ten-thirty. She crept under the security shutters. The lights were up to their full brightness. 'You're late, Ginny,' said a man at the register. The regional manager. He wore a leather eye patch and a shaggy moustache that matched his grey suit. 'Whatever happened to making people read again?' he said, smacking the Mighty Mites with a PVC pipe. He crunched the planes under his wingtips. Nadine and Püd stood against the shelves, their backs stiff against the bestsellers. 'Of course, you'd expect a few peaks and troughs, here and there, because the Aussie public won't read all year round...But this store is abysmal. No sales for a week? Three staff? A theft? What the bloody hell is going on?' 'I'm not going to lie,' said Püd. 'No one reads books. Never have, never will.' 'You're entirely wrong, mate,' said the manager. 'They'll start reading if you slash ninety per cent off and tell them you're closing down.' He pulled an iPad from his briefcase and logged onto the Reynolds portal. 'You two will rearrange the store,' he said. 'I'm going to download the closure papers and get the clearances approved. Miss Anton is going to take herself a breather.' He strode into the backroom and locked the door. 'I want to yank his fucking mo off,' said Nadine. 'How could he speak to us like that? What a wanker.' Ginny ducked under the shutters and wandered into the mall, past a girl in the Lego Store tossing bricks at a little boy, past a kid decapitating a Bionicle, past a woman unspooling tickets from the deli dispenser. She ran through the Hoyts lobby and out to her old balcony, unlacing her Doc Martins and flexing her toes on the ledge. She rolled a cigarette as the traffic banked on Princes Highway, a line of windshields wobbling in the sun, surging from Chadstone to the edge of the suburbs. She opened WhatsApp. 'What would y'all say about meeting in London?' she wrote. 'England? It could happen, honey,' wrote Klein. 'Really? You promise?' 'We'll look at tickets.' 'I'm in,' said Gordon. 'Me too,' said Shelly. Next week Ginny would be unemployed, boiling Jim's eggs for his lunchbox, spooning her cereal into her cage as Betty drafted the caption for her latest Instagram post. 'I really need y'all,' wrote Ginny. A magpie swooped from a tree and arced over the highway, beating its wings over the cooling vents, landing on the balcony railing with a small brush in its beak. The bristles were stiff with pink paint. The magpie squawked, blinking an amber eye. It soared into the shaft, talons zinging like laser beams on the steel. She peeked over the lip and smelled something putrid. Paint thinner. Rotten tunafish. Spoiled spinach. She spluttered, dashing back to Chadstone, her phone singing in her pocket.

Reynolds was open. The shelves had been arranged in spokes to the register so that every aisle led to the POS. A panopticon, she thought. Only instead of a prison guard there was the lone register, constantly monitoring them no matter where in the store they tried to hide. A poster hung over the entryway. 'Closing down!' it read. 'Everything must go!' Some books were discounted by eighty per cent, others by ninety-five. 'He wants us to clear everything as quickly as possible,' said Nadine. 'No matter how cheap we have to go.' 'You know what's going to be sick?' said Püd. 'We only have to work this week, but we get our pay for the next four months. My mate used to work at Toys 'R' Us and when they tanked he got his pay cheque for six months.' 'Are you serious?' said Nadine, waving her orange duster in circles. 'We're alright,' he said, hoisting Nadine on the register, her heels clacking against the woodwork. She giggled, wringing Püd's palms until the veins bulged out of his fingers. 'We're alright,' he repeated, drumming his hands over her belly. 'Maybe you can treat that mystery boyfriend of yours to a nice steak dinner,' he said. 'Maybe you can eat a dick,' she said. 'Maybe in December?' wrote Gordon in the WhatsApp group. 'London sounds cool, but I need to finish my grad school application. The winter holidays are hella busy. January, even?' The store filled, and filled, the aisles flooding with customers. As they scanned the books, contemplating their weight and their covers, or shuffling the pages like a deck of cards, their eyes flickered up to Ginny, hunched over the register on her elbows, and with every short glance they drew closer, one foot after the other, encroaching on her from every direction and no direction at all, like a cell in apoptosis. 'You'll need to sign off on this,' said the manager, leaning through the backroom door. She pushed past the customers and towards the locker bay, swallowed by a whirl of antiseptic and floor polish. The manager rearranged his tie in the reflection of the window. 'Your store's always going to bother me,' he said. 'I'll never forget it. Not for the life of me.' He pointed at the newspaper clipping. It had been severed in thirds on the desk. 'That's Maha Sonpate, isn't it? Not the kind of loony you want in your store. Not going to inspire the best work ethic. And all these bloody paper planes? This isn't arts and crafts, Ginny. Or Melbourne Girls' Grammar home economics. My best advice, for wherever you land next, is to keep the ship afloat or the men will have to salvage the wreckage.' She signed the Foreclosure Notice and he slipped the form into his top pocket. He swivelled in his wingtips, swinging his tartan briefcase by his side as he marched out of Reynolds. His fading footfalls reverberated up the wires of her brace, and she sat stiffly on the stool, her breath swirling across her top lip.

'Sonpate,' she said, sliding the newspaper fragments together and tracing her finger over Maha's face. A second photograph showed a door to a dim lair. There was a copy of a note. 'Dear degenerates,' it read. 'I am insufficient. I am ill-equipped. I am leaving, forever, to the Red Plains.' She imagined a fugitive whirring through Melbourne's back streets, past the bars and the restaurants, to the shifting boundaries of the city. A nirvaasit, thought Ginny, remembering S.S. Sonpate's story in the overalls. One who made her own way. Her phone chimed. 'In winter I'm touring Europe,' said Shelly. 'But July?' 'That's high season for TMP,' said Klein. 'Have to be after. Ginny, can't we wait here? It's NY or nothing, right?' Ginny dropped her phone. She guided the shreds of the article into place, feeling no sadness at her friends' broken promise, not as she expected, but a simple solid hope, the possibility of an unseen truth. Slowly she joined the pieces, one after the other, blowing softly, her spit congealing in the scraps of paper. She clutched the edge of the table, hovering over the restored icon, descending until the pigment swallowed her eyes. She felt Maha's follicles on her lips, the gaping slit of her mouth, the breath swirling under her nose. She had Maha's tongue; she tasted as she tasted, breathed as she breathed. Those cauterised ankles became Ginny's, too, in one shared suffering: the Reynolds closure, the defunct New York dream, the pitiful robbery, one long cycle she had entered at her birth. All she had ever wanted was elsewhere. On an evening months ago, across the world in her Manhattan, she had tricked herself into seeing somewhere to belong. But it shouldn't matter where she ran. Really, it never had. All that mattered was moving. As she melted out of Maha, the ache left her scalp, and she was overcome by the truth of escape. Ever upward. She was held in the blue tint of Maha's sunglasses, like take-off in an endless sky.

266

For a week, the customers hurried through the aisles, phoning their friends to relay the titles on sale, only to realise that every book was discounted. Parents zipped between the shelves, cooing to children sitting on the picture books. 'We can have a fireplace,' said one woman. 'We can ditch the telly.' 'You seen those prices, hey?' said a man at the biographies. 'It's a bargain alright,' said his friend, hugging a box set of fantasy novels. 'Daylight robbery.' There was such a racket that Püd killed the radio and plugged his ears with foam buds. Nadine piled the Reynolds paper bags at her feet, unlocked the register and left the keys jangling in the socket. 'The more we keep the customers keen,' said Püd, 'the more they'll buy and the quicker we can close down.' The customers dumped their loot on the register and leafed through spiral-bound cocktail recipes and Outback Travel Guides, stammering into their phones as Ginny pumped the credit-card reader. 'Use the chip, yeah,' said one woman. 'Don't go goofing up my card.' 'Would you do this set for twenty bucks?' said a man holding a box of dictionaries. 'What about the Little Black Classics?' said another. 'My daughter wants them in her waiting room. She's a dentist now. Says they'll calm her patients down.' 'Could I do this as a coffee table book?' said a woman flipping a King James Bible. 'Actually,' she said, 'could I have the coffee table, too?' 'Yeah, easy,' said Nadine. 'We're selling *everything*.' Püd scribbled on a block of Post-It notes: 'Name a price and I'm yours.' He hurried from the register and stuck them on the shelves, couches, lamps, speaker sets, tables. Then he hunched in the entryway, faced the ramen bar and limped back to the register with a note stuck in the zipper of his jeans. 'You're such a happy cunt,' said Nadine, stacking more books in a bag and giggling. 'God help us.'

There were twenty-one steps from Ginny's car to the escalator. She kept her head down, counting along in her restless mind. Twenty-one steps and she'd be through the automatic doors and could disappear into the crowd of shoppers. How many so far? Eight? An ant crawled over the concrete and stumbled into a can of Fanta. She crunched the aluminium beneath her boot, scraping the edges of the metal under her heel. But the ant carried on, crawling out of the wreckage and along the painted crosswalk. Eleven? Twelve? She lost count and ran into the mall. She hobbled into Reynolds between two teenagers pointing at covers and yelling out to barter with Püd. They stopped talking when she walked through the aisles. The bookshelves bent and wavered, the posters whirred through the air and the books flapped under the harsh white lights. When a shelf emptied, Ginny lugged it across the store and piled it by the entry, like rolling a boulder over the mouth of a tomb. Püd barged out of the backroom, waving a black dry-fit polo shirt in arcs over his mullet. 'Guess who's starting at Nike next week?' he said. 'This fella.' He patted Nadine on the back and pinched her bum. 'My mate just started as Assistant Manager. He's given me fifty per cent off my kit. So come in, yeah, and ask for my discount.' Nadine left Reynolds with her hair tied taut behind her head, two crystal earrings nipping her collar, and returned in half an hour with tears in her eyes. 'I'll be starting at Prada in a fortnight,' she said, shaking Ginny's hand. 'It's a big career move. A pivot. But you know what I read about joy? It's out there all along, and you have to go and get it.'

That night, as Ginny tottered up the driveway, Jim stood at the corner of the patio, his arms crossed. Betty's possum eyes hovered in the gloom of the hallway, flaring white and blue as she scrolled through her Facebook feed. 'Tracy from your mummy's old AA group called today,' said Jim. 'She was passing through Chaddy, looking for treats for Winston after his cataract operation, and she walked into Reynolds, and, well, I don't need to explain the rest.' 'It's true, isn't it?' said Betty. 'I wasn't going to defend your reputation until I could hear the truth. Your daddy called the store but the line was disconnected.' 'I thought we were getting everything together,' said Jim. 'I thought we were done with the secrets.' Ginny climbed the stairs, her brace rattling around her neck. Her breath whistled from her lips. The scab tightened in her nostrils. 'I've thought about your next options,' said Jim, wringing his arm around her shoulder. 'It's best that you get set up somewhere soon, otherwise that mind of yours will start to wander. Cousin Georgy has a writing job you can do from home. You won't even have to leave your bed.' He followed her upstairs, breathing into the prickly hairs on her ankle. 'I'll tell you what, Gin, it's really well paid. Twenty-eight dollars an hour. Have you ever heard anything like that before?' She spun on the landing and angled her face through the metal cage. His compassion was only a guise to make her feel indebted: he wrapped his love around his possessiveness. 'Like a shining apple with a rotten core,' she said. 'You'll never understand.' 'What do you mean, Gin? It's a reputable insurance company. Life insurance. Everyone dies, so everyone's going to need it. You can start saving. Maybe you can join your mother on her trip to Los Angeles. There's a YouTuber who wants to fly her over there.' The breath snorted in her nose and the scab turned crustier, a waxen seal. He yelped, veering backwards, catching the bannister

271

for balance. She gently closed the door behind her, pulling her blouse over her head, slipping her pants around her ankles, and stood in her mismatched underwear, her bra straps twisted, her panties strangling her pubic hair. She stepped towards the mirror and nuzzled her face to the cool surface, leaving a crimson smudge where she kissed the glass. She sorted her clothes into a pile, pressing her pants leg over leg, sifting through her sweaters, folding them sleeve over sleeve. She dragged her suitcase from her wardrobe, unzipped the case and upended the pile of *New Yorker* magazines. The mesh lining trembled with her totems: a plastic Lady Liberty, a MetroCard, a passport. All those props of that old performance.

Moments before dawn, Ginny lay on top of her bedspread, filled with the phantom feeling from Titch's flat. This bedroom, that window, those concrete lions, they too seemed like props in a play. But that could only mean that she was being watched, that somewhere an audience waited. As she murmured at the ceiling, she felt an unearthly comfort, a miraculous hope, that she had not been alone in all these catastrophes. A witness was all she wanted. A companion down those Brooklyn streets and along the halls of Chadstone mall. That morning, Ginny trembled off the end of the escalator and floated towards Reynolds, drifting between the potted palm trees and the bouncers outside Louis Vuitton. She opened the Reynolds register and spread the week's receipts on the counter. They had sold enough books to clear a year's surplus stock. But such a pity: the books would never be read, and the sales were only an echo of a raging success. Püd shimmied from the backroom, pumping the air with a clenched fist. 'The payout came together,' he said. 'Going to sort out my rent. Get a new dog-o for Mum.' He jived through the customers, his backpack slung over his shoulder, clucking around the crowd. She checked the CommBank app on her phone. He was right. The payout had landed. Six thousand dollars in reparations for months of blocked schedules and 'emotional turbulence'. She sailed into the backroom, whistling through her mane of matted hair. Maha loomed on her shrine above the lockers. Ginny knelt before the icon, her body tingling with possibility, her skin itching with the ascent.

'We all want people to guide. I'm joyful because I have two. They're not perfect, but we're getting there. They're beautiful and they're smart. They won't take no for an answer. And they're the best young women I know. Love, Betty Anton. A mother and a mentor.' Jim nodded emphatically and Marg changed the filter on the photograph. 'I could tell them my own daughter lost her job,' said Betty. 'That she has depression. They'll find the vulnerability very refreshing.' Squinting at the image, Ginny noticed the edge of a streamer, the dainty blush of the floral wreath, the family portrait from Betty's rebirth party, and she turned and climbed the stairs to her bedroom. She unzipped the suitcase and unpacked yesterday's clothes, rifling through the things she now saw as mementos. She let herself survey the MTA map, tracing her finger from Bay Ridge to Union Square and up to Astoria. She fingered the mauve pages of her passport. The whole plot, she thought, of an aspirational American life. All that precious pining. She crooned, dulling the screech of the early-summer cicadas in Carnegie, and hugged the suitcase through the night, watching the spindly silhouettes of the acacia branches caress the ceiling. She dragged her luggage downstairs, pausing at every step to listen for Marg and one of her playdates. But it was Monday; Jason had left his sportscar in the driveway overnight, the doors unlocked. She settled the suitcase in the passenger seat, slinging the seatbelt across the purple casing. The sun rose, flaring up the eucalyptus tree and the retro swing set at Lloyd Street Primary, and the few speckled clouds glowed umber in the dawn. She paced up the stairs to find Marg pouting before the mirror, her hair turbaned in a towel. 'You got that insomnia again?' she said. Ginny pivoted, crept backwards down the stairs and filled a glass with water at the kitchen sink. 'Think of this as the end of a chapter,' said

Jim, rubbing his hands on her shoulders. 'I know you're disappointed, I know you're hurt, but there's always another day on the horizon. There'll be less stress on your body in this new job. Less socializing. Fewer occupational hazards.' 'I might even have some work for you,' said Betty, patting a charcoal facial on her cheeks. 'I'll be needing an assistant. I got sponsors writing to me now. Yoga studios. Cold-pressed juice. Dieticians.' Ginny lifted her thumb at her parents and glided through the house. She shut the door, zigzagged through the albino lions, crossed the weeds in the median and slipped into the Nissan.

Across the parking lot, the Coles busboys unloaded the day's produce from the trucks and the cleaners sat on milk crates sharing roti and jars of mango juice. The sky was open, azure. A perfect day for flying. Her phone chimed. 'I know you been a bit lonely,' wrote Marg, 'but there's this guy you have to meet. I met him at gym. A really good deadlifter.' 'After work?' 'OMG. Yes.' At Reynolds, the shelves, lamps and tables had been sold. The posters of new releases and the cardboard boxes were gone. Only the register remained, bolted to the ground, the computer disconnected and the drawer empty. Nadine sat cross-legged in the middle of the room, whirring a fidget-spinner in her hand. 'Are you kidding me?' she said, squealing and jumping to her feet. 'Like, you can't be serious?' Ginny headed to the backroom, but Nadine caught her wrist and said, 'Your mum's Betty Anton? Why didn't you ever tell me?' She opened Instagram and thrust the photo in Ginny's face. 'You look amazing,' said Nadine, 'and she's so strong, you know?' Nadine pulled her closer, easing her into the cushions of her breasts and the stink of Tiger Balm. 'I know we haven't had much to talk about over the years, but I'm here if you ever need anything, okay? It's 2017. Girls got to stick together. Don't stay in the pits for too long, yeah?' Ginny pulled some cigarettes from her tote and showed Nadine, who laughed and said, 'Nah, not today. Maybe another time. You should go for it.' Ginny walked by the ATM and, balling her Bic lighter in her fist, climbed to the roof and stood above Chadstone. The southeastern suburbs spread down the highway and into the Red Plains, like an expanding stain on an ancient rug. She faced the horizon, unflinching, for the first time in her life, and as the distant crimson sharpened into focus, she felt a yearning for oblivion that she had never let herself accept. Again, a magpie fluttered onto the balcony, hopping in circles, genuflecting. Its feathers were grey where the black melted into white. 'He's back,' she said, dropping her cigarette. The magpie's beak was crooked, bent to the left. It hopped into its vent and she followed, hoisting herself over the ridge, crawling through the pipe on her hands and knees. Three feet. Six feet. There was a nest. Her eyes adjusted in the dark. A trail of ants, each no bigger than a freckle, marched between the porcelain eggshells and around the fine twigs. Ginny laid her hand on the nest. The ants ambled over her knuckles, finding her fingertips, yeah, as if to hold her hand. Her cheeks creased in a smile. The nest was built from sticks, branches and prizes from the mall. Milk cartons. A sweet potato. Pink paintbrushes. And twelve Lamy fountain pens. All the tiny thievery, saved for months, out of sight of every guard and shopkeeper and clueless cop. She unhitched the brace from her neck and dumped it on the pile. The ants made the titanium wires into little highways. Then the magpie squawked, unfurling its massive, mottled wings, shooing her from the vent, and she retreated, dusting her palms down her blouse. Pacing along the balcony, she pulled her phone from her jeans. Go on, she thought, typing into the browser. Convince them. One last time. 'Search hundreds of travel sites,' read the Kayak homepage, 'at once.' It would be cheaper if she flew the other way, through Singapore, then Frankfurt and across the Atlantic. A ticket for this evening was only twenty-two hundred dollars. There was one seat left. 'I'm leaving,' she typed, sending a screenshot to the Excelsior chat. 'Ever upward. Tell the whole world.'

'The bossman's back,' said Püd, leaning against the stockroom door. 'He's brought along a copper, the classic piggy sort.' She slid to Püd's side and glanced at his watch. Three-fifteen. Two hours until boarding. She brushed down her blouse, knocking flecks of birdshit and mouldy apple from her buttons. 'He's really ripping into Nads,' said Püd. 'She's not in trouble, is she?' Ginny pushed the door ajar and glimpsed the policeman: a short, skinny man whose oversized uniform flapped around his waist. 'We can confirm he's missing,' he said. 'His landlord went looking for the unpaid rent. His flat's vacant. He uses a number of aliases on social media. Seems he suffers from schizophrenia.' 'But oh-my-fucking-god,' said Nadine. 'We're worried about him, miss. Seems he got caught up in some trouble. What can you tell me about him?' 'He was real quiet, didn't say much. A bit of a weirdo, I guess. You reckon he's legit crazy?' 'How long was he working here?' 'A few months? I don't know. You should ask Ginny, they were sleeping together, and she's the manager.' Ginny shifted from the door and pulled it shut. Her chest swelled, caved, swelled again. Her hand twitched at her side; she opened her fist, but it was bare, yeah, from her knuckles to her nails. 'You alright?' said Püd. 'You look like you've seen a ghost.' 'You're up,' she said, pointing at the door, and as Püd crept to the stockroom, shaking his head with concern, she strode out of Reynolds. She felt light, fleet-footed, burning with the thrill of this escape and the dream of outlasting these suburbs. She was going the long way. She would touch the face of her creator. 'First she flew to Changi,' they would say, 'then to Frankfurt and finally to JFK.' She opened the sportscar door and tumbled beside her suitcase. In a different world, in another time, snow melted over Midtown, caressing tongues and cheeks, and thawing ice dripped and dinged on the streetside scaffolding, and steam burst from laundromats as cleaners unpacked ball gowns and three-piece suits. But here, and now, Ginny turned south on the Monash Freeway. The neon lights glowed under the car, throbbing along the grill, blue on black, blue on red. Her name would echo at check-in and along the polished corridors of the airport. Her family would see the charge in her credit card. They would all have something to say, and share, and post and repost. She rolled down the windows, embraced by gusts of hot air as she roared onto the expressway. The shadows of the exit signs winked on the road, mile after mile. She shut the windows, locked the doors and revved through the red fields, leaving Reynolds and the cop behind, and her mother further still. When it came time to arrive, she skidded the car to a stop. Her phone murmured in her bag, so she tied the handles of her tote and threw it out the window, making a myth of herself at last.

Mansion

BEYOND THE BOUNDARY OF THE CITY, time unwound around Maha. There was no separation between months or millennia. On her first day in the Red Plains, she drove through the dawn, rumbling off the highway, over broken branches and chunks of clay, and as the sun rose, flooding the fields with crimson, she loosened her hold on the handlebars, unravelled her bandages and wiped the water from her face. The breeze swirled between blackberry bushes and reedy shrubs. Telephone lines stitched up the side of the Dandenongs and a digger loomed on the horizon. The suburbs glinted behind her. Somewhere, miles ahead, cattle grazed in open fields. But here, in this in-between, on these impermanent lots that awaited new houses, she drove by scorched gum trees, desiccated fossils and magpies circling in the sky. As the city drifted further behind her, Maha's thoughts settled, and just as she felt herself nodding off to sleep, the Aurora rolled onto a footpath and stopped at a building. It was made of silver stone, five storeys high, with rusted metal netting draped down the walls and maroon paint peeling off the windowpanes. Huge, formless letters, graffiti in black spray paint, ran up the building like scorch marks. Ivy crept along the balconies and corded vines twisted over the stone. A cracked footpath led from the archway to the clay. 'Who's there?' she said. As she drove the Aurora into the shadow of the building, she found her heart pounding, her tongue sticking to her gums. She looked through the lobby window and sniffed the still air in the corridor. The etching over the archway read, 'Sonpate Mansion.' Shaking her head slowly, she remembered her father's life on Dalal Street, the years devoted to the Readymoney building, his endless fantasies of an empire. 'I'm here,' she said, if only to remind herself. Inching through the doorway, she drove across the marble tiles and stopped at a dull gold plaque beside the lift. 'A Temple for the Teller,' it said. She rounded the first corner and reached into the rows of bookshelves that brimmed with notebooks of every kind: leatherbound, moleskin, paperback, hardcover, lined and unlined. Hundreds of blank notebooks had been left on the tables, in the aisles, piled on the tiles, or kept in boxes shipped to Melbourne from Mumbai. The many volumes were covered in cobwebs, loose gossamer strands that broke between her fingers, and a layer of fine red dirt clung to the covers and pages. In the presence of these books, her breathing slowed and, in this sacred, decayed estate, she lost the pain in her legs. The light in the mansion softened from red to yellow. At the end of the corridor, the sun peeked through two thin curtains and lay on the stacks, and outside the broken window, a pit had been dug in the clay and filled with rainwater. Maha slid a notebook from a bookshelf and sat in the sunlight. The cover was made of varnished wood. The blank pages parted over her fingers, awaiting whatever words would be written. The paper whispered on her skin, the sole sound in the mansion. 'And a teller for the temple,' she said, seeing her father years earlier, arriving here on the outskirts of the city, with a box of blank notebooks and the indelible memory of Readymoney Mansion. She saw him paying the surveyors, diggers and bricklayers in stacks of unreported cash, an illegitimate man buying the only property he could find, toiling in secret for so many years to build a home for a daughter who could not yet understand. Sonpate Mansion had found her in the end, see, appearing now without her planning, his gift from beyond the grave. She drove into the lobby and called the lift. The building rumbled and stopped with a ding. The walls of the lift were covered in a plastic membrane and electrical tape. She clutched the notebook to her chest as she ascended, feeling like she had come home for the first time in her life. The second floor was filled with more shelves, more rows of unopened notebooks, thousands of pages awaiting inscription. The third and fourth floors were the same. When she rose to the fifth, her cheeks ached from smiling, and she sneezed so loudly that she swayed in her seat. She found a simple bed made from planks and cushions. She saw her father napping between those long hours of building and installing, longing for Dalal Street until the world outside his eyes reflected his lifelong desire. His greatest work, just see, a library for the divine. All the secret weekends, the thousands of dollars made from the chop shop, and her life from the beginning: a gift beyond recognition, a bloodline borne in books. He had given his life to build her a monument. And just as her tears hung in constellations on her eyelashes, Maha noticed a crate filled with sweets behind the bed. Wizz Fizz. Freddo Frogs. Caramello Koalas. She unwrapped a Snickers and gnawed through the chocolate to the caramel within, her eyes watering, her chest heaving.

But a library should be completely open, she thought, waking in her cot as the sunset filled the room with gloom. A library should be permeable and welcoming, just as a human self, with no essence or core, is really a palimpsest, a multitude, an ongoing iteration. In his life of secrets, her father had misunderstood: there was nothing inside to spend his life trying to hide. She unbound her notebook from the chop shop and lay the pages of the stories in the cot. Then she tore the curtains off their rods, lighting the walls in a purple glow, and folded the material over the bed like a tent. She freed the broken glass out of the window, speckling the courtyard with shards, and made her rounds down each floor, clearing out the windowpanes until the wind swept the corridors and whistled between the cracks in the stone. She swerved into the field. There were trowels and mattocks and rock picks strewn over the clay. She ambled through the tools and reached the pit, which was filled with water in spite of the day's heat. Leaning over the edge, she saw bottle tops and legionnaire's hats floating in the reservoir. Maha beckoned the moon across the sky and it rose over her shoulders, illuminating the pool, and something lapped in the shallows so she drove to the edge and raised her arm above the water. It was a trilobite, awake after an age, swimming to her moon shadow through the mud, starlight flickering in its diamond eyes, currents winnowing through its cilia. She unlaced her shawl, peeled off her clothes and levered herself into the water. Oil sluiced off her neck and her arms. The trilobite frolicked over her ankles, nestling on her knees, tickling her thighs with its antennae. The silt trembled under her back and more trilobites appeared, gliding over the groundwater in a blue-grey flock. She had come all this way, and she was happy, for it was true: she could listen to all beings, ancient and modern, at every stage of the life cycle. It was time to start writing. Leaning on the muddy embankment, she opened the new notebook and wrote, 'Skeater's wake had already started when Titch arrived at the house. The flyscreen door was locked, but he could hear the visitors in the living room and didn't ring the doorbell in case it botched the mood.' The pages in her book were filling fast; her words jostled for space from one sentence to the next, flowing from scene to scene, whole sections contained on the page, and her mind swept through Titch's story as if in a reverie. When she closed the book, she realised another night had fallen. Foxes foraged in the dark. Crickets chirped in the blackberries. She rose from the reservoir, slid into her shawl and climbed onto the Aurora. As Maha drove back to the mansion, the trilobites sunk deep into the clay, their bodies pulsing beneath the land.

On the tenth day, while she sat in her perch by the fifth-floor window, Maha saw a figure in the fields, crawling in the sun by the highway. She stopped munching her sweets and dropped a chocolate wrapper in the cot. The figure was tiny, indeterminate, a backlit silhouette that rippled on the soil with each step, roaming aimlessly like a bug without its head. Maha sat upright. The air whistled over the dry skin on her top lip. Her first follower had arrived. She raced between the shelves, rode the lift to the first floor and whirred off the footpath and onto the rubble. The sun burned her neck. Her pus polished the seat. She trekked across the plains and the topsoil crumbled under her tyres, revealing snakeskins, fox bones and parched tree roots. When she found him, Titch had already turned to face her, cowering behind a pink bicycle, his mouth gaping, his kneecaps bulging on his trembling legs. His hair fell in tufts over his face and his eyes were sunk into his gaunt skull. 'Titch,' she said, humming in her seat. 'Come calmly.' His hands clawed his ribs and grazed his thighs. A nest of branches and roots encircled him. His feet caught in the shrubs and he tripped over the bicycle. He was swathed in her shadow; he was a character of her creation. She clasped one hand on his chest and another on his crusty nose. His forehead burned with fever and his breath stank of chemicals. A poison, maybe, a neurotoxin. She raised him from the dirt and laid his body in her lap. She started the Aurora with a purr, a reconciliatory rhythm, and brought him home to Sonpate Mansion.

Titch's body was breaking down. His pores stank of rotting fish. On the fifth floor, she laid him in the cot and filled a bucket with water from the reservoir. She folded his underwear by the door and extracted the envelope from his grasp, counting nearly seven thousand dollars in red and yellow notes. Slowly cupping her hands in the bucket, she wet Titch's body, dissolving the layers of grit. She scrubbed his feet and plucked the gunk off the webbing of his toes and blistered heels. As she trimmed his nails, he woke, jostling under her touch. 'Up for the Sunday sesh, are we?' he said, sweeping the floor with his feet, brushing a layer of dust from his arms. She rocked the cot and blew on his face until he fell asleep again. She dried his toes and worked over his chest, now more lines than curves, something geometric, striated. She wiped the water off his forearms, his shins, the tendons around his knees. When his body was dry, she moved him through the mansion to the second floor. Inside the drawers of a desk, she found a set of scissors and a folded tarpaulin. She laid him on the tarp, tucked the plastic under his arms, parted his legs and worked the scissors across his body, clipping the hair from his head and the fuzz on his neck. She piled the hair in the corner of the room, rubbing her fingers over the inches she shaved, testing the texture of his skin. 'Be calm, Titch,' she said. 'Nothing to fear.' She found the wax in his ears, the grime up his nostrils and the dirt behind his knees. She wiped her palms down her shawl and gathered him up, folding his legs, crossing his arms, pressing his body to her pores. She felt the stillness in the air, the gift of his life in her hands, and she knew, from the very blood and marrow of her bones, that she would hold him until the end.

She awoke with a start. Titch was asleep, breathing soundlessly beside her, shrouded in the golden morning sunlight. There was a rustling outside the building, muffled voices in the wind, and the sounds of wood clattering on the clay and clinking in the glass. Clenching the Aurora, she stopped at the window and peeked outside. Someone's silhouette stretched across the ground five floors below. Someone else had swept the glass into piles. She heard their laughter and their murmurs. Quickly Maha locked the door to Titch's room and descended through the mansion. The lift opened and there were people in the corridor. Women and men, children too. They trembled under her gaze. A man ran down the corridor and fell at the wheels of the Aurora. 'Mummy Pulse,' he said, 'I never thought I'd live to see the day.' His almond eyes were dazzling. He folded his sleeves, loosened his necktie and lay it in her lap. 'You're here, you are,' he said, and as the sun ascended, she saw his face was mottled with bruises, his teeth chipped. She rested her hand on his scalp, fingering his prickly hair, and saw his father howling on a staircase, punching the framed photos on the wall, and his mother weeping on the landing. Maha inhaled and pulled him to his feet. 'Taz,' she said. 'You've come all this way and I'm grateful.' He quivered, and dried his eyes, and her summons resounded around him and all the others. 'You've all heard my call,' she said, facing her followers. There were ten, for now. 'You're in all the newspapers, on the radio too,' said another man. 'Everyone's starting to talk about you.' She drove between her followers and out of the building and into the field. They had collected the glass, the broken wood, the metal pipes from her father's undone construction. Their cars and bikes and caravans lined the lot. They had left their lives in the city with one prayer: to be with her, to be heard without interruption, to be held without end. A woman pushed through the group, panting and shaking. She was thin and bald, wearing grey leggings and a sports bra. A blonde wig jiggled in her waistband. 'Oh, Mama Pulse,' she sang, her handbag swinging off her shoulder. 'There's a pic of you on Facebook. Riding down the freeway. Got a heap of shares. I saw your name and, well, something came over me and here I am.' 'Vicki,' said Maha, 'after all these years.' She drove over the gravel and back to the shade of the mansion. The pores in her skin began to shine. The earth stopped spinning on its axis. Her followers ran over the clay, behind her, around her, as Maha's magnetism pulsed through the outer suburbs and into the city.

Her degenerate following grew; in only two days, more than twenty people milled through the mansion, waiting at her side to speak their stories. They didn't want her advice or authority. They found freedom simply by being heard. She listened without judgement to all their woes: a woman who smothered her baby boy in her sleep, a girl who cut her thighs each night, a man who gambled away his car and his house. There were drinkers and cheaters, insomniacs and the depressed, grievers and outsiders, the jobless and the runaways; all the people who felt themselves broken, their futures hopeless, whose days in the city were only lures of counterfeit perfection. They brought food and drink to the mansion and shared whatever they had. A man sold his pub, and a woman leased out her flat, and the crowd divided the money evenly among themselves, living together as equals. They scrubbed the graffiti off the mansion walls, repainted the windowpanes and swept the dirt from the tiles. In the evenings, they lit bonfires between the cars and shared their stories as smoke coated the sky, dimming the stars that had loomed over their loneliness for so long. They explored the library, unpacking the notebooks from their boxes and lining them along the shelves, reading the shipping labels from Bandra and Grant Road and other manufacturers in Mumbai. As she ascended to the fifth floor, kept private from her followers, she wanted one day to write every person's story on these many pages, charged with true chaos and wonder, penned with the music and momentum of all humanity. Titch slept all day in the cot, passing the hours in a fugue. She pressed bread and chips on him, drizzled honey on his tongue, water on his lips. Soon, she thought, he could join her other followers, laughing and talking and listening to their stories. Soon he would be free like the rest.

293

But the next day, at noon, when the sun sliced through the window, Titch woke with a shriek, convulsing in the tarp. Maha hurried to his side, pouring water over his hands and forehead. As his crying continued, she opened the bags of chips and lollies and gave him whatever food he could swallow. Soon he settled, sinking deeper into his shroud, and he slept through the evening as Maha trimmed the stubble on his scalp. But there was a pattern to his agony: the next midday he wailed, and every noon after that, and his cries echoed through the mansion and along the halls where waited her growing commune. 'I'm here,' said Maha. 'I'll always be here.' Her face brightened whenever she looked at him. 'Up for the Sunday sesh, are we?' he'd say, and he would roll onto his back, tense his shoulders and puff the air into his lungs, shaking under an invisible weight, his toes scratching the cement, his heels bashing the floor. He howled and shook in the grip of these mad convulsions. Later she locked the door and left the fifth floor, descending between her followers and plunging into the reservoir, calling the trilobites out of their hiding places. The people lined the pond, standing silently in the gloom, as the creatures surrounded her, their wispy feelers lapping the mud off her body, the oldest confidants she had known. She opened her notebook and continued writing. '...Titch felt at the advent of something newer, nek-level, a chance to become someone else.' The lapping in the reservoir rose to a tide, deafening Titch's cries from up between the bookshelves, and she climbed from the water, passing the people who knelt at the Aurora. She tore out a page and uncapped her pen. 'Dear degenerates,' she wrote. 'We are here in the Red Plains. We are living out past the suburbs and before the farms. This is not a land but a state of mind. We have room for you all. We're waiting. Time is sensitive. Secrecy is essential.'

In another week, the fields around the mansion filled with tents, tarpaulins, laundry lines and smouldering fires. Curlicues of smoke wound up the windows. Her followers, now nearly sixty, tended the fields, planted seeds in the soil and sang anthems and ballads as they waited for Maha to appear. She drove among the people, who asked for her ear, who called her name, who revelled in every curve of her body and whir of the Aurora. 'It's simple,' said Vicki. 'All we want is to be with you.' But one day, after listening to the latest arrival, and driving to the lift over the polished tiles, Maha returned to the fifth floor and smelled the fetid stink from inside the cot. Titch's face had turned from yellow to blue. His skin had sunk beneath his bones. The thirty-fifth day of his diet, she thought. The last steps in his life of wandering. She pressed her hand on his forehead but he wouldn't wake. She drove out of the mansion and into the fields awash with the sunset. The clouds to the north left scars on the soil and the shadow of the building bulged over the path. She wiped the mildew off her sunglasses, each flake lingering on her fingers, and climbed into the reservoir. The trilobites rose to greet her, stroking her chest with their antennae, glowing a deep-sea blue. She heard the history of the fossils: a crippling winter, so cold the clouds froze in the sky and sank into the ocean; tendrils of ice strangling worms and molluscs; and the trilobites, deprived of prey, floundering listlessly at the point of extinction. They waited underground for millions of years until the oceans dried, the clay turned red and the clouds returned to the sky. The trilobites were moved by the flux of life: hungering, feeding and hungering again. No one being was any different, then or now. The water turned cold. The creatures left her chest and shoulders. She heaved herself up, dripping muck over the engine and the tyres of the Aurora, and realised that all her plans had come true, that she had written a full human history, and yet she was still here, hoping and waiting, as Titch suffered. All he wanted was to be reborn, to arrive at the next life, to take on his next form. The eyes of the trilobites flickered in the reservoir. The stars burned with her sorrow. She combed her hands over her face, wallowing in the malodour of her palms, and felt the pettiness of all her hopes. By detaching from his suffering, by clinging to this human story, she had failed her own divinity. She had been nursing Titch selfishly. To stay. To hold on. She had ignored his untimely desire, so apparent from his very first word.

'Where's Vicki?' she said, parking in the shadow of the mansion. 'Vicki?' Her name rang through the fields, out of each mouth and into every ear, and soon she ran to Maha's side, her face red, the scars below her nipples exposed for all to see. 'It's time to spread the word even further,' said Maha, passing the note addressed to her dear degenerates. 'Take this, and tell everyone to share this message in Melbourne, then to every city in the world. Do this for the next two days.' Vicki nodded, flattening the paper on her chest, and some of the crowd, maybe thirty followers, began to leave their tents as they heard the plan. But there were others remaining, more people who wouldn't leave. 'Taz,' said Maha, holding the envelope of Titch's money. 'We'll all need to eat, won't we?' she said. 'Take the others and find the right food. There is much more work to be done.' She led him and the last followers out of the mansion's shade, along the hot clay to the highway. Taz took the envelope, fanning the money with his fingertip. 'She's a baller,' he said. 'Never in doubt.' Her followers left their new happy homes, heading for the horizon. Then she drove back to the mansion, shifting in her seat, and rolled to the top floor to find Titch. His jaw pressed through his cheeks. His skull bulged under his scalp. His neck was blue. His eyes were rimmed with purple bruises. He mumbled, his bloated tongue the size of a fist, cracked along the centre, bleeding down his throat. She ran her hand over his brow and his skin tore under her palm. 'Just a moment, Titch,' she said. She had waited in order to listen. She had waited to witness his anguish. But it was precisely in waiting that she had failed him, perpetuating his pain, ignoring what he needed: a leap into the next life, a chance to be remade.

The clay was softest at the reservoir. She heaved herself out of the Aurora and began clearing a plot of land. Handful by handful, she tossed clods over her shoulder, unearthing coins, pickaxes and rusted cans. The mud thudded around her wheels as the tarps fluttered on the plains. Titch would continue as another character, she knew, a new guise, another loop in the infinite spiral to zero. The clay oozed through her hands, wet with groundwater, as soil splattered over the Aurora. She scanned the horizon for signs of any new arrivals, but the only movements came from the mountains as the Dandenongs shifted in their tectonic dance. She smoothed the tracks behind the cart and swept the clay off the mansion tiles. When she joined Titch, he was lying down, his back arched, his chest heaving. The linen cascaded around his waist. He shivered with his midday fever, his ribs glistening, but his face was cool and still as if in the order of things to come. He opened his mouth and spoke, but she couldn't understand him, and she removed his underwear, folding it in the corner of the room. She filled a new bucket and cleaned away the gunk from his forehead, his chin and his toes. 'To cool off,' she said, licking her nails and resting her fingers on his wrists. Then the convulsions came. His heels dug into the floor. His arms pressed the air, lifting that unseen load. A tooth snapped from his gums and she pried it off his tongue. His pupils widened, darting around the room, and a streak of shit slid down his thighs. He reached for the chips but Maha hid the packet under her seat. 'There aren't any left,' she said, and he fell, gasping, into the cradle of her lap. She laid her hand on his heart as it beat itself to pieces. Then she pressed her fingers on his wrist and listened for the last time.

'...Up for the Sunday sesh, are we? It's a graveyard in here,' said a girl in purple tights. She reached over the computer and scanned the tag. Up in the vacant gym, the blue sky beaming through the windows, a niggling fear filled his chest, his quads wobbling on the walk to the barbell rack. Then came the levers shifted from shoulder to waist height, a glimpse of a lean torso in the mirrors around the rack, blue twenties sliding into place. Then he dragged the bench along the rubber mat, lying down, shoulders digging into the cushions, laterals arched down his body, pressure mounting in his hip flexors, the bar at eye level. 'But hold on, just a sec! I was taking a leak!' And it was

, wiping his hands on his tracksuit, smiling as he pinched his cheek. 'We going to smash it today, or what? Get up and about.' Then

's face glowed, the trim of his carnival-blue underwear peeked through his shorts, and he said, 'Five by five. Simple set. I won't get in your way, but I got you. I'll be right here.' And   stepped out of view before Titch's giant exhale, his chest rising, shoulders digging into the bench, torso turned concave, and the two hundred and twenty pounds descended, tipping above his nipples, and there was the first rep without hesitation, and the second, even firmer, and with the third came the deepest exhale, the air tearing his throat and spit leaking on his lips, and on the fourth the barbell bounced on his chest, triceps aching, breath stunted between two puffed cheeks. But with a push, and a growl, the weight returned to position. One last rep to go.   was there, waiting out of sight. The fifth rep began. One hundred kilograms. Then came the last push, a gasp, the weight rising, then stalling, and then sinking down to his chest, and his energy zapped, power drained, breath wheezed, barbell trapping his neck, and he looked for   above the bench, waiting for his help.

'...Up for the Sunday sesh, are we? It's a graveyard in here.' Back against the vending machine, gym pass slipping into wallet, smiling, yeah, as Nikita tracked sports scores on the desktop. Then on by the machine weights, the kettlebells lined against the plyo boxes, the old fella crunching his abs on the medicine ball, through the squares of sunlight that streamed through the window and quartered the power-lifting zone. And every step filled with the promise of a PB-day, yeah, a hundy kilos on the menu, and a deep inhale with both his nostrils, the air buffeting the upper muscles of his gut, and then righting the rungs of the rack and popping the bench in place. 'But hold on, just a sec! I was taking a leak!' And out came   , his curls glistening with water from the bathroom, his arms open for a hug, his breath a mix of toothpaste and peanut butter. 'We going to smash it today, or what? Get up and about.' And assuming the form, arching on the bench with heels digging the floor, eyeing the plates with cold-steel contempt. 'Five by five. Simple set. I won't   , but I got you. I'll be right here,' said   , retreating as the weight lifted. Nervousness, yeah, and the urge to impress. Flying through the first three reps, as simple as taking a big strong breath, pumping the weight with a snarl on his face, blood rushing every   and   and

          of his skin's surface, groaning at the full extension of the

          , and into the   , for performance's sake, it was a cakewalk. Only nah. It wasn't. It was a hundy kilos. The barbell jiggled over his chest, the momentum stuck—but no stress, two fingers would

          , would   in this half-fledged set.

          would   , just a second   and be there, spot-ting, helping out, come to his rescue after   , as he waited for   to reach over   past the forehead to the weight.

'...Up for the Sunday sesh, are we? It's a   in here,' yelled Niki, tracking the Test scores on the Cricket Australia site. Thank God for the quiet, yeah. Today was a big one, an arvo like no other, the biggest sesh in three months. PB day.   of smashing the incline shoulder press, and the high-volume bench, and the tricep dips, and the pause-hold bench, and the *weighted* tricep dips, and the close-grip bench, and all those finicky breathing exercises. And there came   , his cheeky mug, his chitter-chatter, his smile. 'But hold on, just a sec! I was taking a leak!' Ruffling his hair. Slapping his back. Bursting a cloud of white chalk.   hovered overhead with his   running over the barbell, saying, 'We going today, or what? Get up and about.' As   smiled, a   shard spat out of his   and he cracked his and said, 'Five by five. Simple set. I won't   , but I got you, I'll be right here.' And enough with the stalling, yeah, it was time to hit a motherfucking PB. Pumping the   , the   , the   , but always, like his rig's true test of strength, to   on the   , inching his chest back into position, and an almighty huff, just one last to go, and   , and down it went. Enough with the bloody pretending, just   . But something snapped inside. It wasn't   . Close but no cigar. The caved. The   ached. And where was   ? Then began the   , the   , the   quaking against   , the   the watery   .

'...Up for the   , are we? It's a   in here.' But it wasn't worth chatting to Niki. It was   day. Couldn't she tell? Shouldn't   members? Shouldn't they put up a sign that told all the   and   that real work was going on? But enough, yeah. Chill. Air through his abs and his ribs. Flooding every inch of his body with   . If   too much tension,   too much chitter-chatter, the   would tumble. So don't have a squizz at the   in   mirror. Don't start ogling just yet, yeah. Get the work done   , hey? Yanking the   into place and sorting the   on the rack. 'But hold on, just a   ! I was   a   .' And of course   ,   silly-billy, would   now, the   singlet half-tucked into   , bopping his   as   Aoki's beat went   on   stereo. 'We going to   it   , or what? Get up and   ,' said   , his   poking out of his   .   knew   like the   his eyelids. On PB day nothing else   . Slipping beneath   as the rod put a shadow on his   and the   tumbling dust in midair like fissures   . And   pause. And smile. '   by five. Simple   . I won't get in your way, but I got you. I'll be right here.' And   get on with it,   : one rep   , the second   , the third   , the fourth   , nothing to be   —but already four-fifth's there? And no worries   all? But of course, yeah, worry   , it   hundy bloody kilos.   barbell wobbled   .   tension   ligaments of   wrists and flared   burned. Trapped waiting for   . Searching   help. Where was   ?   , look.

Titch stopped shouting. His body softened and Maha opened her eyes. It was dusk. The sun was setting. Something else arrived, a presence outside all articulation, spreading up her scalp and down her neck, over her shoulders, pinning her arms to the Aurora. Ants crawled over Titch's body, exiting his arms and legs, spilling from his mouth and ears. They marched across her lap and down the stumps of her ankles. They were one radiant maelstrom. Moonlight refracted off their bodies; their antennae gleamed, their abdomens glowed. Reaching between the ants, she found Titch's skin was stiff. His eyes had sunk into their pits. A breeze swept into the mansion, rising up the floors, unfurling the shroud. She folded his body over her lap, waiting for the ants to leave this in-between. When the room had emptied, she rolled through the cold corridors, out of the stone building and by the laundry lines. The vacant tents creaked in the wind. Buckets and shopping bags glittered beneath the moon. She parted Titch's fringe, cleaned the spit from his lips and brushed the blowflies off his shoulders. She closed his eyelids. The linen slid off his face, and his chest, and his thighs, and when at last she rounded the reservoir, she laid him in the ground. The stars to the west dwindled beyond the mountains, and with the constellations hidden behind the ranges, the plains plunged into darkness. 'Here, gone,' she said. The clay filled the pit, one scoop after the next, and she chewed the inside of her cheek, patting the mud to send him on.

On her way to the mansion, Maha stopped beside a circle of garden chairs, their stiff plastic arms splintered at the joints. She drove between the chairs and across a tartan rug strewn with the things her followers had left: a tambourine, a purple bandanna, a baby's blue sock. She ran her hand through a pile of chicken bones and Styrofoam cups. Picking up a lidless pot, she pressed a finger through the brown crust and smeared the lentils around the rim. She sighed. In all the miles between the mansion and the highway, the Red Plains had emptied of her people, and the last stars had lost their lustre. She felt an ancient solitude, a celestial ache known only by the sun and the moon; human lives never did last for long. Then she opened her notebook and read the sections of Titch's story: the grog, the cryptos, the granny. For all of her care, and for all of their days together, she had misunderstood; his was really a story of unbecoming, stuck for years loving an absence, wading through his days searching for   , that nameless space that could never be filled. She could see this now, after letting him go, having witnessed his passing on. She shut the notebook and creaked in the Aurora, pulling the sun over the horizon and calling her followers back from the city. They had spread her message, walking down roads and back lanes, across bridges and tram lines, heading home to this edge of reality that they had all been taught to dread. But they were learning not to be afraid, to welcome the awaiting emptiness. She smiled when they returned, happy to hear their voices again. There were more than ever before. Hundreds of people had come to meet their god. A girl ran across the field and sat in Maha's shadow. Her father paced between the stalled diggers and piles of clay, weeping, his hands enfolding his head. Then came the mothers and their babies, old men with unruly hair, the grieving, the forlorn. A long line of shopping trolleys, each brimming with groceries, plastered with newspapers and tied with hessian rope, snaked across the clay. Hundreds of wheels rattled in their sockets. The wind ruffled the sheets of newspaper. Taz hauled the supplies into the mansion. 'The others are on their way, Mummy P,' he said. 'They're getting some fridges. Some generators, too.' She asked him for the pens and papers. 'Please and thanks,' she said, leaving her followers with the food as she hurried to the fifth floor.

'   's wake had already started,' she rewrote, 'when Titch arrived at the house. The flyscreen door was locked, but he could hear the visitors in the living room and didn't ring the doorbell in case it botched the mood.' His story needed many more pages. For a short life, he had maintained a long love, building so many hopes, making so many choices, all in the shape of a bottomless hole. He had lost the only person he had ever really known, the only one who had known him in return. That absence loomed over everything. It could not be heard or spoken; it had to be seen on the page. 'At first,' she rewrote, 'Titch was always on the lookout for   .' She told Taz to pass the pages to her followers, to make copies of Titch's story so others could read it too. 'Why don't I get some helpers?' he said. 'A team effort.' Taz lined the followers along the corridor, twenty new arrivals who sat on the tiles and transcribed. They filled the books with Titch's story and stacked them on her father's shelves. The mansion echoed with the sounds of shuffling papers and scratching pens. Soon the fields rang with Titch's life, and others held him in their minds as she had, and after those hours hunched over the pages, exhausted from erasing and rewriting, Maha went to the reservoir and sat in the water, laying her head on his grave. Her nostrils flared and the cosmos quivered over her head. The texture of her skin shifted, a mix of sweat and ink, a viscous wash of words. The trilobites spiralled up her chest and lapped at her lips and she slept. She had captured his human life. No one would forget it. No one would neglect him again.

The night passed. A hand caressed her face, curled a lock of hair over her ear, and she woke up in the reservoir. 'Mama,' said Vicki. 'Do you want to see this? We've started an archive. You can hear what the stiffs are saying back in town.' Maha hauled herself into the Aurora and followed Vicki across the property. The followers sang by firelight, laughing in the shadows, and they waved as she passed, hoping, she knew, to be heard from start to finish. Vicki had lined the newspapers along the wall of the mansion. The pages were taped to the stone, pink at their edges. There were photographs of the chop shop, the piles of letters, the tiny bed from her childhood in the back of a broken truck. Articles had been written about her, theories and explanations. The police had made a statement, warning that any trip to the Red Plains was unquestionably reckless, a selfish way to disappear, that there would be serious penalties for anyone caught spreading her message. A doctor called Maha Sonpate delusional and dangerous, a predator of the mentally ill, a con artist of the highest order, and that anyone concerned about their psychological wellbeing should find professional help. A deacon said Mother Pulse's followers were naive heathens, possessed by an exotic Eastern spiritualism, ignorant of Australia's true religious origins. 'There is only one God,' he wrote. 'There is only one who sees all. And He is the only miracle worker.' Vicki scuffled her feet, coughing in the quiet shade. The articles were endless, filled with so much mistrust, and by dawn Maha smiled at the scale of their scorn. 'Best we keep writing,' she said, turning to the fields as the sun rose on a new day to work.

The edge around the hours had already faded. Time was shifting, and Maha sensed the close was coming, that she was ready to start again. She trundled through the commune, watching her followers in their makeshift homes as they read Titch's story. Taz enlisted two boys to polish the Aurora and replace the drained battery. Vicki cleared the field behind the mansion and planted tomatoes and potatoes. Even more followers arrived. Cars lined the roadside. Backpacks and duffel bags dragged across the dirt. There were more people than Maha had ever seen in her adult life. That afternoon, she found two motorcycles lying in the clay. She slid her fingers along the frames, up the dusty forks, over the worn tyres, feeling as if her father had been with her until the end. 'Busy-busy,' she said. 'Many-headed.' She realised this world would continue unveiling itself to her, would make itself known from one sentence to the next. Her smile outsized the crescent moon. She sighed, and in that breath a sportscar skidded to a stop beside her. A bag thudded onto the dirt. Maha sat up in her seat. A woman hunched at the wheel, panting in the dark, tears leaking from her eyes. Her breath hissed in her lips. Her nose was plugged with dried blood. Maha leaned into the window and saw the woman had long orange hair, pale skin and purple rings under her eyes. That stare, yeah, from a lifetime of sleepless nights. Maha knew it all already. She reached inside the car and felt the woman's shoulder. 'Ginny, isn't it?' she said. 'Ginny Antonopoulos.' The woman tilted her head, slowly leaning her cheek on her seatbelt. 'You've made it. Your great escape,' said Maha. The woman trembled, and nodded, and then she let out a high, lavish laugh, one note that carried all the joy of recognition, the miracle of being known. The notebook shifted on Maha's seat. Her mind would find monsters, seen and unseen, near and far. She would see over fields and oceans, down shining skylines and snowy avenues, along sidewalks and sakuras, into every crowded house that craved her name. It was time to keep writing. The followers gathered around the car. The children chanted, running in circles around her. Every one of them saw Ginny's face, the shine in her eyes, sensed the weight of her untold story, and watched Mother Pulse guide her past the tents and trolleys and towards the mansion. 'Start from the beginning,' said Mother Pulse. 'Your means of freedom.' They watched her drive by the pages of Titch's story. She was their creator. Their divine writer. They knew that Mother Pulse had dreamed them, her people, and set them in motion. It was true. Their longing had pulled them from their jobs, their families and all the plans they had once trusted, but it was all a means of being remade: to be written with compassion and care. They would let go of their pain, their loneliness, their judgement. Here, gone. 'What can I say?' said Ginny. There was so much to make, so many meanings to create, but here, ringed by these growing roads and building sites, their days without disturbance were numbered. Mother Pulse unwrapped a new notebook, smoothed the pages and opened a pen. The crowd followed as far as they could, snaking past the tents, climbing on the cars, applauding as they walked. Then the two figures vanished into the mansion. The walls whittled away their voices and their forms shimmered in the shadows, lost between the light and the dark.

Acknowledgments

Many loving people have fashioned this book, and its author, in ways seen and unseen; neither this novel, nor its writer, would have prevailed without them.

Thanks to Susan Golomb, for shepherding this manuscript through its past and future lives, Peggy Boulos Smith, Sasha Landauer and the folks at Writers House; to Penny Hueston, for her unwavering belief and honest edits, Michael Heyward, W. H. Chong and the team at Text Publishing; to Lan Samantha Chang, Sasha Khmelnik and Jane Van Voorhis for the time and space of the Iowa Writers' Workshop; and to Adeniyi Ademoroti, Adams Adeosun, Ren Arcamone, Reyumeh Ejue, Ben Mason, Mathilde Merouani, Valentina Ríos Romero, Gemma Sieff, Olivia Speier and the many other daring writers and loyal confidantes who shared the Dey House.

Thanks to my friends and family whose experiences informed my inquiries, travel and research in Mumbai, particularly Fayeza Hafizee, Shiv Kathuria, Avinash Kolhe, Prisca Mordon, Sanjeev Sane, and, especially, Ritika Prasad; to Robin Hemley, Lawrence Ypil and all the artists who outlasted Yale-NUS College; to Aaron Kurzak, Zach Mahon, Rakesh Prabhakaran and Kaushik Swaminathan for looking onward to see the light; and to the teachers of Vipassana Meditation, as led by S. N. Goenka.

For their patience and persistence with those early drafts, my deepest appreciation to Or'el Anbar, Andrew Murray Bailey, Dan Briere, Tara Dear, Alexandra Grimwade, Ally Love, Blair Mahoney, Dini Parayitam and, especially, Cam Delaney, Michael Liu and Brian Mukhaya. For their unending generosity and advice, many thanks to Kevin Brockmeier, Jamel Brinkley, John Clement, James Coleman, Elizabeth Cuthrell, Hunter Panther Deerfield, Chris Drago, David Kambhu, Sharlynn Koh, Swaminathan Krishnamoorthy, Nam Le, Ben Mahon, Joan Ongchoco, Rhett Richardson, Lakshmi Swaminathan, Aditya Talwar, Elise Topazian and David Urrutia.

This project has been assisted by the Australian Government through Creative Australia, its principal arts investment and advisory body. I appreciate the support of the American Australian Association, the Elizabeth George Foundation, the Ian Potter Cultural Trust, the Kittredge Fund, the La Napoule Art Foundation and the Yaddo Corporation.

To all my loved ones, named and unnamed, in this life and the next; thank you for showing me a new way to listen and a richer way to live.